# ʰe

# Island

Anna Ralph was born in Thornaby-on-Tees in 1974. She worked as a bookseller, in public relations and in journalism before writing full-time. *The Floating Island* is her first novel. She lives in Durham with her husband.

## Praise for *The Floating Island*

'Anna Ralph's debut novel is moving, astute and arrestingly readable. I couldn't put it down.'
Miranda Seymour

'A straightforward, frankly sensual debut that explores dependency, responsibility, guilt and desire with assured clarity.' *Guardian*

'Strong and evocative, with a rewarding depth of emotion. Her writing has a direct, sensuous feel which I liked very much. It's impressive to find characters who are so embedded in their physical world; it has a touch of D.H. Lawrence about it. I felt as if I was standing – or sinking – on that floating island.' Helen Dunmore

'Compassionate and beautifully written'

D0260047

9080000068329

*Also by Anna Ralph*

Before I Knew Him

# the
# Floating
# Island

## Anna Ralph

arrow books

Published by Arrow Books in 2008

2 4 6 8 10 9 7 5 3

First published in Great Britain in 2007 by Hutchinson

Arrow Books
The Random House Group Limited
20 Vauxhall Bridge Road, London, SW1V 2SA

www.rbooks.co.uk

Addresses for companies within The Random House Group Limited
can be found at: www.randomhouse.co.uk/offices.htm

The Random House Group Limited Reg. No. 954009

A CIP catalogue record for this book
is available from the British Library

ISBN 9780099505358

The Random House Group Limited supports The Forest Stewardship
Council (FSC), the leading international forest certification organisation. All our
titles that are printed on Greenpeace approved FSC certified paper carry the
FSC logo. Our paper procurement policy can be found at
www.rbooks.co.uk/environment

Typeset by Palimpsest Book Production Limited, Grangemouth, Stirlingshire
Printed and bound in Great Britain by CPI Bookmarque Ltd, Croydon CR0 4TD

For Pat and David, with love

# 1

I swallow hard, sweat prickling my back as the blue Fiesta coughs into the space next to Mum's Volvo. A woman, more of a girl, gets out and walks across the gravel to where Mum waits. Still I'm thinking *no way*. The girl can't be Sarah Bell 'cos carers don't wear black boots with clumpy heels and laces that go halfway up thick, white calves. And they don't have *red* hair. I close my eyes, seeing her, first as a blood-red flash on the back of my lids, then against the white tiles in our bathroom, flitting around me like a robin that's come in through the window.

When I open my eyes, Mum and the girl have gone from the drive. I push myself along the landing, listening for their voices. The front door closes. Still I talk myself a different story. She's too young. Too loud. Too . . . red.

'There you are.'

A guest, yeah, that's it. The tap'll be dripping in Briar Cottage again. She'll want Mum to fix it.

'Matt?'

Or no bog roll.

'This is Sarah.' A smile spreads over Mum's face like butter. 'Say hello.'

'Hello.' Sarah Bell. Big teeth. Big tits.

'Hey there, Matt.' She flicks gum round her mouth. 'How you doing?'

She looks like a gypsy; a scarf with tassels on the end and a corduroy skirt, charity shop. She has earrings, too, hoops that go all the way up her ears, big, bigger, biggest.

'Shall we come up?' Mum asks. 'Or do you want to come down? I know, we'll come up. Then you can show Sarah your room.'

Sarah looks at the chair lift, then at me, or rather she looks at the blanket that covers my legs. And not even that subtle, she just stares right at it with big, goggly eyes that've got too much of that black stuff round them. I know what she's thinking, it's what everyone thinks, what do cripple legs look like? But before she can give me one of those 'it doesn't faze me, I've seen a million cripples' smiles, I swivel round on my wheels and head back to my room. Behind me I can hear Mum, pulling at the chain around her neck and talking, too quiet to make out the words, but I clock the tone.

Having a carer's her idea. Sarah the Carer will be the first one to live in, but the third we've had in as many months. The other two, Neal the Wimp and Scabby Janet, only came for a few hours each day and were gone after a week. Two—nil. Victory to the cripple.

But we have to compromise and Sarah's a compromise. The old-man pants Mum bought for me yesterday, they're a compromise. They're the sort with a door for your willie so you don't have to drop them to take a piss. A bit like Y-fronts – in fact, they probably *are* Y-fronts. Perfect if your legs don't work. I throw a sweatshirt over them, still inside their cellophane wrapping, and put myself over by the window.

The top of Cat Bells is visible today and if you squint you can just make out the ant-lines of walkers following the tracks short of the summit. I can see for miles from here – the three hills popular with walkers, and the lake, of course, stretching from Lyman's Point to Finkman's boat yard. At the bottom of our garden there's a jetty and a narrow pebble shoreline with a wood at the end of it. Inside, where the trees are thickest, is where I built my secret pond. Emperor Pond. Maybe it's dried up, or so overgrown you can't even see it. I can't get to it now.

Sometimes people find their way through the trees and stand on the jetty to take pictures. They're not supposed to because technically it's private property, but Dad never told them to get lost. Good for business, he said. Random people traffic. He had four engine boats for hire, three rowers and one seven-seater which he kept at Finkman's. Sometimes he'd look up at my bedroom window and wave. And I'd wave back. Then he'd be off, skimming the silky water.

Sarah's talking non-stop as she makes her away along the landing. It's a polished wooden floor, the type with a fancy name that's as old as the house. Her boots are loud on it. Clump. Clump. She's loud. The weather. Hot. The journey. Long. Blah, blah, blah. She comes over to the window.

'Wow! You've got your own pier.' The bracelets on her wrists jangle. 'That's yours? The pier? Hope my room's got a view like this, Mrs Logan.'

Her view's nothing like mine. Mum's putting her downstairs in the laundry room. OK, so it's got a bed and a TV, but it was a laundry room way before anything else and it's still where Mum washes the linen from the holiday cottages. The air's damp and warm and reeks of fabric softener and the view is of a rusted barbecue and one of those worm bins that converts household waste into compost. Oh, and yeah, somewhere, past the trees and overgrown flowerbeds, is the *pier*.

'These are brill. Did you do these?'

I turn around to see her holding my drawings, flicking through them, smearing them with grubby fingers. Her nails are short and painted, mushroom colour.

'Yes. They're mine.'

I take them off her and place them neat and flat as they were at the top right corner of my desk. Dr Finch used to make me draw, but I didn't do landscapes then. I'd sit for hours in his office drawing houses and people and cars while he picked at the skin on his fingers. He had certificates on the wall and an old map of Britain in an expensive frame, but the glass was cracked. When I'd finished he'd ask questions . . . 'Who's the boy looking out of the attic window? Did you feel happy or sad when you drew him?'

'Photography's my thing,' Sarah says, brushing away the silence. 'You know, pictures. The light's amazing around here, isn't it? Maybe we could go for a walk around the lake, you could take—'

'Matt doesn't go near the lake,' Mum says.

I don't *walk* either, but Mum's got it covered. I haven't noticed it before, but she looks pretty good when she folds her arms. Her skin's papery, like moth wings, so it comes across as kind of scary. Well, pretty unfriendly anyway.

'Right.' Sarah chews her gum and tucks it away at the back of her mouth. 'Well, I'm sure there're lots of other things we can do.'

'Oh, yes. Lots of things.' Mum flashes another butter smile. 'Matt loves to draw, as you can see . . . and his computer, he's a proper little whiz on the computer. The Internet, and – what's that game you like?'

GA Speedboat.

'You could show Sarah how to play . . . you know the one . . .' She looks at me. 'What's it called?'

GA Speedboat. GA Speedboat. GA Speedboat.

'I swear he's never off it sometimes. You must be tired, Sarah. Such a long drive.'

'A bit.'

'You can change the curtains, bed linen . . .' Mum leads her out of my room. 'Add whatever touches you like, really. You've got the laundry there, of course, but . . .'

'Nice to meet you, Matt.' Sarah places a hand on my shoulder, showing teeth and gum squashed between molars. She stinks of cigarettes. I glare back, the most evil look I can summon. Her eyes absorb the pain of it, then she smiles, chews, jangles a bit more. I look away, listening as she follows Mum. At the door she pauses to look back, most likely wondering why I'm not falling over myself to be nice. Too right. Sarah the Carer. As good as gone. Twenty-four hours, two days maybe. Max.

'So where is she?'

Mum unties her apron and puts two place mats on the table. We don't eat in the dining room any more. We used to, Mum and Dad at either end, me and Tom on the long sides. It's nicer in the kitchen anyway. Even if my wheels don't fit under the table.

'Can you manage?'

'Yep.' I drop the armrest and use my arms to slide across into a chair, then Mum tucks me in. That's the only thing I can't do, tuck in, I can do everything else. My arms used to ache all the time, now they're strong. 'So where is she?'

'Unpacking.' She dishes out a spoonful of shepherd's pie. Homemade.

'Doesn't she eat?'

'She had something on the way over from Newcastle.' She holds a breath. 'You might have made more of an effort, Matt. Why don't you ask her if she'd like a sandwich? Or some apple pie.'

'Is that homemade?'

'No. It's bought.' She stops, counting seconds in her head. 'Can't you just make the best of it, for once?'

I don't want to fight, I want to talk. Part of me's still thinking it's not too late for negotiations; you know, talks like governments have right before they get the big guns out and blow everyone away. She pats my hand with hers, shiny nails with square, white tips that'll be in the bathroom bin come changeover day.

'We do all right.'

She stares at the food on my plate.

'Mum? We don't need anyone.'

'We've been through this.'

'She's a girl.'

'It doesn't *matter*.'

'She's my age.'

'She's eighteen. You're fifteen. Do you honestly think she won't have seen it all before?'

I pick at a scab, a fresh one on a knuckle on my right hand.

'Please don't.'

'Don't what?' So much for negotiations. I go for my wheels, but I've parked them too far back from the table.

'*Ask*. You want your chair?' She gets up.

'No. Leave it.'

'Where? The toilet?' She snaps off the brake and pulls it to within reach.

'*Leave* it!'

'Sarah's the only one who applied.' She sits down again and rubs a hand across her forehead, dragging the skin into wrinkles. 'The only one.'

I want to scream, but I don't. I want to get through to her somehow, because there's just us and we do OK. We're OK. I reach out my hand to stroke her hair but I'll mess it up and she won't be able to get it back to how it was and she'll shout and . . .

'I can't cope, Matt. Can you appreciate what that means? You knew the summer holidays would be like this. I can't not go to work, can I? I can't be with you all the time.'

She looks at me, waits, but I can't meet her eyes. I focus

instead on her mouth, willing away the lines that get tighter with every word.

'You know how much I have to do. How am I supposed to manage the holiday cottages, guests, the house, not to mention doing it on half the income? Since your father—'

'Don't slag him off!'

She raises an eyebrow.

'I bet he doesn't even know about her, does he?'

'He isn't here.'

'You said we'd look after each other. *We. Us.*'

'Things change.'

'Get rid of her.'

'No.'

'Tell her to *go*.'

'NO!'

The silence that follows is made all the more empty because she shouted. I open my mouth to fill it, to say sorry. Sorry. Sorry. But the air's too heavy for any more words. Then I hear music, a soft rhythmic thud like a heart-beat coming from Sarah's room.

'It won't be like last time.' She walks over to the cupboard next to the sink. I can't see the bottle, but I hear the cap being unscrewed. 'Sarah'll help with the cottages. She'll be around, that's all . . .' She pours the whiskey, stops, fills the glass some more. 'To help you, when you need help. Certain things, not everything.'

The scab starts to bleed, fresh blood charting a course through the tiny hairs on the back of my hand. I want her to say what the certain things are, but she doesn't. She picks up a photograph on the dresser, the one of Tom standing in the middle of his train set, face grey and swollen from an asthma attack he'd had the night before.

'You could get a cleaner to help with the cottages. I'll do more, I can put washing in, or—'

'Eat. It'll be getting cold.'

'*Please*, Mum.'

'NO! I make the decisions.' She takes a gulp from the glass. 'I do the best I can, don't I? *Don't I?*'

I stare at her, holding back tears. She looks again at the photograph and then presses it close to her chest. Her lips move, but I can't hear the words. I wait for a glance, a softening in her face just for me, but it doesn't come.

When I get back to my room I wait, light off, sure I'll hear her coming up the stairs after me. At first there's silence, then the clank of plates, homemade shepherd's pie being scraped into the bin. She won't be mad for long. That's how it is when you need someone for things. She can't stay angry while she undresses me and puts me to bed. Lifting, pushing and pulling legs into the right place, we have to touch. I take the pants she bought me, remove the wrapping, and fold them into the drawer of my dresser.

An owl hoots, loud like it could be close. I go to the window and pull back the curtain, wrapping it around me to make a cave. Sometimes, in the dark, it's as though the outside isn't behind glass at all, but right beside me. I swallow over belches of anger and tears, staring at the patterns the moon makes on the lake until I hear different noises, Dad working on a boat, the pull of an engine cord, over and over. And Mum, going out to give him a drink. Ice chinking in the glass. Dad's footsteps on the slats. A laugh.

I look at the jetty, rusted rings punctuating the long sides. No boats. No sound. When the lake's sucked in the light and taken it under, it'll be black, impossible to see where the jetty ends and the lake begins. I imagine feeling my way along to the end, arms outstretched to the quiet breathing of the water, where I'll wait, like I've done a million times for real, and now, in my head. First the darkness is a shroud, then my eyes adjust and I see them. Hansons. Brigg. Fortlowry. Otter. And the fifth island. The floating island.

They say it's coming back. Before long the moon will find a shadow under the lake. Bubbles will rise and the shadow will spread to a stain. Then, in the night, in the dark, the floating island will surface. Here again. As it was a year ago. The day Tom died.

# 2

Sarah set about arranging the contents of her suitcase into piles on the floor. Clothes, books, her camera. Rooting around in her canvas bag, she found the half-eaten cheese and pickle sandwich she'd bought at a service station on the way over. It didn't taste any nicer at the second attempt, but it was better than going hungry and infinitely better than walking in on a family row. It hadn't been possible to make out what Mrs Logan and Matt had argued about, the odd word, maybe even her name a couple of times, but she couldn't be sure.

She forced down the last bite of the sandwich, discarding the crust, and glanced up at the window. It was almost certainly a non-smoking house, no ashtrays in any of the rooms she'd been shown around, only bowls filled with pot-pourri in colours to match the furnishings.

Her room was considerably less formal; bare, magnolia walls, but for a single picture above the bed, a watercolour of the lake. It looked out of place, too good to be stuck in a guest room. At the end of the bed a door, glossed white, led into another room, an en-suite at one time maybe, now the laundry. Pink sheets made slow turns in the washing machine. Above it, there was a long, wide shelf with detergent and several bottles of fabric softener. An ironing board, the cover criss-crossed with burns, stood in a narrow gap, and, next to it, a skyscraper of towels, duvet covers and pillowcases. No wonder Mrs Logan needed help.

It had been a shock to discover she worked when it was quite obvious they were loaded. Something managerial for one of those large holiday complexes that did archery and climbing and had spas and tropical waterfall swimming pools, all under one, golf-ball-shaped dome – *Leisure World* or *Pleasure World*, something like that – she hadn't chosen to elaborate.

Unpack. Sarah cleared a space on the window sill for her French language book and dictionary, a selection of photography books from the library, several months overdue, two Catherine Cooksons that belonged to Nanna, and *War and Peace* – it was supposed to be good, once you got into it. As she lifted them up a postcard fell out of the dictionary. It was a print, a coloured drawing by someone called Tregor, an artist, but not one she'd heard of. Curving over the stone arch at the centre were the words 'L'Artistes Université'. Gargoyles glared from either side, some with fists pulling at their mouths, others obscured by large, heart-shaped ivy leaves. On the pavement, chained to iron railings, were bicycles, the old sort with baskets, and behind them, obscured by a thicket of rhododendron bushes, other buildings, classrooms perhaps, dark rooms and studios. She flicked through the pages of her *BBC Beginner's French Course*, well-thumbed, but not as any indication she'd learned anything, then slung it in the bin.

Even if she got the A Level grades she needed and saved enough for rent and food she wouldn't be able to manage the tuition fees. It was supposed to be the best art school in Europe which is why it was so expensive, but without Julian it just wasn't possible. Having failed to apply for anywhere else she'd have to rely on clearing and take whatever she could get. She put the postcard back into the dictionary, unable, quite, to bring herself to throw it away. A fortnight ago Julian had been prepared to leave it all. Surely that counted for something?

Except he hadn't chosen her.

In the end.

'It's the best thing, for you, your future,' he'd said.

'No, Julian. For *you*. *Your* future.'

He'd chosen a café in town. He knew she wouldn't react there, wouldn't make a scene, scream and yell and beat the shit out of him. You can say I'm sorry, I'm a bastard, I love my wife, and nobody has hysterics. Sugar granules on the table he'd pushed into a line. God, he hadn't even been able to *look* at her.

She picked up her mobile, thought about dialling his number, then switched it off.

*This* was home. This town, this room, this life. She held up her clothes on their hangers, witnesses to her renewed sense of conviction, and took them over to the wardrobe. It was one of those old-fashioned ones made from dark wood; by far the largest item in the room. She peered inside, a fusty smell, and something else, fainter and harder to identify, but almost certainly perfume. She hung up three skirts, packed because she'd considered them to be an appropriate length, and two dresses which she wouldn't wear, but were at least summery. In the first of two deep drawers at the bottom she put everything else, trousers, jeans, T-shirts, shorts, and – not that she expected there'd be an occasion to wear it – her red and white bikini. The second drawer was missing a handle and she had to put her fingers in the gap and tug hard before it opened evenly, then only halfway. It was lined with thin, brown paper that disintegrated to ash in her fingers when she tore it out. She reached to the back, surprised to find something solid. It was an old book, a hardback copy of *Tom's Midnight Garden* with the front cover missing and strands of curled glue stuck to the spine. In the top corner of the title page, written in red ink, was a child's scrawl.

T. Logan.

A knock at the door. She returned the book to where she'd found it.

'Yes? Come in.'

Mrs Logan put her head around the gap. 'Just wondered how you were getting on?'

'Oh, fine.'

She didn't come inside straight away, but stood uncomfortably, one hand on the door frame, the other smoothing fine, blonde hairs around an impossibly neat chignon.

'It's a lovely room.'

'Good.' She came inside and pulled on her necklace, a gold chain with a starfish-shaped pendant. 'I won't keep you. I just wanted to apologise for earlier. Matthew . . . He's very independent.'

'That's good.'

'What I mean to say is I'm sure he didn't intend to be rude when you were introduced. He takes time to adjust to new things, that's all. New people.'

'Oh. Don't worry, we'll be best friends in no time, I'm sure.'

Mrs Logan seemed to think this unlikely. 'One other thing. The lake. Perhaps I ought to have mentioned it to you earlier. There was an accident, you see, a boat, Matt fell in and . . .'

The washing machine stopped, changed direction, gathered speed again.

'It's how he got like he is. A virus from the hospital or the water, we're not sure. Anyway, I thought I ought to say something because you mentioned going there with him.'

Five minutes into the job and she'd already put her foot in it.

'He's quite frightened of the lake now, I'm afraid.' She dropped the chain from round her neck.

'Right. No lake. I'll be sure to remember, Mrs Logan.'

'You can call me Gill.' She looked around the room, taking in the radio and, propped on the dresser until Sarah could find a more suitable spot, the Johnny Wilkinson calendar her brother Josh had given her for Christmas. Gill continued her exploration, finally settling on a dress hooked over the door to the laundry. It was Sarah's favourite, red velvet, bought at a PDSA shop. 'There's not much in the way of things to do round here, I'm afraid. Sometimes the hotel puts on a disco.'

'I wasn't sure what to pack.'

'Dinner dances every second Thursday, a quiz once a month. The first Monday, I think, or Tuesday, well—'

'I doubt I'll even wear it.'

'No.'

She was a tall woman, and slender, with an introverted, slightly childish expression. Occasionally, as Sarah had noticed once or twice during her tour of the house, Mrs Logan's mouth tightened, as it did now.

'Well, I'll leave you to spend the evening as you choose. I'll take you around the two holiday cottages tomorrow. It's changeover day so there'll be a few hours in the afternoon when they're empty.'

'OK.'

'We'll do the first one together so you'll know what to do.'

'Thanks.' Sarah searched for something to say that was less formal. 'Have you lived here long?'

'Sixteen years. Is it? Something like that. Andrew and I moved here when I was expecting Matt, so it must be. It was my father's place before that. No holiday cottages then. We did all that ourselves.'

It was the first time she'd mentioned a husband. He probably worked in a city and came home on weekends.

'Perhaps we'll see you a bit later? Don't feel you have to. There's apple pie if you're hungry.'

'Thanks.'

'Goodnight then.'

When she was sure Mrs Logan was out of earshot, Sarah breathed out. She'd long since abandoned the idea of privacy, suspecting she'd be required to join Matt and his mother in the evening for meals and afterwards, to do whatever it is they did until bed. Only, now she had some solitude in the shape of her room, she wasn't inclined to leave it. He appeared to be the typical teenager, sullen, dark hair flopping over a malevolent gaze, but as he'd said virtually nothing, it'd been difficult to see what, if anything, lay behind it. She'd assumed it was cerebral palsy or muscular dystrophy that had put him in a wheelchair. The fact that he'd endured some sort of accident, and was frightened of something, made him a friendlier prospect.

It didn't much matter. She'd make it work. Brighten the room up a bit, take the money and do the job.

A thin, green curtain covered the window. She pulled it back and lifted the latch. A light drizzle had sharpened the smells; warm, dew-damp air, and pine from the trees that circled the house. She listened, heard a car up on the main road, a trickle of water somewhere.

She'd tried to imagine what Loweswater would be like on the way over in the car, conjuring a collection of child-hood memories gathered on school trips to Hadrian's Wall and the likes. Not that Newcastle lacked fields and hills; they were just too far away to mean anything, like token bits of countryside dropped on to the horizon. She'd explore tomorrow.

A glint. Something swaying. Startled, she jumped back. Whatever it was hit the window frame and bounced off again. A branch? None close enough. Again, another thud. The sight of a square of Blu-Tack was so foreign as to render her stupid for a moment, but having decided it was safe to touch, she reached out and took hold of it. It immediately fell loose into her grip, suggesting it hadn't been tied, but held. There were thumbprints along the

# 3

She'd have to be wimpier than Wimpy Neal to leave because of a note. But it's the cumulative effect I'm counting on and by the end of today all my cumulating's going to add up to quite a bit. Mum's decided to give Sarah a lie-in on her first day (her totally see-through plan of leaving us alone together in the house in the hope that I'll suddenly decide she's my friend).

But I'm not stupid.

Phase One – unscrewing the door handle to the bathroom – is about to have its effect. Cheap trick, sure, but she's been in there twenty minutes and any second now she's going to start yelling to be rescued. Then, I'm not sure, after an hour, maybe three, whenever she's cried herself silly, I'll suddenly hear her and maybe I'll do something about it, just as Mum comes back and sees what a lazy—

'Morning.'

Sarah. She pads, barefoot, across the kitchen to the fridge, yawns, stretches her arms out behind her and takes out the orange. I half-expect her to drink straight from the carton, while scratching some whatever under her teddy-bear pyjamas, but she doesn't. She gets a glass.

'Remind me to tell your mam the handle on the bathroom door's bust. Or it was.'

'*Was?*'

'I fixed it.' She rubs her eyes and yawns again. 'Well, it works anyway, thanks to my hairbrush. Screw's come out; you know where your mam keeps them?'

'I'll take care of it.'

'Things were always falling to bits in our house.' She bends down, showing off her tits, not all of them, just a glimpse of the top bit, the cleavage. 'Got so I was a dab hand at DIY-type stuff, sort of a Handy Andy, you know, him off that programme.'

'I *said* I'd take care of it.'

She looks at me, widening her big, sleepy eyes till they look like they might fall out, then carries on opening cupboards and drawers. She looks different without her make-up, skin paler and freckled.

'Is she here, Mrs Logan, your mam?'

'No.'

'Know what time she'll be back?'

'No.'

'Want some breakfast?'

'No.'

'Know any other words?'

I smile. 'Do you like your room?'

'Sure. It's—'

'Someone died there, the old woman who owned this house before us. It was ages before anyone found her and when they did they had to scrape her off the bed. Sometimes, when you think you're asleep, but really you're not, you can hear her moaning.'

'Really?'

'Yeah. She fell over her cat and broke her ankle on the way to bed. Couldn't get to the phone and she didn't have any friends or family so she just lay there by herself and starved to death.'

'Poor woman.'

'A lot of people have died in this house.'

'Have you got lots of equally gruesome stories about those?'

'I might.'

'I thought this used to be your granddad's place?'

'Who told you?'

'Your mam and dad took it over, just before you were born, and renovated it. That's right, isn't it?'

I shrug, feeling a hot flush rise to my cheeks.

'Where's your dad? Does he work away?'

'You ask a lot of questions.'

'Just making conversation.'

'He's very important, an astronaut. He's on a research mission at the moment, actually. Mars.'

'Hell of a commute.'

'Is that supposed to be a joke? Because if it is then it isn't funny.'

'Right,' she says, flicking the switch on the kettle. She looks out the window to the garden. Birds twittering and, in the distance, the bump of a boat on the lake. She starts to hum.

'He lives in Hayden Bridge with a woman called Laura. He sells photocopiers. Not that it's any of your business.'

'Why are you being rude, Matt?'

'Rude?'

'Playing games.'

'I can't play games. Maybe you haven't noticed.'

'You know that's not what I meant.' She turns to face me and lowers her voice. 'I'm sorry you don't want me here. That's right, isn't it? You want me to "Go home"?'

What have I got to be embarrassed about? *She's* the one poncing about the place like she owns it. *She's* the one who—

'Got your note.'

'Huh?'

'Your *note*.'

'Dunno what you're on about.'

'Your room's directly above mine.' She stands over me, tits like air bags. I open my mouth to speak, but get the warm, sleepy smell of her instead.

'Look, Matt.' She brings two bowls to the table and starts to fill them with cornflakes. 'Reckon I'd be pretty gutted if someone moved into my house to take care of me whom I didn't—'

'Do I look like I need *taking care* of?'

It happens in a second, too quick for me to do anything about it. I spin my wheels round, knocking against the table, and the milk jug rolls on to the floor. I stare at the shattered pieces.

'Sorry,' I say, before I can stop myself.

'Just an accident.'

She gets some kitchen towel, a few sheets first, then she takes the roll off the dispenser and kneels down in front of me. There are tiny, blonde hairs at the bottom of her back. I want to tell her to get up, get away, but I'll sound like a nut. She makes a neat pile of the pieces of jug and mops up the milk with the towel, pausing briefly to tuck strands of red hair behind her ears.

'It was a bet,' she says, glancing up at me. 'What do you think?'

She feels big next to me, not that she's fat, well, maybe chubby fat, just big.

'You're probably right.' She tugs at her fringe. 'Reckon all I need now's an orange jumper and green trousers and I'll pass for traffic lights.'

Ha-de-ha. Do tell another.

'I'll get dressed,' she says, her smile fading. 'Maybe once I've done the cottages with your mam we can go out?'

'Gan doon the toon? No, thanks.'

'Course not.' She stands up, two damp patches on her knees, and chucks the sodden kitchen towel in the sink.

'You're right,' I say, hardening at her tone. 'I *do* want you to go home. Piss off back to Newcastle. I never wanted you here in the first—'

Mum's key turns in the front door. I swivel my wheels around and head into the hall.

'Hello.' She smiles at me. Her face is sweaty, eyes shining like jewels. 'Have you had some breakfast?'

'No.' I take one of the carrier bags out of her hand and put it on my lap.

'Never mind. You can have some now. How've you two been getting on?'

'OK.'

'Just OK?'

'Sarah broke the milk jug.'

'Oh.' She comes into the kitchen just as Sarah's dropping the shattered pieces into the bin.

'Sorry, Mrs Logan. I'll replace it as soon—'

'Don't be silly.' She's out of breath, smiling slightly wildly. 'If it's the one I think it is, it was a gift from my sister. Awful thing. Help me with these bags, would you?'

Sarah lifts the bags on to the counter. Her eyes, dark and narrow before, are now filled with relief. As I watch them unpack the shopping, the two of them engrossed in an unnecessary conversation about what can be done with me for the rest of the day, I search for the rush of satisfaction that should be mine. But it doesn't come.

# 4

At the end of the woods the path opened out to a narrow shore. It looked possible to walk the entire circumference of the lake, but Sarah would only do a small section of it today. The water was calm and still, a glass eye that both absorbed and reflected light. It was supposed to be the second largest of the lakes and had four islands, the largest of which was visible to her now. The others she assumed would be further along. She tied the sleeves of her cardigan into a knot around her waist and took her camera out of her bag. Although the heat was fierce, so much so that she'd considered turning back more than once, she was determined to see something of where she was.

Had she been too firm about the note? Made too much of it? Locking her in the bathroom was pretty backward. She knelt down, lit a cigarette, and loaded a film, glancing up every so often at the lake. He wasn't at all what she'd expected – weedy looking, glasses maybe, the sort of kid you'd feel sorry for. Nothing like that, in fact. He looked older for a start, a large Adam's apple, dark eyes with thick lashes, a fuzz of hair on his top lip. His chest and forearms were well-defined, shoulders broad – for someone his age. Were he to sit up straight and smile, he'd probably be quite attractive. It was only when you looked down, past the waist, you got the sense of him being out of proportion, the thin, muscle-wasted legs that hung puppet-like from his frame.

The way ahead was partially blocked by a network of tree roots stretching out over the pebble shore. She bent down, running a hand over the moss glove that covered them. Further back, on the trunk, lichen grew, peppering the bark like stubble. She wiped sweat from her top lip and looked through the lens to adjust the focus. Julian had told her she had talent, enough to really make something of herself, but it hadn't been about that, not to begin with. She hadn't thought of her photography in terms of a job or a career. Looking through the eye of a camera she was able to lose herself in her surroundings. Close up, out of context, it didn't matter where you were or what you were looking at. Everything was beautiful.

The changeover was easy and even though Mrs Logan had gone through all of the tasks quickly, there wasn't anything Sarah considered daunting – housework mostly, and she was used to that. When she wasn't busy doing stuff related to the cottages she could concentrate on the main house – by this she assumed cleaning – and on Matt. Her duties with him were far less exhaustive and seemed to consist of 'whatever he needs'. In the evenings she might be needed to carry things downstairs if he was tired, or put his clothes out for the following day. These, the only two examples provided, seemed to have been chosen from a far larger, unspoken list, but not wishing to appear stupid, Sarah hadn't pressed her. Matt wasn't shy, nor was he completely dependent, so he was the best person to talk to about what he wanted help with and what he could manage on his own.

By the time she reached Finkman's boat yard, the heat had reached its midday peak, fusing with the sound of bees and birds. She glanced at her watch. She'd better get into town if she wanted the pictures developed and back today. The path from the shore led through to what appeared to be a scrap yard, littered with engines and upturned boats. A young man with overalls turned down to the waist, nodded a greeting.

'Can I get up to the main road from here?' she asked.

He had blond hair, darkened on his forehead with sweat. He stopped work on an engine stripped into parts on a bench in front of him, and came out from the shed.

'I was looking for the town,' she added.

'You must be Sarah.'

'Yes.'

'I heard she was hiring someone.' He looked at her closely, wiping his hands on his overalls which were already black with oil. 'David. I'd shake your hand, but . . .'

She caught a whiff of diesel and something else, Pot Noodle. It wouldn't be his place; he was too young, mid-twenties at most. She looked around, but there was no one else. Normally men would allow their eyes to wander, a glance down to her chest or legs, or, these days, her hair. But he looked directly, confidently.

'The town's a mile that way.' He signalled behind him. 'Follow it up to the top and you're on the main road in. It's signposted from there.'

'Thanks.'

She walked on, felt him watching, but didn't look back. She had to remind herself that in small towns like this everyone knew everyone else. Mrs Logan would be well known, not least because she owned two holiday cottages.

At the main road the traffic queued, cones reducing it to one lane. Those that edged past her showed red-faced passengers, arms resting on the hot metal. She kept going, feet slipping in her sandals, until she reached a row of houses. Almost every one appeared to be a bed-and-breakfast and many had signs in the window that said 'No Vacancies'. Further along, the houses became shops, half a dozen that sold outdoor clothing, most with sales on. By one there was a large sign on the pavement she had to step around, 20 per cent off walking boots. Tackle shops, too, with nets and rods in plastic buckets in the doorways. She stopped to look through the window of one, a tray of feathered hooks, in every colour and size.

At traffic lights she crossed over and turned into a side street, hoping she might see somewhere to get a drink. It was cooler, a thin breeze blowing up the road. She lifted the strap of her bag off her right shoulder so the air could get to the skin underneath. It felt raw, the sun having concentrated itself most brutally there. She stopped outside a shop window, hoping the extent of the sunburn might be obvious from her reflection, but was drawn instead to several large photographs in frames. They were all of the local area. One of them, black and white, showed a Girl Guide standing on what appeared to be a small, flat patch of ground in the middle of the lake. In one hand, she carried a flag. The caption read: Floating Island. Odd. The only island she'd seen had trees and was much bigger. She passed an antique furniture store further along with a small table outside that displayed second-hand books, but none of the titles grabbed her. An elderly woman, who sat behind a desk at the back of the shop, peered at Sarah over reading glasses. She had a sense of how she might look, student on a camping trip, an eccentric American tourist. Not what she was anyway, a resident. Just as she was about to give up and head back to the high street, she saw a café across the road. Relieved to be out of the sun's glare she ordered a tall glass of fresh orange at the counter. It felt like a long time since breakfast so, after checking the money in her purse, she added a portion of black cherry gateau.

'You're lucky.' The girl nudged it on to a saucer with the tip of her finger. 'It's the last piece. Mrs Davis isn't due in until this afternoon.'

Sarah nodded, unsure how to react. She gave what she hoped was a friendly smile and took a seat by the window.

A man now stood outside the entrance to the antique shop. He kissed the woman from behind the desk on both cheeks and, cupping her at the elbow, helped her inside. When he appeared again, several minutes later, he was carrying a brown leather satchel, scuffed and worn at the corners. He walked across the road towards the café, running the last few steps to beat a car. Dark hair, the odd grey.

Forty? Forty-five? He came inside and ordered coffee. Just as she was about to take the first forkful of cake into her mouth, he dropped a coin. She covered it with her foot to stop it spinning.

'Thanks,' he muttered. 'One of those days.'

'You should have some of this then.' She held up the cake on her fork. 'Oh, but shit, you can't. It's the last piece.'

'How mean of you.'

He had a soft, low voice. Nice. He took a seat at a table not far from hers, and pulled out an A4 notepad from his satchel. A clean jaw stippled with a day's growth. Athletic body, broad shoulders.

'I LOVE cake,' she said. 'Especially black cherry.'

He looked up. 'You don't hear a woman say that very often.'

His eyes were distinctive, a rare, deep green. They suited his expression, slightly amused, like a cat presenting prey to its owner.

She scooped another forkful into her mouth and swallowed. 'Did you really want some? You could have a bit if you want.'

'I wouldn't dream of depriving you of it.'

'OK.' She downed the last of it. 'I don't suppose you've got a light on you?'

He took a folder of matches from his satchel and stood up to hand them to her. She reached for her packet of Marlboro Lights; Lambert & Butler or rollies at home, but not here.

'Keep them,' he added. 'I don't smoke, must've picked them up by mistake.'

She read the advert printed on the back of the matches. 'Wellman Hotel and Spa? Sounds like a health farm.'

'It's not, thank God.' He took some papers out of his satchel and spread them out on the table in front of him.

'You work there, then?'

'No. I'm a guest. I'm having the windows replaced in my cottage.'

She leaned forward to retrieve an ashtray from the table in front of her, pausing briefly before leaning back into her seat.

'Easier not to be there,' he finished, a little late. 'You're not from round here, are you?'

'My accent?'

'I noticed it, but no, it wasn't that.'

He'd live in a nice house and have a wife who did the gardening in a dress. She checked the finger. Tan line but no ring.

'The hotel's pretty well known, that's all. Does all the big things round here, weddings, conferences—'

'Dinner dances?'

'The odd one.' He smiled a little into his mug of coffee. 'Hard not to know it anyway, unless you've just arrived.'

'Yesterday.' She glanced at his papers. Important work. A lawyer, or an accountant. Something flash. 'I'm distracting you.'

'This? No. I think if I was serious about doing it, it would've been finished long ago.' His eyes darted, resting finally on her camera. 'Are you a photographer?'

'Sort of.'

'You don't see many of them now.'

'Photographers?'

'Cameras. Proper ones. They're all digital now, aren't they? No . . .' he groped for the word, '. . . film.'

'I tried using one for a while,' she said. 'No . . . fun.'

He smiled again. This time she felt it deeply, a hot flush across her chest.

'What's your name?'

'Sarah Bell.'

'There's a gallery the other side of town, does the odd photography exhibition, Landscapes of the Lake District.' He hesitated, a moment's uncertainty, then the expression passed. 'Might not be your thing, but you should take a look while you're here. If you've time.'

Not an invite. Or was it? He licked his lips. Polite. Contained. She looked away, but his mouth stayed with her, soft, full, a film of sweat across his top lip.

'You didn't tell me yours,' she said, looking at him through curls of smoke.

'My what?'

'Name.'

'Oh. Robert.'

'So will you take me, Robert? To the gallery.'

'Me?' A flame of red around his collar. 'You're very direct, Sarah Bell.'

'Try to be.'

'You've rendered me almost speechless.' He laughed. 'Now that's rare.'

'You're lucky, happens to me all the time.'

'I doubt that.'

She smiled, picked up her camera and walked over to his table. 'There is one thing you can do for me. Is there anywhere round here I can get films processed?'

'Boots.' He swallowed. 'Up to the high street, then left, about halfway along. There's a couple that way, I think.'

'Thanks.' She paused, wondering whether she should ask him for his number. She'd heard 'no' – unspoken, but definitely no. 'Good luck with your work and . . . um . . . I'm sorry about –'

'No need.' He got up and took her hand firmly. The skin was warm, dry. 'I'm flattered, I mean pleased, pleased to have met you, Sarah.'

'I meant the cake?' She laughed. 'Sorry about the cake.'

# 5

She's got no idea what's going to hit her. Stupid Geordie. This is probably the only job in the whole world she can get which is why she's still here, but it doesn't matter because she hasn't got a clue. She's making eggs for breakfast, a special kind with pepper and Worcester sauce, except we don't have Worcester sauce. And there's orange juice. And coffee. She's looking for tomato ketchup, only she calls it red sauce.

'Aren't you hot?' she says, putting a plate of scrambled mess in front of me. 'With your jumper on, I mean?'

'I don't like eggs.'

She pulls out the chair opposite, scraping tiles.

'I said—'

'You don't like eggs. I heard.'

'So make me something else.'

'Make it yourself.' She stuffs her mouth and opens a magazine on the table.

'You're supposed to get me things. That's your JOB.'

She ignores me. It's a woman's magazine with pictures and hardly any words. A woman on a beach in a swimming costume and floaty material tied in a knot around her hips. Banish Your Beach Bulge.

'Banish your beach bulge,' I say. 'Eggs make you fat.'

'Don't care.'

'You're a girl.'

'Pleased you've noticed.'

'Girls . . . diet. They're always dieting.'

'Not me.' She licks ketchup off the back of her hand and turns the page. Tits. Pump them up Wonderbras.

Whatever. I wheel myself over to the cupboard, a low, easy-pull drawer where Mum keeps all my stuff. My own bowl, plate, mug, cereal. I take out my Frosties and tip some into the bowl. The effort makes me sweat, and I could do it now, but it isn't the right time. Not yet. When I get back to the table she's closed the magazine.

'What?' I shrug off her goggly stare. 'The people who write for those magazines are liars. Fat people are fat, that's it. They can't change. It's genetic.'

'What have you got against fat people? It's . . . what's the word . . . there's a name for it, like racism, only . . .'

'Fattism. Discrimination against people who are overweight. Don't they have schools in Newcastle?'

She takes her plate over to the sink.

'You know Alan Shearer?' I ask.

'The footballer? Not personally. Why? Do you like football?'

'I suppose you support Newcastle United?'

'Yeah, course. What about you, which team?'

'Football's for yobs and chavs.'

She doesn't bite.

'I was thinking, there's an art shop in town. I thought we could go, get you some new drawing stuff?'

'You thought wrong.'

'It's the school hols, don't you want to make the most of them?'

'I don't need you to babysit me.'

'No?'

'No.'

'What about your mates?' She squirts washing-up liquid into the sink. 'Haven't they got any plans?'

'Course they have.'

'So?' She waits. 'What've you got to lose? I wouldn't embarrass you if that's what you're worried about.'

'Look in the mirror.'

'It wouldn't kill you to . . .' She turns to face me, curling up her toes on the tiles. I feel it now, me getting to her. 'I was only thinking you might like to get out somewhere, that's all. Do something. No big deal.'

Which means it is.

'What about your dad? Do you still see him?'

'No.'

'He doesn't come here to visit you? You don't—'

'I don't visit him and he doesn't visit me. Anything else you'd like to know?'

'I know what it's like not to have a dad around, that's all.'

'You a bastard?'

'Matt.'

'If you're looking for something we've got in common, forget it. There isn't anything. You're just some lackey my mum hired because we can afford it.'

'I'm *trying* to be your friend.'

'I don't need a friend.' I wheel forward in my chair. 'When are you going to get it? I don't need *you*.'

'Hey, you're sweating.' She comes over, wiping her hands on a tea towel, and kneels beside me. 'What's wrong?'

'Nothing.' I straighten up and take a breath. 'I mean . . . I do feel a bit funny. Do you think you could open the patio door?'

She slides it across, coming back for me, but I'm already right behind her.

'Better?' Sorry on her face. 'Why don't we get this jumper off?'

'No!' I wheel myself outside as far as the gravel. 'I mean, just some air. Take me to the jetty?'

'I dunno, Matt.' She looks at me, at the lake. 'How about I make you a drink? Ice. I really think if you took—'

'Please. I'm not afraid.'

She thinks for a moment, then her face softens and I know she's working it out. Just this one thing to turn things around. Sarah the Carer and her friend, the cripple. Happy. Happy.

'Five minutes then, yeah?' She pushes me over the gravel and along the path at the side of the garden to the gate at the end. From there it's mud for about fifteen yards, brick hard so easy to get across, and then down to the wooden slats of the jetty itself. It's early, but already hot, heat glazing the hills with colour, like they've been painted on to the sky.

'All the way, to the end of the jetty.'

She's out of breath by the time we get there. I wait for her to start yapping, but for once she doesn't say anything. She doesn't spoil it.

'I think I will have that drink,' I say. She comes to the side of me. 'Please. If you don't mind?'

'Sure.' Relief on her mouth.

I listen for her footsteps on the slats behind me, the quieter slap of her flip-flops on the path, then the gate swings open and I'm alone. The lake takes tiny breaths, iron blue under the sun. I fold my arms on to my lap, close to me, like wings to make myself thin so that when I half close my eyes there's just me and a cocoon of water. It's as though I'm suspended above it for a long, slow second when everything's calm and still. Then it happens, a flash of something passes through me and I feel myself changing. The laughter I hear in the distance, children playing, a faraway boat bumping the water, everything bright and sharp like I'm hearing it and feeling it and seeing it all for the last time.

Then I do it. I release the brake.


A smack of cold water. Bubbles escape from my mouth, twisting and twirling away from me as I sink deeper. The water stings inside my nostrils, pressing into my eyes and contracting my mind until there is no sound. Only the thud-thud of my heart.

And dark.

I open my mouth, lips slack to the fog around me. A memory of dive-bombing off the end of the jetty, dripping on to the slats then going again, getting further each time. I made it as far as the reeds once, green eels that tickled me around the waist and swam through my legs. I pulled them up in my fists and waved them above my head and roared. I think about going there now, going deeper, but then I hear a scream, distorted yet loud enough to jolt me. A chain hangs loose from one of the jetty posts. I reach for it, stirring up a cloud of silt from the lake bed. Sarah's splashing. I wait, a second longer, then her arms are on me. Pulling. Urgent. Shouting.

'MATT! Jesus! HELP!'

Her eyes are black, glazed like a rabbit I once saw in a trap in Hopper's Wood. I gasp.

'HELP me somebody!'

Her hands pinch the skin under my arms as she hauls me to the shore, only a few feet, but she must be strong to have got me any distance at all. I cough.

'Matt? *Oh God.*'

She grabs me by the shoulders and pulls me forward into a sitting position, legs still in the water. Then she smacks me hard on the back, hard enough so that my body jerks forward. Wet air bags. I can see her nipples through her T-shirt. My mouth stays open, marvelling at the feel of one on my cheek.

I recognise the next voice instantly. It isn't as loud as Sarah's but that's because she's further away. Mum. I imagine her at the front door first, calling me as she comes through into the kitchen and discovers the patio doors open, then seeing two figures down by the jetty, backs shining like beetles.

She's beside me next, out of breath, pushing Sarah aside, a proper shove too. It sends her stumbling backwards into the water.

'Matthew? Oh, baby!'

I splutter and spit lake water on to her crisp, white blouse. 'I'm all right.'

She kisses me, pressing her lips hard to my forehead and for a second I'm irritated, like someone's scrubbed itching powder on to my skin, but then she holds me, talking in fast whispers. '*Oh God. Not again. Not again. Oh God. No, no, no.*'

'I'm not hurt. Nowhere hurts.'

I sip air, imagining how I might look to her, like Tom having an asthma attack, grey and cold as a fish.

'You're going to be all right, Matt, do you hear me?' She turns to Sarah. 'Lift his legs.'

The tone's fierce, a million accusations as yet unspoken, but I know they'll come. Later, when I'm in bed and I've drunk hot tea and Mum's stroked my hair until I fall asleep, she'll want to know what happened. She'll want to know what Sarah the Carer was doing putting me so close to the lake. Because you don't put someone in a wheelchair at the end of a jetty, brake off, and leave them there. You have to be on your guard, always, because of accidents.

They grunt and lift, faces screwed up with effort, Mum's heels getting stuck in the cracks between the pebbles. I watch their heads bob up and down against a cloudless sky.

'You'll have to get the wheelchair.'

'Yes, Mrs Logan.'

'What were you *thinking*?'

Several rooks lift off the large maple at the side of our garden, whipping the air and sounding their alarm.

'Look at me, Matt. Look at me.'

I don't remember falling asleep, but I suppose I must've done because when I open my eyes again I'm in bed and Mum and Sarah have gone. The door on one of the kitchen cupboards slams. Heels on tiles. Mum's voice, louder than Sarah's, but too faint to hear. I'm propped up on crisp, white pillows and there's a duvet tucked in tight under my arms. Not mine, Mum's, doubled over to make it thick. She's brought me her white throw, too. She used to give it to Tom when he had a chest infection, wrapping him up so tight you could only see his head.

Tired. I start to drift off again, thinking about Tom and all the times I've managed not to. I don't remember, that's how it is; I don't remember and I don't care. He's dead. That's all. Dead and gone and that's all there is. Only, now, I can't get him out of my head. It's as though he was there, waiting for me on the bed of the lake and I've brought him back. Here, his baby shampoo smell on the throw, calcifying me, following me, slowly into sleep.

# 6

Sarah waited for her to come off the phone to the doctor's surgery. 'Mrs Logan, I don't know what to say. I'm sorry.'

'I don't wish to discuss with you the details of what happened, only to say that it was extremely irresponsible of you to leave Matt unattended.'

'Mrs Logan—'

'*Please*.' She raised a hand. 'Dr Hardy will be here shortly.'

An overreaction. Matt was fine.

'What did you think you were *doing*? I told you he doesn't go near the lake.'

'I really am very sorry.'

Things had been going OK – not brilliant, but she'd accepted Matt's resistance and was confident that, with a bit of work, she'd get him to tolerate, if not truly accept, her. It was just a case of figuring out what he was comfortable with her doing and what he wanted to do for himself. There was middle ground and she'd told herself all she had to do was plant her feet firmly on it and Matt would ease up. Now this.

Mrs Logan was far away, unreachable. She'd made herself a drink – port – and changed into cords, but still wore the same blouse, a spray of water stains up the front.

'I really am very sorry. I shouldn't have left him alone, but—'

'After I told you about Matt not going near the lake. I *told* you, I said, "Matt doesn't go near the lake."'

'He wanted to go. He asked me to take him and then he said he wanted a drink so I put the brake on the chair and came back to the house to get him one.'

She had put the brake on. Years living with Nanna who was forgetful, clumsy, seriously accident-prone, had made her acutely aware of such things.

'I'm disappointed in you, Sarah. I don't mind telling you that you're younger than I would've liked, but you seemed mature enough to cope with the responsibility.'

'I put the brake on.' The only way Matt could've ended up in the lake was if he'd released the brake himself. She looked outside to the scene they'd not long left, but it showed nothing of what had happened, garden blanched in the oppressive heat. 'I realise how it looks, but Matt was wearing a jumper. Remember? A thick one. You took it off when we put him into bed. Yet it's really very hot. I think—'

'He's not supposed to go near the lake, Sarah.'

'Yes, but—'

'Accidents happen when you're not paying attention.

43

You clearly weren't. What was it? On the phone to your boyfriend?'

'I went to get him a glass of water.'

Sarah took herself through it again, the moment of panic when she glanced towards the jetty and saw Matt gone, wheelchair gone. Then the water, agitated, and the swell of panic she'd felt on realising what had happened. 'I think I was set up.'

'Found out more like!'

'Right.' The tick of the grandfather clock echoed through to them from the hall. 'Perhaps it would be best if I made a start on packing, Mrs Logan.'

'Wait.' She pressed her hands together to stop them shaking. 'Do you want to go? I mean, is it what you *want*? What if I said I wouldn't fire you? Would you tell me the truth?'

'If you want to fire me, fire me, but I'm not a liar.'

'No.' A laugh that dissipated quickly. She got up and walked across to the patio doors, tapping her nails on the side of her glass. 'You said he *asked* you to take him to the jetty?'

'Yes.'

'Why would he do that?'

'I don't know.'

'Was he frightened?'

'He didn't seem to be.'

'What then? Did he say anything at all?'

'He said he felt unwell.'

A long silence followed during which Sarah concentrated on the tasks ahead. It wouldn't take long to pack; she'd have to get whatever wages she was owed, barely enough to cover the petrol home. Or not home, another job . . .

'I knew he was down, depressed, but I didn't . . . I guess I didn't want to believe it's come to this. I had another son. Tom. He died in the accident on the lake. Almost a year now.'

Sarah was drawn to one of several photographs on the kitchen dresser. A small boy, fair-haired, fragile-looking. She'd noticed them before, when she'd been shown around, but for some reason hadn't thought enough of them to wonder who he was.

'Matt survived, obviously. Tom . . . He was seven.'

'I didn't realise.' T. Logan. Of course. 'I'm sorry.'

'Each of us grieves differently.' Mrs Logan took a breath, seeming for a second or two, not to be entirely in control of herself. When she spoke again her voice was harder. 'I think Matt may have meant to take his life.'

'*Suicide?*'

A car crunched on the gravel. Mrs Logan calmly rose to her feet and went to the door. Dr Hardy was over-weight, middle-aged, with a red face. He wiped his feet on the mat and mumbled a greeting. In his right hand he carried a large, leather holdall which he dropped at his feet, expecting to sit down first, perhaps, only Mrs Logan began to climb the stairs.

At first Sarah wasn't sure whether she should go with them or stay behind in the kitchen. In the end she took position behind Dr Hardy on the stairs, eyes fixed on the wide expanse of his back. The combination of his sweat and aftershave was so pungent she had to pause outside Matt's room to take a breath. She then stood quietly beside Mrs Logan at the end of Matt's bed while Dr Hardy opened his bag and took out a stethoscope.

'Now take a breath for me. That's it. Deep breath. And out again.'

Matt obeyed, his face turned up like a baby bird.

'I'm presuming he didn't lose consciousness?'

'No. Very tired though.'

When Dr Hardy had finished Matt sat back, and folded his arms. The colour had returned to his cheeks.

'Well, his chest sounds OK.' Dr Hardy wound up the stethoscope and put it back in the holdall. 'Keep him indoors and warm for the rest of today, and tomorrow he should be fine.'

'Doctor?' Mrs Logan lowered her voice and stepped away from the end of the bed. 'So he's fine . . .'

Sarah looked at Matt. His eyes were fixed on her, apparently in some close examination of her face. Just as she was about to look away he slowly and deliberately opened his mouth, stretching it wide as you'd normally only do for the dentist. He had a short, moist, fat tongue.

'Matt, love?' Mrs Logan turned to face him. 'The doctor would like to ask you a few more questions.'

'I'm *fine.*'

'If you've been feeling down, Dr Hardy can give you something to make you feel better.'

'I'm not down. I don't want any more pills.'

'The nightmares—'

'I'm FINE. Sarah took me to the jetty only she didn't put the brake on and I fell in. That's it.'

Dr Hardy sat on the bed again. 'You're quite sure about that, Matthew?'

'Positive.'

Sarah shook her head.

'She's lying! It was her fault. She——'

'All right. I think you've had enough excitement for one day, don't you?'

Sarah backed away from the bed and looked around casually. She didn't want to leave as she might still need to defend herself, but nor did she want to be obvious. A crunch. She'd trodden on his pencil case, a flat tin that now appeared to have a dent across the middle. She picked it up along with several drawings that lay on the carpet.

'How about you relax for a bit, get some rest?' Dr Hardy said.

'I'm just tired, that's all.'

'Of course you are.' He stood up. At the door he made a sign with his hand that suggested the three of them go downstairs to talk.

Sarah hastily put the drawings and Matt's pencil tin on the bed beside him and lost no time in following. Once in the kitchen, Mrs Logan pulled out a chair for Dr Hardy, but he refused with a polite wave of his hand.

'What's your take on it?' he asked, facing Sarah.

'I'm sorry,' Mrs Logan said. 'This is Sarah Bell. She's Matt's companion.'

Sarah nodded, vacant at this description of her role. She'd assumed she might have been introduced as Matt's carer, a title which had rather more importance than 'companion'. 'I'm not sure I can add anything. I mean, I'm not sure I could say anything useful about his . . . state of mind.'

'What about the brake?'

'On. Definitely.'

47

Sarah considered adding that she thought the whole thing was a ploy to get her into trouble, perhaps even get her fired. There'd been the note, too, and had it not now been somewhere at the bottom of the wheelie bin outside she might have produced it. But a lot had happened in a short space of time. A brother dead. Another one apparently suicidal.

Dr Hardy rubbed his palms together, polished skin, suggesting it was a habit. 'What do you think about Matt giving the therapy sessions another go, Gill?'

'Can't he just talk to you?'

'He needs to see a specialist.'

'He won't go back to Finch. He won't see him. Not after last time.'

'Somebody else then?'

'I could be wrong.'

A long silence ensued, but which didn't feel empty at all.

'Perhaps I'm reading too much into this,' Mrs Logan added finally. 'I don't know what he's thinking half the time. We've been doing fine without therapy.'

'Even that's a bit of a contradiction, don't you think? I'd say he's not being entirely open with you about how he's feeling.'

'You spent five minutes with him. How can you possibly know?'

'Just my impression.'

'Have you forgotten how it was with Finch?'

'There are others.'

'They're all the same.'

'I'll come up with an alternative.' Dr Hardy picked up

his holdall. 'The bottom line, Gill, is he needs to see someone. Do you agree?'

'Thank you for coming out so quickly.'

'Would you like me to talk to him about it now?'

'No.' She rose to her feet, brushing down the front of her cords with the palms of her hands.

'We could do it together?'

'No. Thank you.'

He paused, a moment's silence, then he followed her to the front door. There the conversation continued, quieter than before, but Sarah could still make out Mrs Logan's tight, defensive tone. Relieved not to be in the thick of it any more, and unable to say anything of use, Sarah made tea.

Several minutes later, Mrs Logan returned. 'I *swore* I'd have nothing more to do with them. I said I'd never go back. But I suppose I have to now, don't I?'

Sarah waited, unsure whether or not she was being asked for her opinion. If she wasn't fired, still unclear, then she supposed she ought to be in possession of all the facts. 'Have some tea.'

Mrs Logan stared at the mugs on the table, lost, suddenly, with the absence of any task to attend to. She slumped into a chair, motionless for a second, then began smoothing crumbs off a place mat.

'Who's Dr Finch?'

'A psychiatrist.'

'Someone Matt saw after the accident?'

'He couldn't remember what happened. It was Finch's job to get him to remember. There was a time I could've shaken it out of him, to know, but I've come to think

49

some things are so terrible you shouldn't have to remember them. It's pretty obvious what he and Tom were doing anyway. They rowed out to pitch a flag on the floating island. They found—'

'I've seen it. I mean, I think I saw a picture of it.'

'Probably. It's a local attraction, a small section of lake bed that rises to the surface periodically and sinks again a few weeks or months later.'

Sarah recalled what she could of the photograph she'd seen in the shop window. A Girl Guide waving a flag. Mrs Logan took a book from the dresser, leafed through the pages until she found what she was looking for, and handed it to Sarah. It was the same one, black and white, the figure of a girl in a wide-brimmed hat holding a Union Jack.

'It surfaces at the end of summer, not every year, usually after a particularly hot spell. It belonged to the Girl Guides originally, then someone else pitched a flag and it changed hands. Traditionally, whenever it appears someone claims it.'

Sarah put the book back.

'I promised Tom we'd do it one day, row out with our own flag. We didn't, of course. I was always waiting until he was well enough. He had asthma.' She drummed her fingers on the table. 'He couldn't run around without bringing on an attack, couldn't play outside if it was too cold, too hot. You know, normal things kids his age were doing.'

'I'm sorry.'

'I tell myself he was doing something he'd dreamed about for years.'

Sarah sipped her tea, but it was too hot and she drew back when it touched her lips. 'What happened with Dr Finch?'

'They said the therapy would be difficult, but it was more than that. I used to sit outside the room and wait while they talked. One day I heard screaming.' She narrowed her eyes on the kitchen door as though imagining herself there again. 'I burst in, wondering what the hell was going on, and there's Matt, sitting in his chair, screaming and screaming.'

'God.'

'Finch had just told him there was nothing wrong with his legs. That the whole thing, his paralysis, was in his head.'

'Made up?'

'Psychological.' She busied herself, furiously brushing the table with the palm of her hand. 'A mental reason for his condition instead of a physical one.'

'But he's in a wheelchair.'

'Someone mentioned a virus, but they dismissed that more or less straight away. Finch kept pushing for more therapy and I kept pushing for more tests. You've seen him.'

Sarah nodded, unsure as to what else she should do. It seemed to be the right response.

'The more therapy he had, the worse he got. Upset, hysterical at times. I didn't like what was happening to him so I brought him home.'

'What are you going to do now?'

'I don't know. He couldn't tell me how he was feeling and now this. It was the only way he knew to get my attention. I have to do something about that.'

Sarah was on shaky ground, searching for something

to say. She rolled the bottom of the mug over her palm, struck by a memory of Matt greeting his mother at the door. He'd tugged on the belt of her trousers, to attract her attention, but she was talking on her mobile and had ignored him.

'Do you want me to leave?' she asked.

'What? Oh. If you put the brake on, as you said you did, and he asked you to take him, then I suppose none of this is your fault.' She paused. 'I do know how persuasive he can be, Sarah. Sometimes you'll have to stand up to that. Can you?'

'Yes.'

'Well, then. We could certainly do with the help.'

# 7

'I can't, stupid!'

Tom's words or mine? I lie still, disorientated, checking for sounds, but there's only my breathing, heavy and fast. I hold it in my lungs, irritated by the noise of it, because I have to hear, I have to be sure. I make a slow arc, analysing the shapes behind the curtains, the floor at the side of my bed. I'm *awake*.

A person looks nothing like themselves when they're dead. It changes their face into an expression you never saw before. And it's weird. Like they're someone else.

'Matt?'

Eyes. Staring. Laced with red. I can't decide whether I'm frightened of them because they look so unfamiliar, or because they're working away at me, searching for something he knows he'll find. Fear.

'Matt?' Sarah lets go of my arms. 'You were dreaming.'

Dark. Night. 'What time is it?'

'Eleven.'

I swallow to wet my tongue. 'Where's Mum?'

'She went out for a while.' She picks up one of my pillows off the floor and puts it behind my head. 'Do you remember your dream?'

'Where?'

'I don't know.' She brushes hair from my eyes. 'It's OK. I'll stay with you for a while.'

'No.' I try to move the covers off.

'Let me help.'

'NO!' The bed feels wet. Sweat, please let it be sweat. 'I'm fine. Go.'

She stands up, but doesn't leave. 'It's not real, you know.'

'Der. I'm not stupid.'

She walks slowly around my room taking in the drawings on my desk, cocking her head to read the titles of books on the shelf above it. 'How long have you had nightmares?'

'Stop nosing in my stuff.'

She looks at a photograph on my pin board. Me and Dad launching the dinghy. It was raining. Wellies and Dad's heavy coat. Our hair's almost the same colour when it's wet. Sarah leans in to get a closer look, notices the fold and pulls it back to reveal Tom standing on the jetty, watching us, a life jacket tied around his waist with string.

'What are they about? Your nightmares.'

'Monsters.'

'What sort of monsters?'

'Japanese-speaking polar bears with machetes.'

'Only asking.'

'It's none of your business what they're about.'

She goes over to the window and looks through a gap in the curtains. The moon shines full on to her face. 'Why did you say I left the brake off on your wheelchair?'

Silence.

'Your mam and the doctor think you were trying to commit suicide.'

'They can think what they want.'

'Even if it means you'll have to see a psychiatrist?'

'You don't know the first thing about me. I won't see the stupid shrink. I don't have to. I don't do anything I don't want to do.'

'Really?'

'Really.'

She comes back to the bed and rests her hands on her hips. She has silver rings on nearly all of her fingers, even one on her thumb which makes a clicking sound when she taps it lightly on her belt. 'Want to know what I think?'

'No.'

'I think you were trying to get me fired.'

I smile.

'Why would you want rid of me so bad you would do something as dangerous as that? You're lucky you didn't drown. I'm not worth dying for.'

'I didn't die.'

'But it backfired, didn't it? You were trying to get me sacked only now everyone thinks you were trying to kill yourself. That's pretty stupid.'

'Finished?'

'Maybe you do need to see a shrink.'

'Piss off!'

'Only one thing I don't get. You could have any wheel-chair you want, you could have an electric one, sporty one, they do all types these days, but you're stuck in that. It's even got Broadman's painted on the back. Why?'

I bite down on my lip, taste for blood, but there's none.

'You're not the first person ever to have a disability. I'm not going to feel sorry for you, or tiptoe around you in case I say something that might upset you. It isn't me.'

'GET OUT!'

'It's like this. Bottom line? Your plan didn't work. I'm not going anywhere. And it doesn't matter what stunts you pull because—'

'Fuck you!'

'Fuck you, too.'

I chuck my pillow at her. She catches it and chucks it back, then she laughs. She bloody laughs. I think about throwing it again, but she's just standing there, grinning like it's a game. I don't know what to say.

'So. What's it gonna be? We got a deal or what?'

'There are no deals. There's only you, walking in here like you own the place, talking like you know me. You're arrogant. And rude.'

'And I'm your carer, or whatever you want to call me.'

'Interfering cow who can't take a hint.'

'I prefer Sarah.'

My head's throbbing, a torrent of words that won't come. She smiles again, comes to sit on the bed beside me. I could smack her one, but I just lie there, dumb.

'Anyway, while you're thinking about it you might as well have this.' She unzips her tracksuit top and pulls out a large, brown envelope. 'Call it a peace offering.'

'Not interested.'

'Take a look.'

Our conversation has diluted me. Why is she doing this? It's just a job, it's not like she owes Mum or me anything. Certainly not loyalty. It's just a *job*. Anger flares, but, like a cheap firework, fizzles out before it comes to anything. With nothing else to do I snatch the envelope out of her hand and tear it open at the seal. It's still damp from her tongue, the glue all warm and sticky. She waits, her eyes flicking from the envelope, to me, and back again. Inside are photographs, blown up to A4 size.

'I noticed all your drawings are of the lake; must get pretty boring doing the same thing all the time, so I thought you could try drawing from these instead.'

I flick through them, quickly, impatiently, then more slowly. I stare at one, a tree branch, or it could be a root, enlarged so you can see all the detail on the moss. Several kinds of moss, too, marbled dew stuck to fibre-like branches, another kind, like a blister, fat and soft.

'I thought you could try looking at things from a different perspective.' She takes the sleeve of her top and wipes it slowly across my forehead and down my left arm. 'Draw the detail, you know? Up close, see if you like it.'

Up close. Tiny hairs on my arm rise to greet her touch, like static, then fall away, rolled flat by the weight of her fingers.

'What do you reckon?'

The next photograph is of a large, chiselled stone, big enough to be one of the boulders that line the lake shore. There are marks on it, lime-green scabs.

'It's lichen.'

'I know what it is.'

The photographs blur in front of me, come back into focus again. She takes the ones I've looked at and taps them together. The rings on her fingers are the kind I've seen in the town hall when they put on the arts and crafts market. Two for a fiver, three for £7. Some have skulls with gems in the eye sockets, but she doesn't have one of those. She has one with two dolphins that meet at the middle, and another that's a snake, its tail zig-zagging as far up as her knuckle.

'So do you like them?' she asks.

They're pretty cool, but I'm not about to go all gushy. The last in the pile is a close-up of pebbles, brown and cream and blue, some almost white. On one, camouflaged so you can hardly see it, is something I recognise. I lean across to my lamp and hold the photograph under the light.

'What is it?' she asks.

My eyes meet hers and, for a second, I'm unable to look away. All I can think is blue eyes, a shade that looks as though it ought to be common, but I've never seen it before. Her breath on my cheek and a smell, not sharp and sweet like before, but different. Not perfume. Maybe just her, her smell.

'I'd have to look in my book to be sure, but it looks like it's a Mayfly larva. This is the shore?'

'Yep.'

'They live in the water usually. It must've been picked out by a bird and dropped or something.'

'Yeah?' She squints, tries to see what I see. 'Do you think you can draw from them, then?'

I shrug.

'Don't flatter me or anything.'

'They're OK.'

'Almost a compliment I suppose.' She gets up to leave, pats her knees. 'You'd be amazed what looking at something from a completely new perspective can do. Sometimes you get a surprise, something in the detail you weren't looking for.'

She pauses, giving her words a chance to sink in, then turns towards the door.

'Sarah.' The photographs are unexpected, and I want to say I haven't seen anything like them before. It's art, I suppose. Art that's just for me. 'All that stuff you said . . . about the nightmares. I know they're not real.'

'Thank God. I'd shit myself if I saw a Japanese-speaking polar bear waving a bloody machete.'

Her sense of humour is improving. 'Cheers anyway.'

'Don't mention it.'

'I'll see what I can do with them.'

She nods and turns towards the door.

'I'm not weird, you know. Whatever you might think.'

'Course you are. Get some sleep.'

# 8

Robert pulled up in front of the cottage and switched off the engine, pausing for a moment before getting out of the car. Better to survey the progress from outside first; he didn't want it to seem like he was checking up on them, though of course he was. The front bay window was out, boarded up, but not too well. He stepped out of the car, walked up to it and gave it a nudge. Seemed secure enough, but any burglar with an ounce of determination would be past it in no time.

The front door was open, junk mail in a heap behind it. He put it on the hall table to look at later. He'd developed a taste for it − tablets that made pond water clear, key rings that spoke to you when you dropped them − a solution for every need he didn't possess and none for those he did, but still he looked.

He went downstairs to find Derek Bowman. John, the younger of Derek's two boys, was sweeping the kitchen floor, or rather moving a large pile of debris and dust while he swayed his hips to the radio. Gary, John's brother and two or three years his senior, stood at the back door smoking a cigarette.

'Come to see how we're getting on, sir?' Derek climbed down a stepladder and shook Robert's hand. He was a small, muscular man with thick-rimmed glasses and a pointed chin. 'Turn that bloody racket off, will you?'

John switched the radio off and joined Gary outside.

'I was just passing,' Robert said. 'When do you think you'll get the glass in the front?'

'Can't touch it until someone from the surveyor's department's been to approve the work. Said they'd try to get here tomorrow.'

'Ah. I didn't know I needed approval.'

'Old windows. Need permission. I'll give them a call in the morning. Won't take us long to get it in once they've been.'

Maybe he ought to spend the night. 'The front door was open. Perhaps you—'

'Gary?' No answer. Derek yelled again. 'You been out the front?'

Gary put his head around the back door and gave a nonchalant shrug.

'When do you think you'll be finished?' Robert asked.

'All of it? Well, there's the roof.' He rubbed the back of his neck. 'We'll start on that when we've finished the windows. In here shouldn't take too long. Two weeks ought to do the lot.'

Had Derek been asked to tear down the cottage and build it back up again from scratch he'd have said two weeks. If he'd said three, or even four, for the work that needed doing, Robert might've believed it. The sooner the better. He longed for the work to be completed so he could get the For Sale sign up. They'd shared a lot of happy times here, he and Elizabeth. Except for a few weeks last August, their visits had always been in the winter months and as such his memories were tuned to brisk, cold walks beside the lake and numerous silent hours spent working beside the stove while she painted vases and plates. It ought to have made coming back now, at the height of summer, easier, but he still heard the wheezing of the potter's wheel, still saw her face, cheek-bones smudged with clay dust. In the end, after two nights in which he'd barely slept, he abandoned the idea of living at the cottage while the work was being done and booked himself into Wellman's, surrounding himself with comforting, impersonal space.

He climbed the stairs to the master bedroom. The mattress was bare, stripped down after their last visit. He longed to press his face against it and breathe deeply in the hope that some of her smell remained locked in the fibres. Instead he sat on the floor. The sadness at her leaving, in its simplest form, wasn't anger or bewilderment over the choice she'd made, but certainty, the physical reality of what it meant, her absent voice, the soft pad of her feet across the landing, a flush of the toilet downstairs. It was still capable of overwhelming him, suddenly and without warning, like grief. At times he had to remind himself Elizabeth was still alive, not dead, just somewhere else, living another life, or as it often felt, the other part of his life.

He forced his mind elsewhere, to unrelated thoughts and feelings powerful enough to jolt him. Curiously his thoughts turned immediately to the girl in the café. Of holding her breasts while she sat on top of him, fucking him on the bare mattress, of her leaning down and feathering his pale chest with her red hair. He cupped his hands over his balls, both alarmed and ashamed by the sudden arousal, yet eager to hold on to it. Not to endure the pain of guilt and inadequacy that infected each day, but to feel something else, pleasure, joy. Something.

Sarah Bell. He caught his breath at the thought of her slow lean across the table for the ashtray, the provocative gaze that rested on him while she lit her cigarette. An obvious, almost hilarious display of flirtation, and yet he'd been reeled in, almost struck dumb. He wondered now whether his discomfort was due to being toyed with by a woman, a young woman at that, or to his inability to capitalise on the opportunity.

And yet he'd chatted, made noises of encouragement and interest, done all the things he was once good at. For a few minutes he'd climbed out of the refuge he'd carved for himself and forgotten his life. He'd seen only Sarah. She was beautiful in a primal, fleshy way. That big, placid mouth, liquid eyes. Now, as the corny image of her finger circling the plate for leftover cream repeated itself in his mind, he felt both aroused and, at the same time, hollowed. He thought of the empty evening ahead, of all the empty evenings that would follow it. He stood up, heart pumping hard. She was simple and sweet, but not a serious prospect.

Outside it had become cooler. He decided to leave his car at the cottage and walk the mile or so back to the hotel where he'd grab a quick meal in the bar and retire to his room to read. Despite the intention it was an unlikely prospect; he was much more inclined to lie in bed nursing a brandy on his chest and watching endless repeats of the news until he fell asleep.

'Robert?' A car pulled up beside him. Terence Hardy leaned out of the driver's side window. 'God, I thought it was you.' He switched off the engine and got out to shake Robert's hand.

'Terry.' He ought to have phoned. 'Good to see you.'

'How are you?'

'Oh, fine. Fine.'

'When did you arrive?'

'Not long ago. How's Jane and er . . . ?'

'Laura. She starts medical school this September. Still wants to be a GP like her dad if you can believe it. Tried talking her out of it, of course.'

A memory of a teenage girl building a snowman in Terry's back garden. Thirteen, fourteen perhaps. He tried to widen the image so that it included Elizabeth, but he saw only Terry, thinner, laughing as Laura chucked hand-fuls of snow at him. They'd seen Terry and Jane more recently of course. Last summer? As long ago as that. He'd kept in touch at first, the odd phone call, but it had been months since the last.

'You're staying a while?'

'The cottage needs a bit of work before I can put it on the market.'

'I am sorry, Robert. You and Elizabeth seemed so . . .

solid.' He shrugged off a moment's uncomfortable silence with a glance to his watch. 'Still, the cottage ought to fetch a good price. Why don't you come and have supper with us?'

'Ah . . .'

'Jane would love to see you. Tonight?'

Cornered.

'Around eight?'

'Of course. I'd be glad to.'

'Excellent. I'm on call, so I better get moving. See you tonight.'

There were papers spread out on the passenger seat and, unusually for Terry, he looked flustered. He lowered himself awkwardly into his car and wrestled with the seatbelt.

'See you.' He tapped the roof of Terry's car and watched him drive away, but before he'd even reached the end of the street Robert found himself thinking of excuses to cancel. There was comfort huddled in his dark fog, making no demands of himself. He functioned in the ways he needed to function and felt content. He didn't call friends any more. He read a lot, book after book until the stories merged together. And he worked, without the dedication he'd once displayed, but giving a good seventy to eighty per cent to his patients most of the time. Dinner would mean sustained conversation, an internal prod and poke, and, worst of all, an acknowledgement of his new, single status.

Ironic that had he and Elizabeth stayed together, he'd feel exactly the same. She'd seen the twins once, shortly after they were born. What would they be now? Three? He'd hoped she'd eventually be able to see them for what they were. Not a reminder, not pain, the injustice of Jane, in her forties, one child already in her teens, suddenly, and unexpectedly, becoming pregnant again.

On reaching the hotel he went up to his room, poured himself a vodka, neat, from the drinks cabinet and ran a bath. When the water in the tub was as hot as he could stand it, he climbed in. Terry and Jane were good people, kind. Dinner with them was perfectly ordinary, but nevertheless the thought was exhausting. He let his head fall back and allowed himself to drift, finding distance from the evening ahead in that formless place between asleep and awake.

He was brought to his senses by a ringing, an unfamiliar, alien sound that he disregarded until he gained a sense of where he was. He sat bolt upright, cramp shooting down the back of his thighs, but before he could get out the ringing stopped.

Perhaps they were phoning to cancel. Bugger.

He lay back and looked at his body, overlaid with black hair, thickest on his chest and funnelling down his stomach to his groin. The head of his cock rose up from the foam and broke the surface. He held it firmly, gratified to find it hardening and closed his eyes, allowing out of curiosity, the image of Sarah to return to his mind. Pink, pliant lips, the blue and grey dolphin tattoo he'd noticed on her right shoulder, shimmering under soapsuds. Then looking up at him, eyes cheap blue, and that unremittingly playful gaze.

By the time he'd shaved and dressed it was almost seven-thirty and suspecting the phone call wasn't Terry – he'd not mentioned he was staying at the hotel – he walked the mile or so to their house. It was a former mill they'd restored themselves and whenever he visited he was astonished at the care and attention they'd lavished on the place.

He stepped over a yellow digger on the driveway, feeling, as he did so, a familiar twinge. He still wanted a child; saw him on the shoulders of other men, balloon in one hand, ice-cream in the other. Snapshot heaven. Only now it was removed from possibility and, at times, after hours or a day when he wasn't reminded in some way, the weight of the longing was absent too. He wondered whether it wasn't through Elizabeth's eyes he saw the digger. Her pain.

'Robert!' Jane kissed him warmly. 'It's so good to see you. I was quite cross when I heard you were here. Why didn't you ring?'

He held up the wine he'd bought on the way. 'It's only from Spar, I'm afraid.'

'Come in, come in.' She led him through to the lounge, glancing back at him. 'You look great. But then you always were pretty fit. One of Laura's words, everything's either *fit* or a *nightmare*. Red or white?'

'Red, thanks.'

'Terry's on bed duty. He won't be a sec.' She looked tired. Upstairs he heard the heavy tread of Terry's feet followed by the light patter of the children's. A few moments later he appeared in the lounge, out of breath.

'Robert, you made it.' He sounded surprised. 'Got a drink?'

'Thanks, it's coming. The twins are three now, right?'

'Four. Sleep about twenty minutes a night, draw on the walls the rest of the time.'

'Once,' Jane said, sailing between them. She handed Terry a pint of bitter and Robert his wine. 'They're good boys.'

A thud of something hitting the floor.

'I'll go,' Terry said.

'Stay, dinner's nearly done.'

'Can I do anything?' Robert asked. He hoped he couldn't. He got up, only to sit down again when Jane touched his shoulder. She disappeared upstairs.

'How long are you taking from work?' Terry asked. He slumped heavily into the armchair opposite, pulling at the cloth between his thighs which had stretched tight.

'A month at least. I'm owed a fair bit. How's the practice?'

'Well, at the moment. I've just taken on a new partner. A woman.' He paused as though considering it. 'The idea is I spend less time at work and more time at home, but it hasn't quite worked out that way. I seem to have combined the whole thing with the installation of a new computer system. Mayhem.' He took a large mouthful from his pint, leaving a crest of foam on his top lip he seemed happy to ignore. 'Actually, now we've got a minute. I wondered if I might trouble you for a favour.'

'Oh?'

'A patient. You remember Tom Logan, the kid who drowned in the lake last summer?'

'Vaguely.'

'It's his brother, Matthew.'

The name was familiar. He and Elizabeth had come to the cottage to recuperate, reeling from the failure of their fifth IVF cycle. He'd gone to the newsagent to buy milk and seen a picture of the floating island on the front page of the *Lakeland Echo*, the dark shape of the reeds that knotted its surface. He hadn't mentioned it to Elizabeth on his return to the cottage, though he must've told her at some point.

'He's been wheelchair-bound since the accident. No damage to the spine. Mother believes it was a virus, but there's no evidence to support that. Anyway, he threw himself into the lake last week. Survived, but—'

'Suicide attempt?'

'Looks like it.'

A door closed upstairs.

'I'd appreciate your take on it.'

'I'm not here to work.'

'It would mean a lot. Anyway, you're always working.'

'Except when I'm on leave.'

'We could talk it over tomorrow? Talk. A drink after work?'

'Yes. All right.' He tried to keep his voice light, but felt a stab of irritation at having given in so easily.

'I thought we could eat in the conservatory,' Jane said, reappearing. 'I do love these warm evenings, don't you?'

Over coffee the inevitable questions about Elizabeth arose, but Robert, with several glasses of wine inside him, felt surprisingly relaxed. He poured another glass for himself and Jane while Terry disappeared into the kitchen to load the dishwasher.

'Don't mind him,' Jane said. 'You know what he's like with this sort of stuff.'

He presumed the 'stuff' meant infertility talk. He'd thought it was a macho thing at first, but Terry just didn't know what to do with the information. It wasn't part of his repertoire. Jane did birthday cards, teacher–parent meetings, baby-related stuff. And, it seemed, friends with dodgy sperm.

'Do you hear from her at all?' Jane asked.

'Now and then.'

'At least you've managed to keep things amicable.'

'Oh, more than that.' He shrank from Jane's words. 'I just think the resentment got too much for her.'

'Resentment of you? That isn't fair.'

'No. But the fact is she wanted a child and I couldn't give her one. Even if we could've made ourselves go on, the next treatment would only have had a five per cent chance of success. Someone had to say "stop". It was me.'

'And she can't forgive you? I don't know, Robert, is that what it really comes down to? It's not like you got married to have children.'

'No.' He hadn't. Elizabeth might've done.

'You can't make something of your lives together? Just the two of you?'

'I think it was the treatments that kept us together. The hope. I've often thought we were comrades, more like two soldiers coming home from a war than man and wife.'

'So that's it?'

'I guess so.'

'It doesn't work, so you separate?'

'Your witness, m'lord.' He tried to laugh, but he'd sounded too sharp. 'Sorry.'

'I don't mean to interrogate. It just seems so unlikely.'

He smiled at this.

'Did you try talking to someone, counselling?'

'I wanted to, she didn't, couldn't. Think you can cite lousy sperm on divorce papers?'

'Robert.'

'That's what it amounts to.'

'You're angry.'

'Yes, I suppose I am. I don't want to be.' He swallowed. 'Anyway, there it is.'

'Terry says you're selling the cottage?'

'And the house, though I'll keep it on for a while. I'm not looking forward to that. It's going to be quite a job just to clear the cottage.' An image of the Christmas tree at the bottom of the garden, bald branches. 'It all went to shit pretty quickly in the end.'

'Bring her things here, if you like. I've got to go to Newcastle in a couple of weeks I could—'

'She isn't there. Moved into her sister's flat in London five, six months ago.'

Jane squeezed his hand.

'I'm fine,' Robert said, reaching for his glass. 'Honestly.'

'You can't blame yourself. You don't, do you?'

He shrugged.

'You're still young.' She tapped him playfully on the arm. 'There *are* possibilities, Robert, not—'

He raised an eyebrow.

'Not *every* woman wants children. It shouldn't stop you having relationships.'

'It doesn't.' He thought of his brief foray into Newcastle's Bigg Market one Saturday evening a few months back. A sea of stretch-marked midriffs that had sent him out on to the street gasping.

'Early days,' she said, after a silence.

To his relief Terry came back into the room, setting down a fresh bottle of wine. 'I hope you'll take a look at my latest project before you get too drunk.'

Jane rolled her eyes. 'He's bought a fountain, enormous

71

bloody great thing it is. Cost a fortune. I don't know what he was thinking, sent him out for a paddling pool and he came back with bloody Niagara.'

Robert smiled, glad the conversation had moved on. Yet later, walking back to the hotel, he felt frustrated. It was easy to oversimplify what had happened to his marriage. They wanted a child; he was infertile so she left him. Edited down, that's what people thought. Relationships broke down because people drifted apart, not because they got too close. But that's what had happened to them. In the white heat of their misery he and Elizabeth had welded together, becoming a shapeless mass – the damage to their marriage had been inflicted not by distance, but by excessive closeness. And he couldn't explain that to anybody. Except Elizabeth. And she didn't need an explanation.

# 9

I wet the bed again last night, the third time this month. If it wasn't for the fact that Mum saw to it instead of Sarah, stripping the sheets and washing me down, I'd still be there, in my stinky piss room, too ashamed to come out. Certainly not here, watching Sarah get ready. We're going to the Bird of Prey Centre in Harley. It's exactly twenty-three miles away so if she drives at an average speed of forty miles per hour, we'll have forty minutes together in the car as well as the hour-long session with Matilda. She's a European Eagle Owl, their star attraction. The website says they often have a wingspan of two metres and can live to be as old as forty.

I listen at the door to Sarah's room, holding my breath as the last song ends, Abba's 'Thank You for the Music', and the next one, 'Waterloo', starts. A gap in the door, only a few centimetres wide, shows me glimpses of her as she moves to and from the bed. She joins in at the chorus . . . 'Couldn't Escape if I Wanted to . . .'

She has their greatest hits. Volumes One and Two.

It's weird how right in the middle of things getting messed up, you can feel normal. There's a new psychiatrist, someone Dr Hardy knows, and Mum says I've got to see him or she'll go out of her mind. That's what she said. And yet now, in a minute that seems to last as long as I want it to, I don't have to think about that. I'm awake. I don't have to go to school. And I've got 'Waterloo', and watching Sarah dance in pink underwear.

'Are you sure you won't come, Mum?' I ask, several minutes later when we're ready to go.

'No, love. But you two have a nice time.' Her hand feels rigid on my shoulders. 'And enjoy yourself, hey?'

She probably didn't get back to sleep after she returned to bed. I made her worry, but now I want to say, 'It's OK, see.' But it isn't.

'We'll probably stop off on the way back,' Sarah says. She takes the keys for the Volvo from a bamboo basket on top of the fridge and waits, glancing at me, then Mum. 'Have some lunch, if that's all right?'

'I can stay. I'll stay with you, Mum.'

'Don't be silly, Matthew. Besides, you know I have to go into work. That'll be fine, Sarah. Here's a bit extra.'

She hands Sarah a twenty from her purse and the moment has gone. They're buzzing around me now, talking about the best route, where's a good place to stop for lunch, somewhere with a beer garden, Sarah'll take her camera. But what if something happens? What if we have a car accident, and the car catches fire and I can't get out? Or we get lost, we run out of petrol and Sarah's phone doesn't work and—

'What on earth's the matter?' Mum looks at me, exasperated.

I open my mouth to speak, but nothing comes out.

'Don't worry,' Sarah says, pushing me out of the door. 'We'll have a great time, won't we?'

And then we're outside, engulfed in a wave of heat, pushing tracks through the gravel to the car. Me and Sarah. Going out.

'I saw a great pub on the way over here. I think that had a beer garden. We'll pig out, eh?'

Till our bellies burst. And we'll drink lager and smoke cigarettes. She opens the passenger side door, unaware Mum usually puts me in the back. It's an easier angle because I can hold on to the seat in front and lower myself in. But I want to sit up front.

'Lean on my shoulder. That's it.'

I hold on, a slow dance. Her cheek brushes against mine and I smell her deodorant, a spray kind in a thin can called Impulse, which she keeps on the dresser in her room next to two lipsticks called Sugar Rush and Plum Dandy. My other arm searches for something, but the dashboard is smooth and flat and she struggles to hold me. I fall in and knock my head on the handbrake.

'Shit. Sorry, Matt.'

'It's fine.'

I try to push myself with my arms, but they're trembling, no use. I can only wait, staring into the footwell at Mum's driving shoes, breathing in mouthfuls of their old sweat, while Sarah lifts and turns my legs into position.

'There!' She secures the wheelchair in the boot and gets in the driver's side, fiddling with unfamiliar knobs until she finds the one for the air-conditioning. At first it just blows hot air over the sweat on my face and neck, but as we pull on to the road at the end of our drive, it gets cooler.

'Do you want to listen to some music?' I ask.

'Yeah.' She stuffs two oblongs of chewing gum into her mouth. 'Why not?'

Mum's tapes are all over the place, some inside their cases, others loose in the glove box. Some lipstick, too, but in a colour I haven't seen before, and a small bottle of perfume. Most of the tapes are classical with pictures of green landscapes on the sleeves. I should've brought my Black Eyed Peas, but of course it's on CD and Mum doesn't have a CD player in the car. We brake suddenly and I'm pushed into my seatbelt.

'Nearly missed it!' Sarah takes a sharp left, signposted Harley, and accelerates along the narrow road. This is the scenic route, and longer, but I don't think she knows. I grip the handle on the door as she approaches another corner, fast, braking hard just before it. Once around the bend she picks up speed again, scuffing over bumps and bends in the road like they're not there. Gear up, gear down. All the while she's chewing, pausing when she gets to a bit where she has to concentrate, chewing again when we're on an open stretch. It makes me want to laugh. I take a breath.

'You all right?' She glances across.

'Wicked.'

'Wicked, hey? Good to get out of the house?'

'Yep.' I set the radio to scan, stop it, and go back when I hear a song I recognise. 'Money, money, money, it's so funny . . .'

She laughs.

I made her laugh. 'Abba's brilliant.'

'No way?' She grins. 'I love Abba. I like all the old ones. What else are you into?'

'Old ones. You know . . .' I try to think of some. 'Elvis, and what's his name, Billie Holiday, stuff like that.'

She gives me a funny look.

'So where did you learn photography?'

'Nowhere. My dad bought me a camera for my birthday. Some bloke offered it to him in the Rose and Crown, it's this pub at the end of our street. I don't think he knew what to get me. Does the job till I can get something better.'

I picture her house, Yorkshire pudding mix bubbling in the oven while Dad's down the pub, and Sarah, in her bedroom, dancing. 'You should send him the ones you took of around the lake. I bet he'd like to see them.'

'Yeah.' She hesitates. 'Only he didn't just *buy* the knock-off stuff, know what I mean?'

No. She turns back to the road, different, eyes narrowed and a frown. She opens her mouth to say something else, but stops and a silence opens up. I want to know if she means her dad's in prison, but the moment passes and I turn to look out of the window, feeling I must've crossed some line. At the side of the road the fields fall away, a steep descent to the River Sway, glistening a snail trail through the valley.

77

'There are five species of owl in the UK, did you know that?'

'No, I didn't.' She smiles. 'You know a lot of stuff like that, don't you? Like that insect, what's it—'

'Mayfly. Most people just think creepy crawly, you know? But insects are amazing. If we died out, like got a virus that nobody could cure and it wiped out the whole of the human race, they'd take over. Insects. Rats, too, probably.'

'Yeah?' She bullets her chewing gum out of the window. 'I hate rats.'

'You wouldn't if you knew more about them, you have to admire something that can live anywhere, eat anything, and still thrive.'

She taps her fingers on the steering wheel.

'You can smoke a cigarette, if you want to. I won't tell Mum.'

She looks surprised, like how do I know she smokes. 'I'll leave the window open then. Your mam'll freak if the car stinks of tabs.'

I smile at our secret and at the thought we might have more secrets together. I watch her light it, take a drag. Her lips leave a band of Plum Dandy on the filter.

By the time we reach the Bird of Prey Centre the sky's darkened to slush. A light drizzle flecks the windscreen. Sarah hands me a heavy green waterproof jacket from the boot, Dad's. She must've taken it from the cupboard in the hall thinking it was mine. A whiff of oil on the cuffs and a memory of him working out on the jetty in the rain.

The entrance is too narrow for my chair.

'I'll get them to unlock the gate,' she says, disappearing into a small hut. A moment later she's back with a tall man dressed in camouflage trousers and boots like they wear in the army. He looks young, apart from his mouth which is bracketed by deep creases. He unlocks the padlock with a key from a large bunch, brushing dark fringe out of his eyes.

'There's loads,' Sarah says, skipping over to me. 'All the way along the back there.'

She goes to push the chair, but I wave her off and follow her and the man through the gate. His name's Gavin, he tells Sarah when we reach the first enclosure.

'Ah, Matt. Look, there's an owl.'

'Western Screech Owl,' Gavin says, smiling into his creases.

There must be twenty or thirty enclosures, some low on the ground with just a pole across the centre where the birds sit, others with trees and boxes inside where they can hide. I put a hand up to the wire mesh of the first one, see nothing at first, then a pair of yellow eyes. Gavin and Sarah have already moved along to the next one, but I can't go any further because the path turns to gravel. I roll into it and get stuck.

'You know how you tell what sort of predator they are?' Gavin says.

Sarah shakes her head.

'The eyes. Yellow means they hunt during the day, dark eyes means they hunt at night, and orange—'

'At dawn,' I say, finishing for him. They turn to look at me. Sarah sees the gravel and comes over, sorry on her face. 'Actually, if their eyes are orange, then they're crepuscular – they hunt at dawn and at dusk. Owls' ears aren't the same level either.'

Gavin looks blank.

'Yeah,' I carry on, pushing down on my wheels. 'They're asymmetric. Work a bit like a radar, so they can pinpoint the smallest sound even in the dark, a tiny rustle in the leaves, or under snow.'

'Cool,' Sarah says.

'He'll be after my job next,' Gavin says, flashing teeth at Sarah. 'How'd you like to fly one? You can help with the demonstration if you like?'

'Brilliant! We'd love to, wouldn't we, Matt?'

I check Gavin's reaction, but I'm pretty sure the invitation isn't for me.

'I'll get Matilda,' he says and sprints away up the path.

Sarah and I continue along the line of enclosures, peering into each one. There are no signs to say what the birds are, but I know some of them. A Bateleur Eagle. A Lugger Falcon. A Kookaburra. I tell her about their talons and where the different species come from. Those I haven't read about on the Internet we skip over. She listens, leaning down close to me so she can hear what I'm saying over the crowd gathering at the far end of the enclosures. Gavin catches our eye and waves us over.

The spot where they fly the birds is up an incline, but he doesn't help to pull me up so we have to go backwards, people parting to let us through. When we get to the top I'm red-faced, embarrassed everyone has had to wait, but then he gets the European Eagle Owl on his glove and everybody looks at it instead of at me.

'Say "hi", Matilda.' Gavin strokes her chest and signals for others to do the same, then he brings her down to me. She flaps her wings, settling on his glove. Sarah gets her camera out.

'Put your hand in there,' he says to me, indicating the back of Matilda's head.

I do it, feeling through soft, russet-coloured feathers until I reach the skull. 'Now you, Sarah. It's amazing.'

Sarah does it and laughs, surprise spreading over her face. The rain has darkened her hair, turning it the same colour as her lips.

'Put this glove on.' Gavin hands Sarah a suede glove he takes from his belt and sends Matilda away to another man, older than Gavin, who waits over a fence at the far end of a field. When I turn back I see Gavin's holding Sarah's arm, gripping it tightly with his right hand. The knuckles are dry, nails bitten down to raw cuticles.

'You're going to take her on your arm, OK? Just keep it up, like this.'

Sarah nods, nervous, smiling, and Gavin moves her arm in a short, upward motion, which is Matilda's signal to return. She makes a low, straight glide back to us, wings closing in around our heads at the last second, then she lightly drops on to Sarah's arm.

'She's so light! You wouldn't think she'd be so light.'

Gavin takes more meat out of a suede bag he wears like a belt and lays it across Sarah's glove. Cockerels, culled at one day old.

'Can Matt have a go?' she asks.

'Not sure if she'll register the change in height.' He looks at me, at Sarah, at the group of onlookers. 'We'll try it, though, give it a go, eh?'

'You can't describe it, Matt. It's a brilliant feeling.'

There are cuddles on everyone's faces, loving Gavin for being so nice to the kid in the chair. I want to go back to the enclosures, just me and Sarah like before, not to help with the demonstration, just us talking quietly. Gavin drops another glove in my lap and says something to Sarah, just for her.

'Off you go, girl.'

He pushes Sarah's arm away from her chest. He looks big under his waxy jacket and heavy boots, but I bet he isn't. Inside he's probably thin and weedy and pale.

'OK, mate. Matt, isn't it?'

'Yeah.' I sit up straight in my seat and hold my arm up, like Sarah. Gavin asks the others to stand back, then he waves at the man in the field and Matilda begins her glide towards us. For a moment all I can think about is how amazing she is, feathers curled up to the wind, feet the size of fists, but then she's above me, braking sharply. A shriek from a woman in the group, then an excited giggle as Matilda flaps over their ducking heads, her mouth open to show a pink sliver of tongue. She settles on the roof of an enclosure nearby.

'Now then, Matilda.' Gavin makes a noise, a throaty sound that's not really a word, and she flies back to his arm. 'You've done it before, girl. Not for a while, though, hey?'

The crowd murmur, sympathetic to Gavin, to Matilda, to me.

'Shall we give her another go?'

It's a challenge now. He wants the others to be part of it, to cheer him on. Sarah's lips are tight with worry. I lower my head, feeling the glare of predatory eyes, brown and yellow and orange. Sarah kneels down beside me, her soft breathing becoming quicker, willing Gavin to make it right.

'Come, Matilda!' Gavin waves my arm from side to side, blood-spotted flesh waggling between my fingers. She hovers longer this time, but drops to ground and lumbers across the gravel in a confused panic. A moment's silence, then everyone laughs and Matilda steps up on to Gavin's arm.

'Can we go now?'

Sarah whispers neverminds and doesn't matters and OKs. Gavin creases his face. He tried and he thinks that gets him points with Sarah, but she's not stupid. She isn't going to fall—

'Thanks, Gavin.' She pats his shoulder.

'She's done it before, you know, I don't get it.' A brief glance at me, then back to Sarah. 'It must be the chair.'

'You tried, that's the main thing, and we both appreciate it, don't we, Matt?'

'Perhaps you could come back another day? Perhaps try one of the other birds?'

I want to smash his shag-me face in.

'We'd like that.'

'I WANT TO GO.' They look at me, a blood-red cherry in a chair.

My hands slip on the spokes and I start to roll down the slope.

'Matt, wait!' Sarah grabs the handles.

The momentum of me going forward is too much for her and in the end she's forced to come with me, feet slapping on the path until we reach the gravel around the enclosures and I have to slow down. The sweat's running down my back, between my shoulder blades and into my pants, across my chest too, and down my arms. It isn't until we get back to the car I realise the wet between my fingers is blood, closing around my fingers like a glove. So much of it and so red that it doesn't look real.

'Sorry,' I say.

She takes the sleeve of her top, wets it in her mouth, and rubs around the scab on my knuckle to get a better look. She looks sad, but not for me, just concerned in her eyes, in the tightness of her mouth.

'You must think I'm weird.'

'No, I don't.'

'They do.' I turn my head in the direction of the enclosures behind us, voices, a laugh. 'They'll be thinking, "Check out the kid in the chair, even the birds think he's a freak."'

'You're not a freak.'

She sucks in her bottom lip, wetting it, then it spreads into a smile. Spreading into me. I don't know where to look, except at her mouth, holding on to the seconds as they pass, not speaking.

She still has hold of my hand. 'Does it hurt?'

'No.'

She spits on to her sleeve and cleans away more of the blood. I wonder if she tastes it on her tongue. The thought cools me, a part of the inside of me is touching her. And her saliva, *inside* me. I close my eyes and feel it, Sarah in my veins, coursing up my arms to my chest.

'Let's get you in the car. Ah, man, would you look at that?' She frowns at the sky. The clouds are even darker than before, thick as chimney smoke. 'I don't think we'll be doing our pig-out today.'

She busies herself around me, a frantic rush against the rain. It gets heavy quickly, flushed from the dark clouds above and landing like a thousand tin hammers on the roof of the car. Her touch, ecstasy a few seconds ago, becomes an agonising fumble and jolt of necessary actions. The lift and push and pull of wasted flesh in tight, wet clothes. Once I'm strapped into the car I wait, watching her through the rear-view mirror, face screwed up with effort as she shoves the chair into the narrow space, and slams the boot shut.

# 10

'What do you prefer? Matt or Matthew?'

'Matt.'

We're in the staff room in Dr Hardy's surgery. The lockers, kitchen worktop stained with rings, months-old magazines in piles on the floor, it all reeks of incidental, unimportant chat, a break from important things, rather than a focus on them. Dr Mason sits on one of the low armchairs and turns to a fresh page on his notepad – yellow paper like lawyers use. He writes something, underlines it and rubs his nose. There's a slight indent on the bridge, suggesting he wears glasses. But not all the time. And not today. He's clean-shaven with neat sideburns flecked with grey and his eyebrows are thick and dark, but not wiry like Dr Hardy's.

'It must be nice to be off school, Matt.'

'It's OK.'

'Do you have a favourite subject?'

'Art.'

'What do you like about art?'

'Dunno.'

'What about outside school? What do you enjoy doing?'

'Games.'

'Board games?'

'Computer.'

'You play them with your mates?'

'No.'

'Why not?'

'Got none.'

The fingers on my right hand tap lightly on the spokes. Dr Mason sees it so I stop, then I start again. Finch asked me about school, too. I think there must be a list every psychiatrist uses – ask about school – tick the box – ask about hobbies – tick the box. They don't really care what answers you give – unless you say something that gets the alarm bells ringing, like not having any mates, Riiiiinng! Then they write it down. Dr Mason's writing.

'I thought it might be useful to go over what you can expect from me today. OK?'

'I know what to expect. You ask questions.'

'That's part of it. Does it worry you?'

'No.' I glance at the folder on his lap, a thick wad of pages scuffed at the corners. 'It's just obvious.'

'It makes some people anxious, talking to a stranger, not really knowing what to expect. Is that how you feel?'

'No. I imagine we're talking here because you thought I'd be anxious in your office?'

'Are you comfortable here?'

'I couldn't care less where we talk. I'm here because my mum's on one of her guilt trips. She's lost it. You should talk to her.'

'Why is she guilty?'

'Because she's busy at work. She works at Farnham's Leisure World. "Pleasure you can't measure". It's very important. *She's* very important – runs the place.'

'Is she at work a lot?'

'She's got an assistant manager to handle the day-to-day stuff. Donald Dresden – Deputy Don – but he's useless. Anyway, that's why you're here. Makes her feel better.'

'Why don't you tell me what *you* think some of the problems are, if any, and what you want to do about them?'

He waits, but I don't say anything. He watches me rub at the scab on my knuckle.

'From the chair?' he asks.

'When I'm in a rush. I knock my hands against the sides. It's nothing.'

'Looks sore.'

'I don't mind. You don't live round here, do you?'

'Is that important?'

'Do you always answer a question with a question?'

He stands up, walks across to the window and opens it. I get a whiff of rain, warm drizzle on hot tarmac.

'No, Matt, I don't live here. Not all the time. I have a practice in Hexham and a cottage here in the village—'

'So you're rich?'

'I'd like —

'Married?'

He takes a breath.

'Kids?'

'We're not here to talk about me. I want to understand what's been going on.' He waits, maintains eye contact. I don't look away. Pretty soon we're locked in a staring contest. He looks away first.

'What if I were to ask you what you'd like to change about your life, Matt? What would you say?'

'I'd say I don't want any more do-gooders asking questions.'

'What do you think these do-gooders want?'

'They want what you want. To talk about how I got like this.'

'The accident?'

'I don't remember anything.'

'Yes.' He looks down at my notes. 'You don't remember anything at all of what happened.'

It isn't a question, but I've slipped up all the same. Now I'm where he wants me to be. 'I can't answer questions about something if I don't remember it, can I?'

'How about this, I'll agree not to ask you questions about the accident until you say it's all right, and you might not, and if you don't, that's OK too.'

I shrug.

'Does that sound acceptable?'

'Doesn't leave us much to talk about.'

'What about last week when you fell into the lake? Would it be OK if we talked about that?'

'Mum overreacts, I'm all right. It was nothing.'

'Can you recall what you were feeling when it happened?'

'I wasn't feeling anything.'

'Had something upset—'

'I wasn't *feeling* anything. It was an accident.'

'Were you frightened?'

'No.'

A trickle from a gutter above the window.

'All right, Matt. I'd like you to try something for me if you don't mind. A game. You like games. I want you to close your eyes and think of something.'

'What?'

'It can be anything you like; a holiday, something you play on your computer, one of your drawings, perhaps. You like to draw, don't you?'

I didn't tell him that. He picks up the folder and puts it on the table beside him.

'Let yourself see it.'

I close my eyes, scrunching them as tight as I can and breathing out heavily through my nose.

'Do you have something in your mind?'

'Yep.'

'What is it?'

'An emperor dragonfly. *Anax Imperator*. Male identified by a deep blue abdomen and a green head. Female green and brown. Lives near lakes and ponds. Wing span, four inches. Wing beats, thirty a second.' I open my eyes. 'That's faster than a bee. The young are called nymphs. They live in the water. Want to hear about *those*?'

'That's very—'

'Nymphs. Wingless. Submerged for two years. Excellent predators of water lice and other nymphs. They kill them with extendable jaws which have hooks sometimes known as—'

'A death mask.'

'Yes.'

'Have you seen any around the lake?'

'They're rare.'

'But you've seen them?'

'There's a pond I built. They go there sometimes to hunt. Lots of them. Or there used to be. I don't go any more.'

'I bet it's quite a sight. What do you like about them?'

'They're perfectly designed, unchanged for millions of years. Simple. Resilient. I dunno. I just like them.'

'I used to keep stag beetles. That was my thing when I was your age, perhaps a bit younger. I took them from a log pile at the bottom of our garden and put them in a glass box.'

Now he's telling me stuff about himself, without me asking. Stuff about when he was my age, not a psychiatrist, just a kid rooting around in dead wood for stags. He's not getting me that easily.

'Their jaws, no, not jaws . . .' He thinks for a moment. 'What's the word?'

'Mandibles. Did you ever get bitten?'

'It's a common misconception they bite. So no, I didn't.'

'What are you going to tell my mum?'

'Nothing. I'm not interested in making judgements, of any kind, at least not yet.

He's better than Finch.

'I *am* interested in finding out how you feel.'

'About dragonflies?'

'About everything.' He glances at his notepad. 'I was wondering about your dad.'

'Why?'

'He doesn't live with you any more. He left when you were . . .'

'Twelve.'

'Yes. You were twelve and Tom was . . . five. Do you still see him?'

'Sometimes I get a letter, or a present on my birthday. He has a new family, a girl and a boy. The girl's hers, the boy, Danny, they had together.'

'How old's Danny?'

'Fifteen months. They live in a five-bedroomed house in Hayden Bridge. They have a room with a snooker table and the girl, Charlotte, has a pony called Hester.'

'I see.'

'Dad sells photocopiers. He used to have a boat business. Trips around the lake. He had a seven-seater. Rowing boats you could hire.'

'Do you know why he left?'

'I played on the snooker table once. I put a tear in the cloth.'

'Do you know why he left?'

Because of Tom. 'No.'

'You have no idea why he left?'

'Why don't you ask him?'

'Does it make you unhappy that you don't see him very often?'

I feel resistance rise up in me again, a swell like a bite under my skin. Involuntary. 'Want to know what Daddy got me for my birthday this year? An astronomy set. An expensive one with a telescope that came in a large box made of wood.'

'Do you like astronomy?'

'Not really. Want to know what he got me for Christmas before last?'

He nods.

'Same thing.' I look at the pad, but he doesn't write it down. 'Everyone gets sad.'

'The times you feel sad, Matt, have you ever thought about hurting yourself?'

'This is fucked-up. I can say that, right?'

'What you say to me stays in this room. Between you and me.' He uncrosses his legs and rests a hand under his chin. 'What's fucked-up about it?'

'You, asking me stupid questions like, "have I ever thought about hurting myself?" What do you think I'm going to say – "Yeah, Doc, I've got a shotgun under my mattress and any day now I'm going to blow my head off"?'

'With a lake at the bottom of the garden I wouldn't have thought you needed a shotgun.'

We share a smile.

''Cos I'm paralysed, people assume I want to top myself. Goes with the territory.' I tap the armrests of my chair with the palms of my hands. 'If I wanted to I would. It doesn't scare me. But I don't feel like that.'

'What, then? Something else?'

'Not . . . I don't . . .'

'Take your time.'

'You don't give up, do you? Why do I have to *feel* anything? You people are all the same, you think I've got

93

to be depressed because my dad couldn't stick it and went to live somewhere else, or I ditched into the lake therefore I must be suicidal. There doesn't have to be a feeling for everything, a neat little box you can stick a label on, hundred quid an hour and bingo, you're cured.'

'What couldn't your dad stick?'

'Why don't you ask him?'

'Because I'm asking you.'

'He couldn't stick not being able to make things better. He thought he could, wouldn't just accept things the way they were. When you can't make something right, you can't, that's it.'

'What did he want to make right? Tom?'

'Ever seen someone who looks like they're taking their last breath?'

'Yes.'

'It scared my dad. It scared everyone.'

The trickle from the gutter has slowed to a drip.

'What about the nightmares, Matt?'

'They're no big deal.'

'They don't occur frequently? You don't wake up sweating?'

'If you already know all this, why are you asking me?'

'What about when you go to bed, do you try to stay awake?'

'I read from my insect book. I can't just read because that makes me tired so I have to memorise what I've read, read it aloud, then close the book and write it down. Sometimes it works and I'm able to pick a moment and stay there, other times I can't do it.'

'What happens when you wake up from one of these nightmares?'

'Nothing.'

'Does it feel like the nightmare's still there?'

'I'm tired.' I touch my neck. Even with the window open, and the rain, it's still hot. I suck in a breath of the warm air, feeling the dampness in my lungs. 'I'd like to stop now.'

'We're nearly done. Are the nightmares always the same, or different?'

'*Now.*'

He nods. My hands are sweating. He holds the door open for me, a gesture, rather than help, and we go back along the corridor to the waiting room. Mum's there, fingers knotted around the strap on her handbag.

'OK, Matt, I'd like to talk to you again. I'm afraid I don't have my diary with me, but I'll leave some dates with Dr Hardy and ask him to get in touch. Is that all right with you?'

I shrug. He waits.

'Yes, it's OK.'

'Good.'

'Right,' Mum says. 'Thank you, Dr Mason.'

She ducks under his arm when he holds the door open, wheeling me out in front. At the car, waiting for her to move some shopping off the back seat, I turn around and see him, Doc, standing at the entrance to the surgery.

'How was it, then?' Mum asks. 'You were in there a long time.'

'Was I?' I put an arm around her neck and lean forward.

'What did you talk about?'

'Stag beetles.'

Doc has one hand in the pocket of his trousers, the other raised to wave. As the car pulls away I put my hand up to the glass, a hot palm print that leaves a mark and slowly fades to nothing.

# 11

It was a circuit Robert had done before, eight miles if he looped around White Hare Farm, but he took the OS map just in case. After a mile or so he felt himself relax. The main footpaths were quiet, only an occasional walker who nodded a greeting.

He'd spent the morning packing Elizabeth's things into boxes – a necessary job he saw no reason to delay any longer. In the wardrobe in their bedroom he'd found a photograph of her, taken beside the lake on their wedding anniversary five or six years ago. She stood beside a dinghy, small, red, perfect for fishing, or for rowing over to the islands. Dad stuff. Inevitable that it should trip him up, he'd sat on the bed staring at it for, how long? Too long.

She'd told him once, albeit in a row, that she'd be willing to sleep with someone else to get pregnant. Infidelity was nothing in comparison to the desperation she felt. Only now she didn't have to be unfaithful. She was free to do whatever she wanted, with whomever she chose. So that was how he imagined her, unprotected sex, lying in someone else's bed, pelvis tilted, holding on to the cum.

He pushed on, head down, needing the sound of his feet on the stony paths, the simple chain of decisions of where next to place his feet so he didn't slip, then reaching a stile or a fork in the path, pulling the map from his back pocket to pinpoint his location and studying the contours of the route ahead.

He climbed over a gate, pausing to take in the view before setting his feet down on the other side. To the east there was Loweswater, the tall steeple of St Mary's church standing out against the grey roofs of other buildings, and, stretched along the north side of the town, the lake. He tried to find his cottage, but his view was obscured by a small wood closer to him and he could only guess.

The session with Matt had been surprising. In the waiting room, slumped posture, poor eye contact, fingers interlocked. Then a few moments later, agitated, hostile and, occasionally, charming. But depressed? No, not obviously. The nightmares were clearly something he had to contend with, and there was some bed wetting, according to the notes. He cast his mind back to the short interaction with Matt's mother. She was a small woman with a tight expression and tiredness that looked deep-rooted. Quite beautiful, in a fragile way. But as a parent? Overpowering, strict? Emotionally absent?

He'd told Terry he'd be happy to continue the sessions. Terry's plan from the start, of course. Just until work on the cottage was completed. A distraction, necessary, perhaps.

At the bottom of the valley he reached a T-junction, fields piled up on either side. To the left was Burdon Village, to the right Blackburn Fell and, another mile or so, White Hare Farm, the halfway point. Far away, on the horizon, the sun cast thick rods of light on to the town. He kept going until he found himself there, eventually following the path that circled the lake. It'd been a long time since he'd walked like this, and the first time without Elizabeth. They'd explored a lot of the area together on foot, side by side along tracks, single file on the country lanes, nearly always finishing back at the lake. Today, several times, he'd found himself slowing the pace with the expectation of seeing her round the bend behind him, thumbs hooked under the straps of her rucksack.

When he reached Grainger Pub he bought himself a pint and rested on one of the picnic benches outside. The lake spread out before him, the gentle parade of dusk turning it the colour of tar. He ought to ring Patrick, check on his patients, not that he need worry. He and Patrick had been partners at his practice in Hexham for ten years. 'Take as long as you want,' he'd said. Even so, Robert couldn't justify living in a hotel for much longer. It was an extravagance he could ill afford. Despite its state of upheaval, he'd have to move back into the cottage. The absence of Elizabeth's belongings had made the rooms seem cold.

'Hello.'

A woman's voice. He glanced along the path behind her, unnerved at her sudden arrival.

'You don't remember me, do you?'

'I do. Sarah Bell.'

She looked out over the lake, a moment's unexpected shyness. He hadn't seen that in the café.

'How are you?'

'Fine. Thought I'd take a walk.' She smiled. 'I can't decide whether it's lonely or peaceful.'

'The lake?' He looked at it. Clouds of midges danced tight circles across the surface. 'Peaceful, I think. Exploring?'

'Getting lost.'

'Would you like a drink?' It didn't feel forced, he was, after all, already drinking. She sat beside him on the picnic bench, crossing her legs at the ankle. Trainers, white, small. He felt suddenly gripped, fenced in by the presence of her body so close to him. 'What would you like?'

'Oh, er, dunno. Half a lager?'

'Right.'

He skipped quickly through the patio doors with a great deal more energy than he felt. While the barman prepared the drinks he bolted himself into the gents. He ought to have said lonely, wasn't that what she was saying? Implying? He was hot, sticky from the walk. He pissed, zipped up his trousers, and splashed his face with water at one of the basins. The mirror above was cracked. He stared at his fractured reflection. Old man. His clothes agreed, shabby T-shirt and khaki trousers – old man doing the gardening. He went back to the bar, hastily paid for the drinks and took them outside.

'Cheers,' he said, handing her the glass.

'Yeah.' She took several large mouthfuls.

'How long's your visit?'

'Oh. Not sure really.' She wiped her mouth with the tips of her fingers. 'I hadn't thought about it. The summer, I guess.'

He'd never been able to imagine himself in a new place without knowing exactly how long he would be there, even in his twenties.

'Not much to the place, is there?'

'There's an Internet café,' he offered.

'Cool.'

He leaned back on his elbows and stretched out his legs. Realising that this mimicked her own position, he straightened up again. 'Did you manage to get to the exhibition?'

'That landscapes thing? No, not yet.'

An awkward silence. She'd asked to be taken. So? Take her.

'I like your trousers.'

'Thanks,' he said, sounding as shy as he felt. 'They're for walking.' He wanted to fast-forward to a different scene, in bed, sweated limbs in post-sex sprawl, only that would mean he'd have to be different too. More beer.

'How are your windows?' she asked.

'Done. I was just thinking before you arrived I'll probably move back now they're in.'

A group spilled out into the beer garden, student types, noisy. It made it difficult to hear what she said next. He smiled, nodded. It seemed the right thing to do because she smiled widely back at him. It was enough just to watch her mouth, full of relief and warmth.

He'd nearly finished his pint.

'I do like it here though.' She waved a hand towards the lake. A breeze shifted across the surface, wrinkling, still again.

'Nice when you get off the beaten track, I imagine. I can't get over how many walking shops there are. They're everywhere.'

'Yes, it's big business.'

'Do you walk a lot? You look pretty fit.'

'Oh, not all that much.' He tried to stop himself thinking ahead to what it might be like to touch her, inching inside, part of him maniacally fucking while the other part stood back and marvelled. 'Would you like another drink?'

'Not really. We could walk a bit?'

As they strolled she asked questions, scuffing the path with the toes of her trainers, head down except for now and then when she'd squint at him through the low glare of the sun. He'd got into the habit, with great and deliberate care, of avoiding talking about himself. He was sweating, longing to take off his walking boots, but he *was* doing it, chatting, holding eye contact. They followed the path that lined the lake, him falling in behind her as she made her way along a stretch of duckboard that bridged two areas of marshy ground. After a few hundred yards, he indicated a bench and they sat down.

'It smells so good,' she said. 'I used to live by the sea. All you could smell was fish. I can still smell it sometimes. Funny that, isn't it? How the scent of somewhere stays with you.'

'Where was that?'

'Seaham.'

'Ah, yes. I know it. I taught at Newcastle University for a while. Is that where you studied?'

She looked at him, holding his gaze. 'What you really want to know is how old I am, right?'

'It had crossed my mind.'

'Does it matter?'

'No.'

'I'm nineteen in September.'

He blew a stream of air through his lips. He'd have put her in her early twenties at least. She was lovely, neat, unconscious of herself in a way which was extremely attractive, but, Christ, too young. Too young for what?

'So, what, you're twice my age, three times—'

'Hold on!'

'What, then?'

'Actually, I had it in my mind that I was going to ask you out to dinner.' God, it was crass. Yet the words were his. He had, at least, been capable of them. To his relief she smiled. It aroused him seeing her eyes, bright, exultant, then that flash of shyness again.

'You'd like to get to know me better?'

'Yes.'

She took out a cigarette and lit it, twirling it round and round between her fingers then, unexpectedly, she leaned forward and touched his knee. The heat of her fingertips met the skin beneath his trousers. 'I'd like that. You could show me around.'

He felt himself harden at the thought of what that might mean. Not, he assumed, that she'd meant sex, though he couldn't be sure. He couldn't be sure of anything. He was unravelling.

'So are you here on assignment?' he asked. 'Or a holiday?'

'More like a summer job. It gives me time to develop my portfolio. If it's good enough, I might go to uni.'

'I used to paint. A long time ago. I thought about taking

it up again.' Accurate, though he'd been saying it for months and, as yet, had done nothing about it.

'Are you any good?'

'God, no.'

She laughed.

'I keep hoping I might get better. It relaxes me. I suppose you could say I like the idea of it even though I'm useless.'

She'd changed the shape of everything, just by existing. He talked, listened; sometimes he just watched her mouth. She told him about photographers she admired, artists, too – Gustav Klimt, to his surprise, a favourite of his. He felt like a boy on a first date, obliged to lessen the cheapness of the occasion with talk and yet he wasn't anywhere near capable of anything else.

'So,' she turned to face him directly, legs tucked up on the seat. 'I take it you're not married?'

'Divorced.' He felt the word glide out. True enough. The papers were on the desk in his room. He looked away; hoping he'd disposed of the question.

'Were you married long?'

'Nine years.' Nearly ten. His throat tightened. For all he was made giddy and guilty by the sight of Sarah, he felt the need to convince himself he was entitled. *Was* he twice her age? More? Yes. Old enough to be her father? He tried to do the maths in his head, but the thought unnerved him so much he couldn't focus. Suddenly, she laughed. It took him by surprise.

'You know, when I first saw you, I thought, there goes someone with a lot on his mind. And there you go again, that look, like a cocker spaniel.'

'Thanks. You might at least have said Alsatian.'

The urge to kiss her was strong, forcing him to look for something to fix his attention on. The lake spread out before him, a blank canvas.

She drew him back with a gentle tug on his sleeve. 'I'm free on Friday?'

'OK. Friday sounds good.' A few drops of rain dimpled the surface of the water. 'I think this might turn heavy, shall we head back?'

When they arrived back at the pub he wrestled with the idea of offering her another drink. The patio doors were closed, ashtrays and glasses cleared from the picnic benches. Inside it looked crowded, several groups standing near the bar. No seats. So they'd stand, that was all right, wasn't it? He imagined her leaning into him to hear his words over the music.

'Well, thanks for the drink,' she said. 'Shall we meet back here?'

'Yes, if you like.'

His fear was vivid, crude in its simplicity and yet he wanted her, now, without pause or deliberation. Something inside him had wrenched itself free, fleetingly, but long enough for him to know it still existed.

'Wait. I don't have your number.'

'Friday. I'll be here. Eight.' Then she was laughing, spinning away from him up the path until she was out of sight.

# 12

I don't want Doc in the stinky piss room. Mum says you can't smell it, not on me, or the sheets, washed, mattress turned and covered with plastic. Yeah, plastic, like little kids have. Anyway, I can smell it. It's like a hot, yellow fog that clings to the walls and the carpet, in my drawers, all over my stuff. The hotter it gets the more I smell it. Today is really hot.

'Andrew, his father . . .' The next words carried off on the wind. 'Letters . . . the odd phone call. Nothing for a few months.'

I glance at my watch. Fifty-three minutes and counting. It's not just Dad he wants to know about, he wants it all, school, grades, friends. Do I eat? Do I sleep? Do I keep a diary?

I strain to slow down their voices so I can break up the

sound into words I can understand. Even with the window open – a millimetre, on account of not wanting to wang it open and blow my cover – I only snatch bits of their conversation. Mum's tone, high-pitched, talking fast, set to a background of ice chinking in the lemonade jug. She'll be filling Doc's head with shit that doesn't mean anything, like when I was little and I had to have the landing light left on when I went to sleep. Stuff like that. Or other stuff. He'll probably want to sniff the sheets.

'. . . So yes, the house is a reminder and we could do with the money, but it isn't up to Andrew to dictate where we live . . .'

I wait. Silence from under the window. I guess Doc hadn't figured on Mum hating Dad so much. Doc says something, but a speedboat goes past on the lake, buffing the water, and I can't make out his words. I wait for it to pass, Doc talking, then Mum, '. . . exuberant, cheerful . . . sense of humour . . . remarkable resilience . . .'

I rest my head against the window, relief washing over me. Nice one, Mum. See, 'cos people with resilience don't need their heads looking at. We don't need this shit. Things are all right. Then I hear 'Tom' and it dawns on me. Tom's resilience. Tom's sense of humour. Tom. Who's special. And dead. I want to lean out of the window and scream, but I don't. I close my eyes instead, feeling a sweep of heat spread down my back and paste me to the chair. I'm here. This is now. The past gone, forgotten, dead. Tom dead. When I open my eyes again it's to a coolness on my face. Mum's standing at the door. My turn.

She takes me outside. The air is thick, like jelly.

'And how are you today, Matt?' Doc takes out a fresh notepad, one just for me.

'Fine.'

There are sweat patches under his arms, two damp circles on his crisply ironed, blue shirt. He undoes the buttons on the sleeves and rolls them up. Hairy arms, like Dad's, but his hands are different, smooth, clean nails. Not like Dad's.

Mum appears with a fresh jug of lemonade, homemade, and sets it down on the table between us. 'Wouldn't you like the parasol up?'

'Allow me,' Doc says. It's too late and he and Mum go for it at the same time, knocking into each other. Mum backs off and lets him do it. I wonder if they'd be like that if they had sex, all knocking together and not quite meeting in the right place. I don't know why I think that, all of a sudden, except Mum's wearing a dress and has put her hair in a ponytail.

'I've got some paperwork to do. I'll be in the lounge; you just have to call if you need anything.' She goes back inside.

Doc pulls his chair further into the shade, so he's almost touching my chair, and pours lemonade from the jug into two tall glasses, cautiously, the way you do when you think the ice is going to plop out in a big rush. Mum's put sugar on the rim.

'Sorry we were so long. Is there anything special you'd like to talk about today?' He looks at the notepad I've brought with me from my room, lined, A4 like his. 'Sometimes after a session things come to mind that you didn't think of at the time?'

I shrug.

'I wondered if we could talk about your nightmares? Have you had any more?'

Loads. 'A couple.'

I forgot he knows about them. Now he's got something to do, a reason for being here. Except things are different now, or maybe just one thing.

'You look tired.'

'I'm all right. What did you and Mum talk about?' I look into his eyes for a glimpse of it, but there's nothing.

'I should've explained. That's one of our rules, Matt. Whoever I'm talking to the conversation stays just between us. So when I talk to your Mum, it stays between us, and with you, between us. It keeps things nice and simple and you know you can trust me.'

'Whatever.' I pull my notepad into my lap and turn over the page, make like I'm writing.

'There's something I'd like to clear up before we come to the nightmares.'

I put down my pencil.

'The day on the jetty, when you fell in. You said you weren't frightened and that you weren't trying to hurt yourself—'

'I said I wasn't trying to top myself. I wasn't.'

'But nor was it an accident?'

'I know how deep the water is at the end of the jetty, I know how long I can hold my breath, I know there's a ring with a chain on the end I can use to pull myself round. It was a *wind up*, a joke, you know? Ha, ha.'

Doc scribbles something on his pad.

'Only I guess it wasn't funny.'

'Why do you say that?'

'You're here, aren't you?' I search his face for a reaction, surprise, confusion, but it's blank. 'You don't believe me.'

'I was just thinking you must be pretty brave to take such a risk, just for a prank.'

'It's only a risk if you don't know what you're doing. I knew what I was doing.'

'Why did you do it?'

'I told you, a wind up.'

'Who were you winding up?'

'The new girl. The carer.'

'You don't like her?'

'I *didn't*. She's all right, I suppose.'

Doc looks into his lap. 'Thinking about the nightmares then, the one you have regularly, can you take me through what happens?'

What I remember first is draping Sarah's silk scarf across my face and feeling cooled by it. It stirs inside me, the caress of it on my cheeks, the smell of her being sucked into my open mouth. 'He stands there. Tom. At the bottom of the bed. He wants me to go somewhere with him.'

'Where?'

'Dunno.'

'What do you do?'

'Pull on my trainers and go for a kickabout. What do you think I do? I don't *do* anything.'

'How does he look, different each time or the same?'

'Same.' I rub the back of my neck, prickly in the heat.

'How's that?'

'Like he's been *dead* a year.'

A pause. 'That must be very distressing.'

'It isn't pretty.'

'Is he still there when you wake up?'

'Sometimes.'

'When you're awake?'

'I don't know. I guess I'm awake. I suppose I must be because there's screaming; it's me who screams.'

A blackbird's alarm call drills holes into our silence.

'Last summer, what's the last thing you remember before the accident?'

'We were talking about the nightmares. You're breaking the rules.'

'I'm just interested in what you remember *before*. Is that all right?'

I think about Finch and what he said about the paralysis being in my head. Doc hasn't said it yet, but he will. When he does that'll be two, two people who think I'm crazy. I look at him, trying to measure out in my head why I don't want him to say it. At least not yet. I tell him about the camp me and Jack built in Hopper's Wood. We made the frame out of saplings, big enough for two, then covered it with fern. We'd only just finished it, that morning, and we planned to sleep out in it that night. I want to get the details right, as I remember them, not to impress him, but because, well, I don't know why exactly, maybe because I want Doc to know I *can* remember things. There are things I do remember, exactly as they were.

'What happened when you went home?'

'I got my stuff ready, packed food I thought we could cook on the fire. Then Tom came in and said he wanted to come with us. I said he couldn't and he started crying.

Mum said I had to take him, just until it got dark, then bring him back.'

'But you didn't want him there.'

'The camp was for me and Jack.'

'I had a brother, I was the eldest, like you and Tom. We fought a lot, about little things mostly. Was that how it was with you two?'

I try to imagine Doc as a kid, like me, only it doesn't quite work. His accent's funny, like it used to be something else, before it was posh. He's probably one of those people who grew up on a grubby housing estate, moved away as quick as he could, leaving his rotten family and his rotten brother behind in a scabby council house.

'He got bored, usually when the weather wasn't right for him to go outside, which was pretty much all the time. Like now.' I look around the garden, the air a soup of greenflies and pollen. 'Hay fever triggered his asthma. In the winter it was the cold. I let him play with my stuff. It wasn't his fault he was ill.'

'Can't have been very nice for him, or you, seeing your brother like that?'

'I guess.'

'When you had arguments, what were they about?'

'We didn't argue.'

'Never had a disagreement about anything?'

'No.'

He looks at me, weighing me up or maybe just waiting to see if I'll say anything else. He does it a lot, sits there, waiting, looking thoughtful. The sun's moved round, exposing his neck. I wonder if it'll hurt later. I look down the garden at the flowerbeds, roses bloated on their stems.

Peach and yellow and pink and the red one in the middle of them all. Tom's rose. It's past its best, shedding boat-shaped petals on the scorched earth.

Doc writes something on his pad.

'I suppose you think my dream has a meaning.'

'There are people who believe dreams are an avenue for our unconscious mind to work out problems we can't solve when we're awake. Nightmares are different.'

'Why?'

'Recurring nightmares like yours suggest there's a problem you can't work out, like a blockage. What about you? Do *you* think it has a meaning?'

'How should I know?' My heart thumps large in my chest. 'If he's got something to say to me he should just come out and say it.'

'Have you thought it might be the other way around – something you want to say to him?'

'No. It's him. His cheeks are fat, they get fatter until . . . I think he's full of words, of things he wants to tell me, but he isn't. It's flies. Millions of them in a black stream. The noise . . .'

Doc puts the notepad on the table, several pages of writing I don't remember him doing.

'It doesn't matter.'

'Talking about it might help.'

'When I opened my eyes this morning there was a second I thought you might be able to help. I thought maybe I wanted you to. But I don't.' I think of Sarah, leaning into Gavin, his big army boots.

'You think you're beyond help, Matt?'

'Finch wanted to talk, all the time, talk. It didn't help.

It's me who has to do it all. Not you. You're not inside my head.'

'No, I'm not. What are you most afraid of?'

'You know the party game, the one when you stick your hand into a bucket of something? Sometimes it's shredded paper, or cold beans.'

'I think I know the one.'

'You don't know what you'll get till you put your hand in and dig around. Usually it's a toy. Or a bar of chocolate. Something nice.'

'Yes.'

'Well, that isn't going to happen.' I look at him, searching his face for some sign that he understands. 'The things everyone wants me to remember aren't nice.'

Before he can answer Sarah bursts on to the patio from the kitchen, a washing-basket perched on her hip.

'Sorry,' she says. 'I didn't realise. Oh . . . it's you.'

Doc looks embarrassed. I follow his eyes to the ground, Sarah's toenails are painted ruby red. She breaks the silence with a laugh.

'You know each other?' I ask.

'Yes,' he says, but he isn't looking at me.

There's an awkward moment when nobody says anything, then Mum comes out and she and Doc walk around the side of the house together. I wait a few moments then follow. Doc shakes Mum's hand and gets into his car.

'He's the shrink?' Sarah says, following me. She drops the washing-basket at my feet.

'Yeah.'

She waits for Mum to go back into the house and hops across the gravel towards him.

'You've no shoes on,' he says.

She doesn't hear him.

'You'll cut your feet.'

'They're hard,' she says. 'Fancy seeing you here.'

'Yes. I didn't realise this is where you work.'

'I didn't realise you were a shrink.'

'Psychiatrist.'

'Oh.' She sniffs. 'Nice car. I had you down as a lawyer.'

He laughs. 'What on earth made you think that?'

'I dunno. You've got this useless look about you.'

I can't hear what she says next, but I reckon she's asking him questions, sussing him out for me because that's what she's like. She's not soft like Mum. She swings her hips from side to side, checking him over, not talking, just staring at him until he looks away. Then, only then, she turns to me, sees me watching, and smiles.

# 13

Thank God she was Matt's carer. If she'd been a relative he couldn't have seen her, but dating a carer wasn't the same. Not the same at all. No different, really, to dating a nurse.

He inspected himself in the bathroom mirror, linen shirt tucked into his waistband, pulled out, creased, in again. He'd made the bed. Sheets changed just in case. Just in case. An incredible tension came over him, the need to breathe deep and expel energy. Christ. They mightn't even get there. He glanced at the clock on his bedside table. Nearly half past seven. He wasn't happy by himself, but he was content. Content was good. It made no demands. Get a dog, for God's sake. Anything was better than this.

It was precisely eight when he arrived. Sarah was waiting

at the same table they'd sat at a few days earlier and she'd bought herself a drink, half a lager.

'Hello.' She smiled broadly, making no attempt to hide her relief at seeing him.

'Can I get you another?'

'Sure.' She put a cigarette to her lips, inhaled, and let out a long stream of smoke.

He went to the bar, needing time to absorb how she looked. Incredible. More skin than he'd been prepared for. A deep cleavage, a mole resting on her right breast. When he returned he noticed she'd almost finished her cigarette. She tapped the end of her lighter on the table. She smoked a lot.

'How was Matt after I left?' It wasn't the best subject of conversation, not even wise, but it, or rather he, was something they had in common.

'OK. I'm sorry if I burst in. I didn't know you were coming.'

'Not to worry. We were just about to finish, as it happens.'

She held the cigarette up near her face, rolling it between her fingers before flicking a chimney of ash into an empty cigarette packet. 'Did you know his brother, Tom?'

'Not personally, no, though I think I was here when it happened.' He stopped himself just in time from saying 'we'.

'I don't know how you get over something like that. Maybe you don't.' She brushed hair from her eyes. 'Do you think his paralysis is in his head? I mean, psychological?'

'What do you think?'

'I think it sounds like something a psychiatrist would say. No offence.'

'None taken.' He groped for something that would get them off the subject. 'Are you staying with them?'

'Yes. I have my own room. I like it. It's a beautiful house, in a rather grotesque way. What I mean is, it feels like the sort of place you could easily admire, for hours and hours, without ever actually imagining yourself living there, or wanting to. But the view's spectacular.' She crossed her hands. 'And you. You looked different. Serious. Took me a second to recognise you. Not going to analyse me, I hope?'

'No.' He ran a finger around the rim of his glass.

'So, where are we having dinner?'

'Gregory's, it's a little place just around the corner.' He wondered now whether he'd manage to eat. 'It does a bit of everything. I wasn't sure what sort of food you liked.'

'Any. I'm starving.'

The pub was getting busier, a group of girls on a night out commandeering one of the tables not far away. He imagined what he and Sarah might look like to them.

'Shall we go?' he said. As they started to walk he added: 'It's good that you care about Matt. He needs a friend.'

'What about you?' She cocked her head. 'Doctor Robert. Can I call you Robbie?'

'Not if you expect an answer.' This was worse than he'd thought.

'Robert, then. Do you need a friend? Course you do, everyone does.' She glanced at his hand. 'Nine years is a long time. You got kids?'

'No.'

She hooked her thumbs into the pockets of her denim skirt. The bangles on her wrists clunked together, thick plastic in orange and yellow. 'Didn't pick the friendliest village in the world, did you? I think I've only spoken to a couple of people since I got here, apart from the Logans. You were one of them.'

'It must be quiet compared to Newcastle.'

'It is, but a job's a job. Didn't much care where it was to be honest.' She shrugged, a flash of sadness. 'Want to know what I think?' She smiled again. 'I think you're like me.'

'Oh?'

'Out of your depth. Don't worry, I mean it in a nice way. You've just got this look about you, like you're expecting things to go tits-up any minute.'

'Cocker spaniel?'

'Yeah. Takes one to know one.'

At the restaurant she asked for a vodka and orange. He returned the wine list to the waiter and followed suit, ordering whiskey. They were led to a table in the corner of the dining room, which was almost empty. Tiny lanterns flickered on every table. He ate without tasting and listened as she talked, mostly about photography, the sort of work she wanted to do. He urged her on, relieved not to be talking about himself.

'I'd like to see some of your work, if you don't mind?'

'Why would I?' She blushed slightly. 'Most of my work from home is of people, faces. I'd go to allotments, old people's homes, and just take pictures, you know?'

'I imagine it's quite difficult, getting pictures of people without the pose.'

'Yeah, you have to have a way of disarming them. My mam says I have, she says I talk too much.'

'It's called charm. A great attribute.'

'I don't think that's what she meant.'

He ordered more drinks. The restaurant had filled up since they arrived, changing the acoustics of the room so that her voice seemed further away. He was content, though, fenced in by the table and by her, happy to be whisked along.

'What do your parents do?'

'My dad's a policeman and my mam works from home, her own business.'

'Oh?'

She brought the salt and pepper together on the table, rotating one fat-bellied container around the other. 'What about you? What made you want to get inside people's heads?'

'My grandmother. She had this incredible fear. She never left her house, didn't use gas, or climb the stairs or take a bath. She'd lived like that for years, the whole time I was growing up. I used to go shopping for her, take it in, and then have to fold up the plastic bags into tiny squares and bind them with string. She was terrified I'd get one over my head and suffocate.'

'God!'

'I wanted to understand what had happened to make her like that.'

'And do you, now?'

'She died before I qualified, though I'm not sure what sort of difference I'd have made. She was pretty set in her ways, happy even.'

'I thought about doing a counselling course. If I hadn't have done photography, that is, but I don't think it's something I would've stuck at. Sitting in front of someone while they tell you all their problems, doesn't capture my imagination in the way looking through a lens does.'

'I think you know when you've found your passion. Something you have to do, like breathe or eat.'

'That's right. That's exactly right.'

She smiled and he was pleased to have offered this understanding, even if they'd once been Elizabeth's words.

After coffee they strolled, retracing the steps of the walk they'd done the other day. Light clung to the surface of the lake, an iridescent glow that belonged to neither moon nor sun. He felt slightly drunk. She steadied herself on his arm.

'What time is it?' she asked.

'Do you have to be back?'

'No.'

'We could get a drink at the hotel?' A completely unintentional come on, but there it was. The question rose and hung in the air around them. He didn't mean sex, or at least he thought he didn't.

'We could walk a bit more?' she said.

A few feet into the undergrowth on either side of the path it thickened to total blackness, a faint rustle of an animal moving around, then a car on the road, headlights turning branches into silhouettes.

'You know, you won't believe me, but I was so wound up when I was getting ready tonight. Nervous, I guess.'

'You?' He didn't believe her. 'Not nervous of me?'

'You know what it's like, a big relationship comes to an end and all of a sudden you're on the singles scene again. It's terrifying.'

He hadn't seen her as someone who might've been in a long-term relationship. But then long-term to a nineteen-year-old was probably a few months.

'Was that what it was like for you', she continued, 'when you were first divorced?'

'Actually you're my first . . . date since—'

'A date! Wow, I didn't know this was a date. And your first, too. I like that. It's like something my dad would say.'

He groaned inwardly.

'I'm teasing.' She nudged him. 'It's just you don't hear of people going on dates much any more, do you? Courtship and all that. You see someone in a club, they like the look of you, you like the look of them, and if you still feel the same in the morning you exchange numbers.'

God. 'So you were in a relationship, how long?'

'Long enough to get his number. A few years.' A silence opened up, then, suddenly, she spun in front of him and held him around the waist. 'I tell you what, you don't tell me your heartbreakers and I won't tell you mine.'

'OK.'

'Thank you for dinner.'

'You're quite welcome.'

'Want to give me your number?'

'Yes.'

She lifted her head to kiss him. As his mouth touched hers he felt her lips open, the first touch of her tongue, tentative, then stronger, exploring his. She tasted of orange juice and cigarettes. He had a sense of watching himself in fast forward, seed to bloom in seconds.

She looked at him, eyes widening and closing again, then, quietly, she slipped her hand into his and they continued walking. They turned up from the lake, passed his cottage and, though tempted, he didn't make any reference to it. Besides she was talking, fast, moving from one subject to another without pause. He liked it, losing her hand as she brought it up to gesticulate some point or another, and feeling the pleasure as she found his again. At the bottom of the long drive up to the Logans' house he stopped and she kissed him again, the force of her weight pushing him gently against the trunk of a large conifer. In that dark, damp place, spiced with pine she was more passionate than he'd imagined she could be and when he emerged from the kiss he was quite off balance.

'Goodnight then,' she said.

'Night.' He watched her walk up the drive, turn around once and wave, then, plastic bangles clinking on her wrists, she sprinted across the gravel to the house.

# 14

I count the seconds between breaths, two, three, four,
then I gasp and my body shudders. Awake. A dark room.
Cool air from the window and lake sounds, like a cat
lapping milk. I list shapes, naming them as they come
into focus.

The lamp is real.

The desk is real.

I open my eyes wide, wider, scraping the fuzz of sleep
off my mind. I think of Doc on the patio and the scratchy
sound his pen made when he wrote things down. I think
of what I said to him about Tom, how we never fought,
never argued. I try to move, but my thoughts keep me
rigid. I'm stuck, a fly writhing on a web, between nightmare and awake.

The window is real.

The moon is real.

Slowly, I waggle my fingers, then an arm and with what seems like an enormous effort I pull out the small square of paper, folded twice, from the drawer in my bedside table. I found it yesterday when I was looking through a box of computer games I keep on a shelf in the airing cupboard. Tom's handwriting, letters drawn fat and uneven.

*NOT A REAL WOLF.*

He wrote it after he sneaked downstairs to watch *An American Werewolf in Paris* on the telly. I see him; knees up on the sofa in the dark, duvet wrapped around his shoulders, a loose tooth he pushed forward and back with his tongue. The next day, for weeks afterwards, Mum and me kept finding the notes, in the cupboard in the bathroom, under a tin of baked beans in a kitchen.

*NOT A REAL WOLF.*

His voice jumps off the paper and like a cold breath I suck it in. The note is real, too.

It's lunchtime before I make it downstairs. The air's full of the silence you get after somebody's spoken. I see Tom turning corners, leaving a room I've just arrived in. I hear his steps creaking the floorboards. Mum's left cereal and a bowl and spoon out, but I'm not hungry. Sarah's out too, the keys for both holiday cottages gone from the hook in the hall. I sit in the living room, TV off, and take small sips from a glass of orange. The clock on the video flashes, turning over minutes until, at exactly one o'clock, the doorbell rings.

'Hello, Matt.' He looks different today, no tie. 'How are you today?'

'OK.'

Mum's car pulls up beside his. She gets out, looking flustered, and walks briskly towards us. 'Sorry, Dr Mason. I meant to be here when you arrived. Have you been here long?'

'Arrived just this minute.'

'Have you offered Dr Mason a drink, Matt?'

'No.'

She looks at him apologetically. I would've offered him a drink, but he's only just got here. Like he said. She fusses, pulling out a chair at the kitchen table for him, offering him a drink from a long list of possibilities.

'I'll have Coke,' I say. She brings me a can. No glass.

'The parking in town now is quite ridiculous,' she says, moving from fridge, to cupboard, to fridge. She looks for ice, but there isn't any. 'Don't you find that? I had to park next to the cinema and walk all the way from there.'

Doc accepts a drink of lemonade. He tells her about an article in the local advertiser about a new car park he thinks they're going to build, the site of the old community centre. I watch them tittle-tattling and wish I was somewhere else. Sarah appears in the garden and empties a bin liner full of weeds into the compost bin. There's a CD player hooked on to the belt of her jeans. Her lips are moving to the words.

'I knew you weren't listening.' Mum's face in mine. 'I *said* I'll be giving Sarah a hand. We're going to clear out the loft in Briar Cottage and then I have to pop into work. So you'll be here on your own with Dr Mason, OK?'

'Fine. Go.'

She disappears out of the patio doors, carrying her box of cleaning stuff. She touches Sarah on the arm, which makes her jump. She removes her headphones and the two of them set off around the side of the house.

'It's really a very nice garden,' Doc says. He crosses his legs under the table. 'A lovely view of the lake. Do you have this view from your bedroom?'

'Yes.'

'It must be—'

'Why do people make small talk? Mum and the car-parking and you and the garden. It's not important. Just talk for the sake of talking.'

'Is there something you'd like to talk about, Matt?'

'Not especially. I just wondered if you ever thought about it, that's all. It's what you do, isn't it? Interpret what people really mean from what they say, or don't say. Mum couldn't give a stuff about the parking, she just said that so she'd have something to talk about, so she could hide it from you.'

'Hide what from me?'

'The sadness.' I snap the ring pull of my can. 'I hear her crying. She thinks I don't know, but I've known for ages.'

'Do you ever talk about it with her?'

'No.'

'Why not?'

'Because if she wanted to talk to me she would.'

The dishwasher gargles water then starts its low grumble again. I pick a spot in the garden, the fire plant, and fix my eyes on it. The young leaves are burning red.

'How are the nightmares?'

'Worse.'

'Every night?'

'Most.'

'I think we can get rid of them.'

The bed-wetting, too? I look at him, look away quickly, he doesn't know about that.

'But there's something I want you to understand first. It'll involve talking about Tom. Do you understand that we have to talk about him in order to do something about the nightmares?'

'Makes sense as they're about him.'

'And you're OK with that?'

'Let's just get on with it.'

'I want you to start by telling me something about what your life was like before he was born. Can you remember that far back? You would have been seven when Tom was born, right? Your father was here then, running boats from—'

'He didn't have his own business then. He worked at the boat yard for Mr Finkman – not David Finkman, his dad, Old George. I don't know why he was called that, he wasn't old.'

'Did your dad like working there?'

'I guess. He used to take me to work with him on Saturday mornings and Old George would give me one of his sandwiches out of a packed lunch his wife made. The bread was cut from a loaf, and he had ham, always ham, but not the packet kind; when you took a bite it was meaty.'

'You liked going to work with him?'

'Sometimes I got given parts to clean. Dad would sit me on a bench, high, my feet didn't touch the ground, and I'd work my way through a line of nuts and bolts. I liked the smell of oil on my hands and the look of it, like fingerprint ink. But then Old George had a stroke and his son took over. A few months later Dad lost his job.'

'Go on.'

'That's it.'

'He was fired?'

'I didn't say he was fired. I said he lost his job.'

'Did he find something else?'

'He worked in a supermarket for a while, stacking shelves at night. He and Mum talked about money a lot. The cottages came with the house when she inherited it from my grandad, but they were a right mess. Dad had this idea that if we fixed them up before the summer season we could have guests. Mum did the work. I helped after school, then she found out she was pregnant. I think she was ill a lot, I don't remember exactly.'

'Would you say your memories of that time are happy, mostly, or sad?'

'Oh, happy. Definitely.' I swirl the Coke around in my can, a swash of foam that nearly escapes, then softer, the tinny sound of bubbles settling. 'We didn't have a lot of money and I didn't always get the things I wanted, but it was good. Dad managed to get a loan from the bank and he bought his first boat. I remember him coming back with it one morning, my seventh birthday. It was white with a small 25cc engine at the back and a blue and green stripe that ran down both sides and got wider at the helm.'

'Sounds nice.'

'It was OK to start with. He got champagne on staff discount from the supermarket so we could christen it.'

'What did you call it?'

'Matthew.'

He smiles a little. 'Do you remember Tom being born?'

'It was snowing. I went to bed and it wasn't, not a single flake, then Dad came into my room and woke me up and there it was, four or five inches. He said the baby looked just like me.'

'What did you think about when you saw Tom?'

'Small. He was . . . I can't think of the word.'

'Premature?'

'Yes, that's it. His face was all squashed and his skin, everywhere, was red and thin, like a membrane. You could see all the stuff underneath, veins and ligaments. I thought I could see his heart beating.'

'When did they find out Tom had asthma?'

'I don't know. Later.'

'But you remember him being ill?'

'Yes. He cried a lot, at first, then he stopped and we were always at the doctors. They had a big bin full of toys; you had to climb inside to get what you wanted. Half the stuff was broken.'

A bee comes in through the window, drunk on pollen. It bounces off the glass and flies out again.

'Mum said he was special. She meant he was different. She said I couldn't play rough games with him because he had funny breathing. I didn't want to play with him anyway, he was too young.'

'Who did you play with?'

'Mates from school. By the time I moved up to secondary school there was a big group of us. We kind of owned the woods, made camps in the trees and on the ground.'

'Were you the leader?'

'We didn't have a leader. It wasn't that sort of group. And we didn't *play*. We just hung out, fooled around. Sometimes there was drink.'

'Alcohol?'

'Yeah. Alcohol. Pornos.' I check his reaction, but he just blinks. 'Someone brought cigarettes once. We put it all, our stash, in a hole in the ground.' A memory of sitting astride a branch, late, when everyone had gone home. 'In summer we used to swing off a tree into the lake until someone from the seniors went on it and snapped the rope.'

'What was school like for Tom?'

'I don't know. I don't suppose it was much fun. He was in infants and I was in juniors, then him in juniors and me at comp. I didn't see him. There was a yard in the middle we shared, that was the only time, breaks, lunch.'

'Did he have mates?'

'A couple.' Mum made him carry a note around in his rucksack, in plastic to keep it clean. It had Mum's phone number at work, the names of the drugs he took and where he kept his spare inhalers. No one likes a sissy. 'He got a bloody nose once, but I sorted it.'

'You stuck up for him?'

'Of course. And I tried to include him in some of the stuff I did, but it didn't work. He liked the Teletubbies. He was way too old, but he still liked them. I liked going out on my mountain bike. I put him on the back once; he loved it, but every time I went fast he started wheezing. I *had* to go fast, to keep up with everyone else.'

'What about your mum and dad? You said before that you thought your dad was scared of Tom's illness.'

'Did I?'

'Can you think of an example of your dad being scared?'

I try, but I can't do it. His face appears to me, always the same, deep concentration, bent over some mechanical problem he had to solve.

'He wasn't around much. Never far away, at the jetty, or working in the garage, but he might as well have been out working somewhere because we weren't allowed to disturb him. He said I wasn't old enough to take people out in the boats, it was too much of a responsibility, in case anything happened. But I could've done it. The engines were easy.'

'Did it make you angry?'

'I was used to responsibility. I looked after Tom until Mum got in from work. Nothing ever happened to him, but Dad couldn't see that.' I take a deep breath. 'I dunno. Dad didn't get Tom, didn't get this little kid who couldn't do anything and didn't run around. He couldn't fix him so he just didn't bother with him all that much. Dad can fix anything.'

'Do you think he thinks in the same way about you?'

'Yes.' I think for a moment. 'Now. I suppose Mum's told you I've got to go and visit him soon. He rang Mum to arrange it.'

'How do you feel about seeing him?'

'It's been a while.' I don't even want to think about it. 'I don't know.'

# 15

Robert went into the kitchen to turn the heat down on the lasagne. How long since he'd cooked something from scratch, or bought expensive wine? He poured himself a large glass to drink while he waited. Outside the afternoon receded, lifting the emergency of the day's heat from the garden. Even the regimented lines of red-hot pokers, normally erect as a firing squad, sagged with relief.

He'd looked forward to seeing Sarah, noted his impatience as he got on with the necessary preparations. He felt harboured by her; safe in this new experience he'd created for himself while at the same time aware that he'd abandoned a great many familiar concerns in its favour. The thought unnerved him and he felt strangely disconnected from himself, as though these missing parts might cause him to overheat and eventually shut down.

A knock. She was early. Having hauled himself into a state of supreme confidence, he greeted her immediately with a kiss. It felt awkward at first, his lips on hers. He sensed her surprise, but fearing retreat would appear even more odd, he pulled her closer to him and slipped his tongue lightly through the seam of her lips.

'Nice to see you too,' she said and kissed him again.

Now that she was here, her hands moving over his back, he was pleased to find it easy. Doing it, or rather the concentration required to ensure he did it well, afforded him little room to think about anything else.

Released from his mouth for a second she whispered, 'Let's go upstairs.'

'OK.'

Suddenly they were on a different track, a predictable chain of events he'd initiated, but miles away from what he'd imagined. They were supposed to eat, drink, talk, drink some more, and eventually, cajoled and teased by all the subtle nuances the evening would offer, they'd fuck. Numbly, a child holding on to his mother's hand, he climbed the stairs behind her. She led them first into the spare bedroom, which contained no bed. Instead, there were the crumpled sheets of newspaper and several belongings in various stages of the packing process. She laughed at her mistake and steered them out again. For a fleeting second he thought he was going to have to point the way, but she found the correct room on her second attempt. The bed, innocent and unquestioning, stared up at him in the half-light of the room.

Focus.

Sarah.

She pushed him gently on to the bed and knelt on the floor in front of him to begin work on his belt buckle. The desire for physical contact raged inside him, but was so indistinguishable from fear that when she reached his cock he was surprised to find it erect. Its veined shaft flowered to reveal a purple, glistening head. She smiled, pushed him on to his back, and took it into her mouth.

'Jesus!'

Stop. Don't stop. Christ. He heard himself, a stuttering of effs and ooahs that sounded alien in the otherwise silent room. She sucked, flicked the bulb with her tongue and drove down with her mouth until she'd taken it all. Seconds, minutes, he wasn't sure, but too soon to come. He pulled at her hair, dragging her head up his chest when, out of the corner of his eye, he saw a blue and white dish on the dresser. Lavender. He swallowed hard, pinged away from Sarah like an elastic band. Sensing the change in mood, she leaned back from him and wiped her mouth.

'Sorry,' he said.

Here, in this cottage, in this room, he'd tried to make love with Elizabeth and failed, unable to get over the shame of knowing the sperm he ejaculated were dead, dying or deformed. He watched Sarah's face grow blank; staring past him as if addressing someone he couldn't see.

'Don't worry about it,' she said. 'I didn't bring a johnny anyway.'

He gazed at her, suddenly horribly young. 'I'll make us a drink,' he said, standing to pull up his trousers.

She got up from her knees and straightened her T-shirt. Why did he have to make it so fucking complicated? She wanted sex, not his heart and soul. All he had to do was what any other man would be foaming at the mouth for by now.

He locked himself in the bathroom, splashed his face with cold water, and sat on the toilet. The peculiarity of the bathroom door being closed made the space feel small. Tongue snug against his palate; he buried his face in a towel. He felt as nauseated now as he had in The Room at the clinic, a sensation so familiar; he didn't want to open his eyes in case he found himself there. A room with no name, no sign on the door to say what it was. A sticky pornographic magazine opened to centrefold, rubber gloves in boxes, straddling the sink so he could wash his cock under the tap.

He stood up, heart pounding, and splashed his face again. Sarah required nothing of him, not a child, not even a relationship in the proper sense, and yet the seconds of relief he enjoyed in her company were still marred by his inadequacy. He'd understood, more since they'd separated, why Elizabeth had sometimes said she wanted to cut her arms, so there was something to show for the pain. She'd longed for something that would bleed and, eventually, heal. He felt the same now, wanting to protect Sarah from that part of himself. The infertile part that said 'You're not a man, you're nothing.'

He went down to the kitchen and found her sitting at the table smoking a cigarette.

'I thought you'd have gone,' he said.

'Do you want me to?'

'No.' He stared at his feet. 'Will you stay? The night, I mean?'

The question surprised her, surprised him even more.

Maybe he just needed not to run away. Not to have sex either, or at least not to attempt it again for several hours.

'There's dinner,' he waved a hand to the oven door.

A mistake. He felt old suddenly, heavy and stupid. His heart was thumping so loudly he could feel the blood pulse behind his ears.

'OK,' she said, affording him a smile.

He turned the oven off, wary of looking at her. 'Sarah, about just now—'

'It's all right.' She moved towards him and placed a hand at the centre of his chest. 'I'm not expecting anything, just whatever you can give.'

The statement surprised him. He hadn't expected such kindness, if that's what it was.

'It's just I haven't got out much since the divorce.' The lie floated to the surface and stung the back of his throat. What was he saying? Bit of a dry patch? Out of practice? He'd had an erection, in itself a big improvement on those last perfunctory Sunday morning fumbles with Elizabeth, only that seemed to make it worse.

'It's fine,' Sarah said. 'I mean, we don't have to do anything. I'm happy just being with you.'

He looked at her, a blush spreading in splotches up her creamy neck. He held her jaw in his hands, pushing her head back gently to look at her. Her eyes were woozy, lost in some desire that had grown thick with waiting. She stared back at him, swayed a little.

'Thank you,' he heard himself say. His voice sounded strange. It was as though he'd given her, without her knowledge, the job of refashioning him from clay, and all he had to do was sit back and be moulded into a new shape.

'I'm starving,' she said, suddenly.

'Then let's eat.'

The lasagne, predictably, was a disaster. He sipped at his wine while she poked at the crusted edges on her plate. 'It's horrible, isn't it?'

'I'm afraid so.' She laughed.

'Come on.' He moved everything over to the sink, picked up her trainers, and slung them at her feet. 'I'll treat you to a takeaway.'

'Now you're talking.'

They got fish and chips and walked along the shore of the lake, eating from the bag. He was enjoying himself and for brief moments it was enough just to know he was stepping inside a foreign world that, now and then, felt more familiar than he gave credit for. He was already forming a catalogue of her expressions and mannerisms. She spun in front of him and fed him a ketchup-smothered chip.

'So, come on then,' he said. 'Tell me more about your family. You said your mother has her own business. Doing what?'

'Sewing, alterations. It's not really a business.'

'Do you have any brothers or sisters?'

'A brother. Josh.'

'Older or younger?'

'Younger. Fifteen.' She dropped her chips into a bin and reached for a cigarette, drawing deeply on the first puff. 'Why the interest all of a sudden?'

'Not quite all of a sudden.' It mattered to him to know something about her, something that would give some solidity to what they shared. 'I'm just curious.'

He watched her shrug, defensive suddenly.

'Come on, there can't be that many skeletons in your cupboard.' He said it jokingly, but it sounded patronising.

'My dad's in prison and my mam works in a fish-finger factory in Bensham.'

'But you said your dad was a policeman, and your mother—'

'I lied.'

'Why?'

'It doesn't matter.'

'Of course it does. Why would you lie about it?'

She stared at the lake. A breeze furrowed the surface into a frown that matched her own. It seemed odd she'd bothered to lie – she had such a take-or-leave-me attitude. He thought about trying again, taking a different tack, but then he hadn't exactly been truthful about his own situation.

She picked up a stone and skimmed it across the surface of the lake. It kissed the water twice and sank. Something false had stepped between them, and in the infancy of their relationship it mattered. Perhaps it was better left.

He joined her, picking up several flattish stones, and choosing one to throw. The angle of his wrist was wrong and it gave out a loud plop. 'I don't care if your entire family are in Wormwood Scrubs, Sarah.'

He threw another stone, knowing as he did so it was just right. It tiptoed across the surface producing rings in its wake that slowly spread to the shore.

'Good one,' she said.

'Did you hear what I said? It's you I want.'

She nodded, stealing a stone from his hand.

'Hey! That was my best one.'

She laughed, put a hand around his neck, and kissed him. What the hell. She could have it.

# 16

Sarah rubbed steam from the bathroom mirror and removed her dressing-gown from her shoulders. In the gentle light of dawn that drifted in through the window her reflection looked almost alien. She covered her nipples with the first two fingers of each hand, the skin contracting beneath her touch, and thought of Robert, still at the cottage where she'd left him, features clenched in sleep.

Being near him made her feel incredibly powerful; the polite, constrained way of his, the dark curls that looked like they were never allowed to grow too long, the posh voice groping for the right word. Nothing in the way of polished chat-up lines, and ancient, even by her standards. But something else which was incredibly attractive. Uncertainty perhaps, an expression that suggested he was waiting for something, or someone, to come to his aid.

Unable to join him in sleep, she'd got up to pee and noticed a small reproduction of Gustav Klimt's *Hope*, postcard-size, pushed into the mirror above the basin. It was one of his more striking paintings, the heavily pregnant figure of the young, red-haired woman with death heads and skulls reaching out to her from the dark.

She'd never gone to bed with a man and done nothing before, and she hadn't been inclined to start anything after the puzzling events of earlier in the evening. So she'd lain there while he slept, playing out fantasies of what it might actually be like. His nervous fumble as he undid the buttons on her shorts, touching skin, growing in confidence, warm, short breaths over her stomach, fingernails digging into thighs as he drove inside with his tongue . . .

She turned off the hot tap and started the cold, promising herself a long soak before anyone else got out of bed, but before she'd got one foot in the water she was distracted by a distant murmuring. At first she thought it might be the TV, but the sound grew louder, culminating in a piercing scream that seemed to fill the house. Matt. She waited for the sound of Gill's footsteps across the landing, but when they didn't come she put her dressing-gown back on and went through into the hall.

Gill's car was absent from its usual position on the drive. Where could she be so early? At work probably. Her job often required her at odd times, mostly in the evenings, but it wasn't too much of a stretch to think it might demand the occasional early morning. Sarah climbed the stairs. Matt's door stood open.

'Don't come in!'

'Oh, Matt!' He was sprawled, upper body on the floor, legs still wound up in the quilt. She rushed over to the bed and lifted him up by the arms to rest him back on his pillows, but he struggled violently.

'What's the matter? What's wrong?'

'Get out!'

As she wrestled with him she became aware of a pungent smell. He appeared to have wet the bed.

'Please! Please just go!' He was sobbing, trying to push her away with his hands.

'I don't *care*, Matt.'

Her hands slipped on his arms, wet with sweat or urine. With surprising strength he shoved her hard on the chest sending her stumbling backwards. It threw him off balance, too, and he slid again from the bed, head first, taking the brunt of the fall on his face.

'Jesus, are you OK?'

'Go!'

'Let me help you.'

It wouldn't be possible to get him back into bed, at least not yet. As gently as the situation allowed she took hold of him beneath his arms and dragged him over to the wardrobe where he sat, a puppet without strings, while she stripped the sheets off the bed and took them out to the wash-basket on the landing.

'Let's get you out of these,' she said, coming back to kneel on the floor beside him.

He stared through her, body shuddering with tears. 'Where's Mum?'

'I don't know. Please, Matt. You can't stay like this.'

'How can you stand it?'

'Stand what? Look at me.' She raised his chin gently. 'I don't care, all right? I don't think anything bad.'

'But—'

'No buts.' He was wearing red pyjamas that drained his skin of colour. She started to undo the buttons. 'We'll get these off and then I'll take you to the bathroom.'

'Sarah . . .'

'I'll keep my eyes closed.' She smiled at him. 'The whole time. Promise.'

In the half-hour it took to get him washed she found herself returning to the thought that had entered her mind, first when she'd found him, and then repeatedly as she dealt with the crisis. The task of looking after him and becoming familiar with what he did and didn't need, what he could and couldn't do, left little room for wondering about what it was actually like to live his life. It was, obvious though it seemed, full of restrictions and compromises. As she removed his sodden pyjama bottoms to the sound of his strangled sobs, she found that she, too, was close to tears. Finally, naked in the wheelchair, he fell silent.

His body surprised her, lean, muscular, but with a rawness to it that suggested it hadn't yet found its final form. It was as though his development had been interrupted, man and boy gelled together midway through the change. It wasn't unpleasant, particularly, and there was much, in fact, that was pleasing. His skin was warm, powdery, and the angles of his elbows, shoulders, hips, beautiful. She put a flannel over the flush of his pubic hair, made small talk, ignored the protests, let him do whatever he could manage himself, then took him down to the kitchen and made tea.

'Did you have a nightmare?' she asked, putting the steaming mug in front of him.

'I'm sorry. I'm sorry. I'm sorry. I'm—'

'Matt, stop.' She rested a hand on his arm. 'It's not your fault. It's perfectly natural to—'

'Know a lot of people who piss themselves, do you? I'm *fifteen*.'

'The nightmares, I meant.' The whole experience had shaken her. Even now, dressed in fresh pyjamas with his hair slicked back, he looked ghostly, an imprint of himself that might fade away at any moment.

'Don't feel sorry for me.'

'Maybe if you talked –'

'I don't *want* to talk about them.' He closed his eyes. 'I just want to go to bed and sleep, one night, that's all, one night. Don't tell Mum about this. I don't want her to know.'

'Why?'

'Just don't. It's bad enough . . .'

He looked beaten, emotionally, and from the bruised veins beneath his eyes, physically, too. Robert said that he had a good mind and he did, far more intelligent than Josh and they were the same age. It was, terrible as it would sound if she were to say it out loud, such a waste.

'Would you do something for me?' he asked.

'Of course.'

'Look in my mouth?'

He opened the large cavern, dark inside, and stuck out his tongue. Puzzled, she peered inside as he tilted his head from right to left. She shrugged.

'Nothing? You looked?'

'There's nothing there, Matt.'

'In my dream there are flies. At first they're in Tom's mouth, bulging behind his cheeks. Then they're in mine. When I wake up, there are millions of them buzzing in my mouth.'

'God.'

'Talk about something else.'

'Like what?'

'Tell me something about you I don't know.'

'All right.' Anything she might say about her own life would be trivial in the context of their conversation. 'I can't think of anything.'

He gazed at his hands, taking on an expression of sadness that made looking at him for any length of time painful.

'OK,' she said, finally. 'How about my tremendous, incredibly cool and disgusting party trick? I can burp the alphabet. All of it.'

'No, you can't.'

'A to Z. Even some words.'

'Go on then.' He looked at her, the first meaningful eye contact. She put down her tea, sucked and swallowed several breaths and then opened her mouth. No sound. Spectacular failure.

He raised a single, mocking eyebrow.

'Well, I used to be able to do it. Least I cheered you up.'

'Have you ever been in love, Sarah?'

'What sort of question is that?'

He shrugged.

'Yes. I think so. Why do you ask?'

'The person you loved, did he feel the same about you?'

'I don't know.' It was as though her longing for Julian and the sting she'd felt at the ending of their relationship weren't opposite sides to the spectrum. It was difficult to know what she felt. 'I thought he did.'

'What happened?'

'I didn't belong with him any more.' She felt she would have to elaborate on this vague explanation and yet it felt entirely accurate. For a long time Julian had been home and then, suddenly, he wasn't there. She glanced at Matt, expecting confusion, but saw instead that he was nodding his head.

'I feel like that about the Sunshine group. I don't belong. You know we're having our summer picnic next Saturday? Carers' Day. I don't want to go, but Mum'll say I have to. Apparently I learn things.'

'At the picnic?'

'At the centre. I go every so often to cook, wash clothes, do ironing. Mum wants to know I'll be all right if anything were to happen to her. That I wouldn't be, you know, left to fend for myself.'

'What about your dad?'

'I can't live with other people for the rest of my life,' he answered sharply.

'Of course not. Well, at least there's one thing. You won't have to go to the picnic by yourself.'

'Why not?'

'Carers' Day. I'll be there, won't I?'

# 17

Check me out. I'm the kid dripping piss. I'm the kid washed and dressed and laid on plastic. See me. Smell me. Laugh and shake your head. Then forget me because I'm nothing.

All over my skin burns with shame. Now, sitting here red as a slap, I can still feel Sarah's hands on me, hear her humming 'Waterloo' while she mops me up. What I want, my body can't feel. To be stroked and held and caressed with fingers that don't hide behind a flannel, that don't pull and drag. Clean him up, that's it, turn him, push him, dress his withered sticks in something nice.

I watch her from my bedroom window. She's hanging washing out on the line. A breeze picks at one of the bed sheets, hiding her from me, showing her again. She goes back inside with the empty basket. A few minutes later I hear her on the stairs.

'Hey, you.' She peers her head around the door then comes inside, crouching on the floor in front of me. She rests her hands on my knees. 'Going to get some sun on those lovely legs of yours?'

'Don't.' I tug at my shorts.

'Come on, you can't possibly stay in your room all day. Besides, compared to mine, your legs are gorgeous.'

'Leave me alone.'

She rolls away from me and pulls up the bottom of her jeans. 'See? Turkey legs.'

'Right.'

'You're not looking.'

Her calves are white, a big scar below her left knee that's turned silver.

'See? Manky.'

Beautiful.

'So what's it going to be? Sit up here like a mushroom or come outside with me and get some rays?'

'I'll be fine.'

'Suit yourself.' She gets up, loses a flip-flop and skirts the floor with it to get it back on. 'I'll be in the garden if you change your mind.'

I wait until I hear the patio doors open then go to the window. A scraping across concrete as she drags the sun lounger on to the lawn. By the time I get outside she's lying back, almost flat, her red hair poking through the slats. Her hand, dangling lazily over the side, taps to a beat on her personal stereo. Kssch, kssch, dum, kssch, kssch, dum. I wheel myself closer. She's changed into her bikini.

Her eyes are closed, lids fluttering, lips mouthing words. She makes a circle with her ankle then scrunches up her feet until her big toes crack.

'Bloody hell!' She squints at me. 'You scared the life out of me.'

'Sorry.'

She takes the earpieces from her ears, letting them drop to the grass, and rests her head back down. A bluebottle lands on her stomach and crawls through golden hairs towards her belly button, flexing its wings like it might fly off any second, but it doesn't. It stops, shining purple, and tastes her skin.

'You don't have to be uncomfortable. With your top off.'

'I'm not.' She brushes the fly away. 'What's up?'

'Nothing.'

'You've got this look on your face. One minute you're down in the dumps, the next you're on top of the world. What's the deal?'

'No deal.' I pull my T-shirt off my head, smiling as it passes over my face. Her eyes flick over my chest, following the contours of muscles on my arms and shoulders. I feel like I could pick her up, and I want to, pick her up and taste her.

'So there's nothing wrong?'

'Nope.' I stretch my arms out to the sides, rolling my shoulders.

'What about just now, in your room? You're not in a mood any more?'

'I wasn't in a mood.'

'OK.' She shrugs. 'Look, about last night, if you're embarrassed—'

'I'm not embarrassed.'

She turns on her side to face me, pressing weight into the curves on her breasts and stomach. I stare at a mole on her thigh, large, like a chocolate penny. She covers herself with a sarong.

'Does it . . . help, talking to Dr Mason?'

'I'm not crazy.'

'Didn't say you were.' She closes her eyes and wets her bottom lip. 'Want to know what I think? I think if it wasn't for those crappy nightmares of yours you could tell him to piss off, but you never know. Might be worth hearing what he's got to say. You don't like it, he's history.'

Geordie style. For a second I can actually see myself telling Doc to piss off and me and Sarah, afterwards, laughing our heads off.

'Just hear him out.'

'That's what you'd do?'

'Yeah. What do you talk about anyway, or is it a secret?'

'Not secret. Just boring.'

'That means it isn't.'

'This and that. Nothing really. School. Dragonflies.'

'Dragonflies?'

'In the first session, when he was assessing me, he asked me to think of something nice, my favourite thing.'

'And all you could think of was an insect?'

I laugh. 'An incredible insect.'

'Yeah, they're beautiful but . . .' She shrugs and reaches for her earpieces, pulling them up like buttons on a string.

'I don't expect you to understand.'

'Why?' A playful smile. ''Cos I'm a girl?'

'Are you really interested?'

'Yes. I'm reeeeally interested.'

'Right. Come on then.' I take the T-shirt from where I've rested it over my legs and put it back on.

'Where are you going?'

'Where are *we* going. You can borrow Mum's wellies. They're in the cupboard under the stairs.'

'Matt!'

I don't even know whether we can get to Emperor Pond or not. It'll be overgrown, but I don't care. I want to find out and I want to show her. I go into the utility room and try the door to the garage. Locked. I look around, opening the cupboards next to the washing machine. Paint tins. Wallpaper paste. I pick up one of Dad's old golf clubs, an iron with no head that Mum's used to stir paint. In the kitchen I look for a container, settling on an old coffee jar Mum keeps five pences in. I empty them out on the counter, several coins skidding off on to the floor, and go back to find Sarah.

'Do they fit?'

'They're OK.' She sits on one of the patio chairs to pull on the second wellie. Bare feet. She's put shorts on. 'Have you seen my T-shirt?'

Kitchen. 'No.'

'I'd better find it, or slap some more cream on at least. God, it's boiling.'

'We'll be in the shade. Hurry *up*, I'd like to get there this century. If you don't mind.'

'Where?'

'Wait and see.'

She wheels me fast down the path to the gate, laughing into my shoulder. The sun blazes hot off the shoreline, blasting dry heat up into our faces.

'What do I need wellies for?'

I love that she's excited and I want to drag it out, her not knowing. I hand her the golf club. 'You'll have to go first,' I say, when we reach the edge of the wood. The grass at the foot of the first line of trees is tall, golden wands that whisper coolly on my arms.

'In *there*?'

The path is further in, strewn with brambles and nettles. There's a way through, but it won't be easy. In the distance an ice-cream van stops midway through the tune. 'Hitler Has Only Got One Ball'. Sarah looks at me, the chair.

'I can do it if you lead the way.'

'Matt, I dun—

'Please.' I pull forward into the shade. Suddenly the distance between us seems to have grown. I could reach out, touch her, but it would still feel miles. The seconds pass then, giving me a rub on the back of my head, she sighs and walks ahead of me into the wood.

The first ten feet or so are easy, the ground hard under my wheels. When the undergrowth starts to get thicker, Sarah looks back. I push her on with a smile. My arms ache and I can taste sweat from my top lip, but I don't stop. I won't. I focus on the soft white of the back of her knees. A bramble has scratched her further up, a string of blood beads just below the line of her shorts.

'You all right?' she says, turning around again.

'Keep going.'

Her arms swing from side to side, beating the undergrowth back with the golf club. She takes slow, careful steps through the brambles, snapping their spines.

'Left there, then right at that funny-looking tree.'

My wheels are choked, thorns riding up the spokes and pricking my knuckles. I feel them biting, nettles stinging. If I can just get to the grassy clearing ahead we can rest. Sarah reaches it first, but comes back for me.

'This is madness. Your mum'd kill me if she knew what we were doing.'

'So don't tell her.'

She pushes me the last few steps, collapsing on the grass with her arms stretched out behind her. Her breasts squash out to the sides, filling creamy skin. 'If I didn't like you so much I'd kill *you.*'

She likes me so much. I pick a sticky ball out of her hair.

'And you,' she says, 'your T-shirt's covered.'

She brushes them off then lifts my hand and blows on a nettle sting I don't feel. Her breath is hot. I want to reach out to stroke the glistening film of sweat on her neck. A V of sweat has appeared at the top of her shorts too, darkening them from peach to a deep, burnt orange.

'Feels like we're miles away, doesn't it?' I say, because I have to say something.

She nods. The wood is quiet, but for birdsong and, high up in the canopy of bright green and yellow leaves, the drumming of a woodpecker. I wet my lips, smelling her sweat, tasting my own. The sun disappears behind a cloud, spreading an even darkness, then light again, burning through in pencil shafts.

'It's beautiful,' she says.

'This isn't it, you know? What I wanted to show you. This, it isn't it.'

'It isn't?'

'No. It's over there.'

My hands and fingers tremble when I grip the wheels again. When I reach the top of the bank I see it, the lake shimmering through gaps in the trees and set twenty yards or so further in, with the remains of a canal I used to get the water down to it, the pond.

'Dragonflies. I built the pond to encourage them to breed. Come on.'

'Matt. You can't get down there.'

'It isn't steep. I'll shuffle down on my bum.'

'I couldn't get you back up. No, it's too dangerous.'

'I can use my arms.'

She looks at it again then shakes her head and makes to turn back. 'We're lucky we got this far. I think we should go back.'

'You go if you want.' I drop the armrests. 'I didn't come all this way for nothing.'

I'll show her I can do it. I slide over to the edge of my chair, but before I can lower myself, it tips over and I land awkwardly with my legs underneath it.

'For fuck's sake, Matt. Don't you know when to stop?' She grabs the chair and pulls it off me. Then, with the same severe grip, she takes hold of me under the arms.

'You're hurting me.'

'You can't do this, Matt.'

'I can.'

'Not on your own.'

'Then stay.'

She groans, wipes her forehead, then rests her hands on her hips. 'OK. I'll stay, I'll help you, but only if you promise to listen and do exactly as I say. Don't think I won't leave you here.'

'I'm listening.'

She sits down at the top of the incline and looks towards the pond, weighing it up.

'I could roll?' I say, smiling.

'No, you couldn't.'

'Bum scud then.'

'Bum scud?' She laughs. 'I've never heard it called that before. Why do you have to go down anyway?'

'I want you to see it.'

'I can.'

'I want to catch something.' I reach for the bag I looped over the back of my chair and pull out the jar. 'See?'

'You can't just wade into a pond and fish around in it like you're Tom bloody Sawyer.'

'You're right. I can't do anything. I'm useless.'

'I didn't mean . . . Matt, I admire you, it's just—'

'You do?'

'Yes.'

'Help me, then.'

As we start to slide down the bank, Sarah on her side, straightening out my legs as we go, there's a part of me that doesn't care if we make it to the pond or not, which is weird, because I wanted, in the moments leading up to this one, to get there more than anything. Only now, with Sarah, touching, closer than we've ever been, I just want it all to stop, to lie still, close my eyes and breathe next to her until there's nothing else.

The last few feet are the steepest culminating in a bank of powdery earth knotted with tree roots.

'You'll have to stay there,' she says, sliding down and standing up at the edge of the pond. 'No arguments.'

'It's smaller than I remember it.'

She peers into the water.

'Over by the reeds.' I wave her forward. 'What can you see?'

'Murky green stuff.'

'Go in, to the right. The bottom of those reeds.'

She wades in, jar in one hand, the other held out for balance. Her legs are stippled red, the crusted line of another scratch above her knee. 'What are we catching anyway?'

'Dip the jar in.'

'I can't see anything.'

'At the *reeds*, where they meet the water.'

She fills the jar and looks through the glass, puzzled. I pick up a hard lump of earth and plop it into the pond near to where she's standing. The water splashes up her legs. 'Hey!'

'Anything?'

She tips the water back into the pond. 'It might help if I knew what I was looking for.'

'A nymph. Looks a bit like a moth. Brown.'

'That helps.'

The next time she fills the jar she brings it over to me. 'You look this time. What's a nymph anyway?'

'You've got something.'

'I hope it isn't something that bites. It'd be just like you to omit a crucial fact like that. Anyway, I thought we were looking for dragonflies.'

'You did it!' I check again to be sure. At first it looks dead, then the water starts to clear and I see one of the front legs stretch out. 'There must be loads in there, or you just got lucky.'

'It's called "skill".'

'It's close, see?'

'Close to what?'

'Metamorphosis. Look at the size. I've never seen one this big.' I dig around in the earth beside me. 'Find me a snail. Quick. A water beetle, anything.'

Sarah stumbles awkwardly back to the water's edge and uses a stick to prod around in the water. After a minute or so she drops it, using her hands to move vegetation out of the way. Her hair falls forward, damp around her ears where she's brushed it back with wet fingers. I watch, mesmerised, for a second. She's like a sore patch on the roof of my mouth that would heal if only I could stop tonguing it.

'Got one!' She turns and smiles, waving a snail. 'What's it for?'

I pull the body of the snail through its shell and drop it through the top of the jar.

'You killed it!'

'Watch this.' It happens in less than a second. The nymph senses the movement in the water and strikes. 'Mint!'

'I don't *believe* you did that.'

'I suppose you think the roast lamb we had on Sunday died of old age?'

She raises an eyebrow and sits down, wiping her hands dry on the front of her shorts.

I hand her the jar. 'See the mouth? It ambushes the snail

and stabs it with jaws, kind of like spears. Lightning, wham, and it's dead. Then it brings it up to these really sharp things called mandibles and rips through the flesh.'

'Lovely.'

'It kills, eats, it sheds skin. It waits. Two years it takes. Then one day it climbs up out of the water and becomes a dragonfly. Everything has to be right, the water temperature, the time. They do it at dawn usually so they can dry their wings in the sun. It's called metamorphosis.'

'When?'

'This one? Soon. We can watch it if you like.'

'Whoa there! *We's* already had me wading about in the mud, thank you. If you think I'm staring at that jar for the next God knows how long, you really are mad.'

I shrug, hiding my disappointment. 'I'll do it, I'll wait.'

'You really like them, don't you?'

'Yeah.'

'Nymph. You wouldn't think something that ugly could have such a beautiful name. I wonder what they feel when they're changing.'

'They don't feel anything.'

'Rubbish. They've got to feel something.'

'Insects don't have that kind of brain.'

'And how could you possibly know that?' She turns the jar around in her hands, narrowing her eyes, smiling when she locates the nymph. 'I bet it's feeling something right now. Something incredible. Right this very minute.'

# 18

'Not in the mood for talking today, Matt?'

The bubbles on my pop fizz. I focus on the sound, thousands of tiny worlds forming and dying at the side of the glass. Warm Cola. Not Diet Coke or Pepsi. I take a sip and spit it back into the glass.

'Perhaps you'd like something else?'

No television. No DVD. He doesn't even have a stereo. There's only a cheap-looking clock on the mantelpiece that looks strange, out of place with it's gold-leaf trimmings and silly ball things that go round and round. It ticks unevenly, too. Tick-TOCK. Tick-TOCK.

'It was my mother's,' Doc says.

'Is she dead?'

'Yes, she died a couple of years ago.'

He narrows his gaze on me. I mentioned his dead mum, so I must be thinking about Tom.

'Has something happened since we last spoke?'

'No. I don't want to do this any more, that's all. It's messing with my head.'

'In what way?'

'I can't stop thinking about stuff I don't want to think about. Dad's gone and I was all right about it. I didn't spend every minute of every day thinking about him. I don't want to think about Dad, or Tom; they're gone.'

'But you have nightmares about Tom.'

You'd think having the same nightmare over and over again would make it less frightening, but it's like someone saying they'll give you a shock to get rid of your hiccups. You know it's coming, but you still jump. Except the nightmares are changing. Tom isn't the same. He isn't decaying any more, doesn't look rotten. He's coming alive. If I told Doc it would sound all wrong, like I was having hallucinations or seeing ghosts. But I don't *see* anything. I *hear* his silence. I *feel* his absence.

'You could draw, if you like? Sometimes it helps to draw what you're feeling. You could do that instead of talking.'

I look at the pad and the box of crayons next to it. Yeah, crayons. Fat and greasy like dinner-lady fingers. 'No, thanks.'

'How about this, you can sit there and not talk for as long as you want to, until the end of the session, if you like. In the meantime, I'll talk and if you want to say anything at any point, interrupt. Cool?'

I hate it when he tries to be trendy. You can tell right away he doesn't normally use words like that.

'Cooool.' I wait until he takes a breath to talk again

then I put my fingers in my ears. He looks at me, probably wants to slap my head right off my neck.

'In the last session you took us up to the point where your father moved out.'

Da. Da. Da.

'I'd like to pick up there.'

I don't have to listen. I can stay inside my head. I think about something beautiful – the nymph in the jar on my window sill at home and how, last night, the spines along its back were silhouetted in the moonlight.

'Let's talk about the bed-wetting, then.'

'I didn't tell you that.'

'How often does it happen?'

'You're pushy today. I don't like it.'

'How often do you wet the bed?'

'All you can think of to talk about is how often I piss myself?' He doesn't answer. Voices outside. A car engine starts and stalls. 'I want to go.'

'No.'

'I want to *go*.'

The weird thing is for the last few days I've wanted to talk, but now I'm here I don't want to. It's like I'm right back at the beginning and it's Finch sitting on the other side of the desk, chewing his fingers. The silence is like a balloon filling up the room. The clock on the mantelpiece ticks. A funny sort of grating sound, then it chimes. It's supposed to do two chimes for two o'clock, only the second chime doesn't come.

'It's broken,' Doc says.

I shrug.

'I keep meaning to get it fixed.' He stands up, holds it out in front of him, and places it gently back on the mantelpiece. 'Only I think I might've got used to it. What do you think? Should I get it fixed?'

'It's just a clock.'

He waits.

'I dunno. Yeah, it's broken. Fix it.'

'What about you, Matt? Do you want to get well?'

'I'm not sick.'

'You have nightmares, you wet the bed, you're in a wheelchair.'

'Got a point?' I look at the clock. 'You can't *fix* me.'

He goes back to his chair. 'Maybe I can, maybe I can't. The way I see it, you've got a choice. You can carry on having nightmares, wetting the bed, spending the rest of your life stuck in that chair, or you can take control.'

'Reckon it's you that belongs in a loony bin.'

'Your dad was busy, building up the business, your mum worked late. You had to look after Tom. Your dad left because he couldn't cope with Tom's illness and when he did things got worse for you.'

'I don't remember.'

'Dad wasn't coping.'

'You're putting words in my mouth!'

'Tell me, Matt. How did things change for you when Dad left?'

'Worse, like you said. All right? Shit. Crap. Horrible.'

'How?'

'Because it didn't matter how much Mum worked we never had enough bookings, or enough money, or enough help. She was always busy, trying to keep up the job and managing the holiday cottages. She could've asked him to come back and everything would've been OK, but she wouldn't. It was her decision, but she wouldn't and it didn't matter how much I wanted her to.'

'Do you think he'd have come back if she'd asked him?'

'No.'

'Why?'

'Because I phoned him up and he said so himself.'

'When he left, then, and your mum wasn't around, you looked after Tom, same as before?'

'Not like before. It was all the time.'

'It must've made it very difficult for you to do things with your mates.'

'They didn't want a kid knocking around with them.'

'What about last year, last summer? Did you want to go to the island?'

'I don't know.'

'Did Tom?'

'I don't know. Yes, he wanted it because that's what he always wanted. But he couldn't go because he wasn't allowed. Neither of us were allowed on the lake by ourselves.'

'But you went.'

'We must've done.'

'I want you to think back to when you were in hospital—'

'I don't remember.'

'The doctor told you something about your paralysis.'

He tries to get me to look at him, but I don't want to.

'You had tests. Sometimes, when something terrible

happens, our bodies hold on to the memory. Our minds can't process what's happened so it gets stored physically.'

'It was a virus—'

'No, Matt.'

'A virus from—'

'I want you to listen very carefully. There's no doubt, no other explanation. The cause of your paralysis is entirely psychological. Do you understand what that means? It means it's inside your mind.'

'I know what it *means*.'

'If you can accept that, if you want to—'

'If, if, if, if, if . . .'

'You control it.' He stands up and comes over to kneel on the floor beside me. 'You control it, Matt.' He stares at me, looking right into me like some kind of freak.

'It's rude to stare.'

'Say it. "I control it."'

'You're crazy.'

'I control it.'

'OK. I got it.' I shrug off his stare, but it stays fixed. 'I control it. I control it.'

'I control it.'

If he say's it again I'll smack him.

'I—'

He catches my fist in his hand and for a second we're locked together, him pushing against my fist, me pushing back.

'Let *go*!'

I can't do anything, my face burns, I thrash my head around to try and release the rest of me, but he's too strong. Then, suddenly and stupidly, I start to cry. After a few minutes I realise he isn't there any more. He isn't even in the room. He comes back with a glass of water, packed tall with ice, and puts it on the coffee table. Then he hands me several sheets of bog roll that he's folded into a neat square. I take it, too embarrassed to look up. I wipe my cheeks, stuff the bog roll up my sleeve and sip water from the glass. The cold stings my teeth. 'What did you do that for?'

'Why do you think I did it?' He sits down again.

'You want me to face up to what the doctors told me.'

'That's right. Doesn't make a lot of sense, does it? The mind's a very powerful thing, Matt. But I meant what I said, you have a choice. If you decide you want to get better I can help you. You'd be doing it all, but I'll be here with you when—'

'When I remember.'

'I think if we can unblock your memory of what happened on the lake with Tom, the nightmares and the bed-wetting may go away. No promises, you understand? But, and this is the most important thing, a lot of what we've been talking about focuses on the past, but the key to getting well again is to focus on something in the future. Look ahead.'

The room is quiet again. I want to explain, but all I see in my head is the floating island, rising, coming back to the surface. I see it out of every window in the house, inside every corner of my mind. It's there, like a shadow that falls in and marches beside me. I look up, startled to find myself talking out loud.

'Are you afraid of what'll happen when the island has surfaced again?'

A flash of Tom, arms flailing, then cushioned on air, falling on to a flat expanse of black water. 'I wasn't nice to him. I was horrible. I lied when I said we didn't argue. Maybe there's a reason I don't remember. Maybe I've forgotten—'

'Listen to me.'

'If I forgot, then—'

'Matt.'

A tear rolls down my cheek.

'You're in control. OK?' He glances over to the window, raises a hand. 'Every time we make a choice about something we're more in control than we were before. I think we'll leave it there for today. Try not to worry.'

He stands up to answer the door. I hear Sarah's voice. My hands are shaking. I feel tired, pulled and stretched in all directions. I control it. I say it over and over in my head until the words blur at the edges. But inside, where I need to hear it most, it doesn't reach.

# 19

They'd been going fast, but now everything slowed down. It was a dark night, no moon, just shapes and the taste of her. Her calves sidled up his chest. He slid his mouth down the side of one, leaving a trail of brightness to her knee, a tiny scar on the side, the ticklish underside. She groaned frustration, but he wasn't teasing. He wanted to explore.

Her foot slid down his stomach, clinked over the belt buckle, and rested firmly over the bulge. 'You've made me crazy waiting.'

She started to undo the buttons on his jeans, quietly, confidently, while he fumbled with her blouse. His head felt thick, a feeling that spread to the rest of him. It was as though all the rationalising had made him awkward, but it was Sarah who took the lead, found his mouth, offered her tongue. She undid the last button on her blouse and pushed him back on to the bed to straddle him.

The sight of her, expectant, woozy with desire, gave him confidence. He removed her blouse from her shoulders and brushed her bra straps to the sides so he could trace the lines of her collarbones. She kissed, tongue, lips and teeth on his fingers, thumbs, palms. He pushed her back gently and ran a finger down the centre of her breasts, pulling down the cups of her bra so he could circle up and over her nipples with his thumbs. Her skin flushed in pink splotches where he touched.

She tugged at his jeans. 'Off.'

He lifted his legs into the air while she yanked, the coins in his pockets escaping on to the bed. The jeans were knotted, bunched around his ankles where they'd turned inside out. His efforts to assist made it worse and for one horrible second he thought, 'I can't do this', but she'd already abandoned them and started on his pants. The sight of his cock, springing forward and up, made her smile broadly. All he had to do was not think. Don't think.

He cried out silently as she slid down his cock. He felt the pulse in his neck; her heated lips flutter across it as she leaned over him and began a rhythm. A pool of sweat gathered in his belly button. Unable to move his legs, he had the curious feeling of being pinned, like a lab rat gazing up at the process of being dissected and exposed. He closed his eyes, the darkness tuning his senses to the one, delicious sensation of her moving over him, coming almost all the way off him, then falling again, a deep thrust that made his balls crawl. Her cries were raw, an outpouring of stuttered demands and appreciation that made him dizzy with excitement. He opened his eyes and lifted her skirt to watch her dark bush of hair swallow him until, finally, his body soft except for his cock which was perfectly hard, he came.

Stroking her sweated back while he grew limp inside her, he felt exhausted and lay, shivering, until she reached for the duvet and pulled it over them.

She rested her chin on his shoulder. 'You make me very happy.'

They made love several times that night, coming out of sleep to find each other in the dark. How long since he'd done that? And simply done it?

In the morning, when she went home, he felt her absence acutely. He whiled away the hours reading and listening to the radio, horrified by how empty the cottage felt without her, as though all the air had been sucked out of it.

She returned in the afternoon and they spent most of it in bed, sometimes curled into each other. They drank, ate, talked nonsense. He felt indulged, keyed up, and, at times, deeply uneasy. It was as though he were clutching a fantasy that'd disappear the second he opened the door to the outside world. Poof and she'd be gone; taking the new, fragile version of him she'd created with her. Now, late into the evening, and still in bed, he propped himself up on his pillow to look at her.

'Let's have a bath,' he said.

'What's wrong with here?' She ran a fingernail up the sole of his foot and along and down each toe.

'I want you wet.'

She smiled and reached for his hand, taking the index

finger and pressing it between her legs. 'Wet enough for you?'

'God, you . . .'

He chased her into the bathroom, but they didn't make it as far as the bath. She faced him, laughing, and gripped his cock firmly in her fist before spinning away to grip the towel rail with both hands. It seemed remarkable that he could get so worked up again, but the sight of her bent over, the dark mouth of her cunt gaping, took hold of his breathing and he entered her sharply. Ignoring the stuttering of protests she made at being forced to slow down, he held her at the waist and rocked her forward and back. Despite his efforts, the rhythm grew into a frenzy, sawing, thrusting, the slap of his thighs against hers. After a short time he came and fell forward, shivering, guilty, on her back.

Arching herself like a cat stretching out of sleep, she came off him and staggered to the toilet where she sat down and wiped at herself with tissue.

'Why the rush?' It bothered him. That? Or something else?

She was out of breath. 'Because you drive me wild.'

'I'm serious.' He turned the taps on to fill the bath and followed her into the bedroom. 'Why so fast?'

'I thought you enjoyed it.'

'I did.'

An atmosphere. But it mattered. Not just the quick fuck, there was a time and a place for that and he did enjoy it, but he'd wanted more. He wished suddenly to be alone, to take away all that had happened and break it off into chunks so he could make sense of it. 'You seemed to want it over with.'

'That's ridiculous.' She stared at him for a moment, cheeks flushed, then turned away and sat on the bed to pull up her socks.

'Sarah.'

'What?' She stood in front of him, no bra or pants; socks pulled halfway up her shins.

He looked down at himself, towel wrapped tightly around his waist.

'*What*, Robert?'

'You.' He stuttered over breaths with no words attached. 'This, it's nice, but I want to, Christ, I don't know. Talk.'

'Talk?'

'Slow down long enough to have a conversation. Share something.'

'I thought we were fucking.'

The words entered him like the point of a blade.

'I'm sorry.' She held him around the waist. 'Hey, I didn't mean . . . I didn't mean that, I—'

He retreated to the bathroom and after turning off the tap he went downstairs to the kitchen to fill the kettle. In no time they seemed to have been transported into some quasi-marital scene. What did he want? He was tired. She appeared in the doorway, dressed.

'I suppose . . . Robert, I like you a lot—'

'Please.' He raised a hand. 'Forget I said anything.'

'No, I've upset you. I didn't appreciate what was going on between us. I thought you weren't all that interested in anything serious so I didn't allow myself to want more.'

He had to force himself to slow down his thinking. How had they got to this point, discussing a relationship that hadn't even existed a few days ago?

'Do you?' She was close to him now, nestling her fingers in the palms of his hands. 'Do you want more?'

'I don't know.' He breathed out slowly. He wanted something to counterbalance the sight of her on the toilet wiping away dead sperm. He wanted to know, 'Why him?' Why was she still here and not getting drunk at parties? 'You're eighteen.'

'And?'

'And I don't know. Maybe I find it difficult to understand what you're doing here.'

'So I'll go.'

'No.' He sighed. 'That's not what I meant. It's just that it feels like I don't know anything about you.'

'We talk all the time.' The kettle, silent, now began to stir behind him. She tugged on his towel, loosening it, then tightening it again. He felt like a schoolboy having the duffles done up on his coat. 'What do you want to know?'

'Anything. Why did you lie to me about your parents?'

'Oh, that.' She turned away from him to light a cigarette. 'I don't know. It, they, it's not who I am. I didn't think it mattered. I thought you weren't going to psychoanalyse me.'

'I'm not.' He felt chastened. 'Sarah, anyone can see—'

'I had an abortion, OK?' She sat heavily on one of the kitchen chairs, cupping her chin in one hand. 'No big deal.'

A child. He hadn't seen that. He felt winded. The words tumbled over each other, finding pockets of pain inside him he'd forgotten existed.

'A week before I moved out here.'

He felt the familiar twinge of sadness at the thought of

this unwanted life. There one day, gone the next. He thought of Elizabeth, of the bitter reaction he'd witnessed whenever they were faced with evidence of unwanted, teenage pregnancies. It wasn't fair, she'd said, reduced time and time again to angry sobbing. It wasn't.

'Haven't you got anything to say?' She waited, filling his silence with a sigh. 'That's why I didn't tell you. I wasn't ready to . . . explain it.'

'You don't have to explain it to me.'

'I do. I wasn't ready to have a child, not at my age. I couldn't . . .' Her voice broke, then, suddenly, she lowered her head and began to cry. 'I don't—'

'Oh Christ, Sarah, I'm sorry.'

Her face was red. She wiped her cheeks.

'I shouldn't have bullied you into talking. Come here.'

She rested her cheek against his bare chest, sniffed and coughed. After several minutes during which he felt her try to regain some control over her breathing, she straightened up and lit another cigarette, sucking on it in sharp, uneven breaths.

'What about the father?'

'What about his wife?'

'I see.'

'No, you don't. If you want to know about me, I'll tell you. I'll tell you everything, but before you judge me—'

'That's not what I'm doing.'

She tapped the ash from the end of her cigarette into her hand.

'You're angry. Let's—'

'My dad got sent down eighteen months ago for burglary. My mother's a drunk. My brother nicks cars—'

'Sarah, stop.'

'Me nanna. She's got dementia. Wanders off in the middle of the night, turns the gas on, forgets to light it—'

'*OK.*'

Silence. He handed her a saucer. She ground out her cigarette, keeping hold of the butt to shape lines out of the black ash.

He took a bottle of whiskey from a cupboard above her head and poured large measures into two glasses.

'Changes things, doesn't it?' she said.

'What does?'

'You, a psychiatrist, me, a—'

'No.'

'When I told you . . . don't tell me we aren't different. I didn't want you thinking I was just some kid from a shitty council estate who screwed around and got knocked up. That's where I'm from, a place where all you can do is fuck or get high because that's all there is, but it isn't me, Robert, it isn't what happened.'

'I was shocked, that's all.'

'Disgusted.'

'No.'

'I wasn't fucking around. I thought I was in love.' She stared into her glass. 'I thought he loved *me.*'

He looked out over the garden. Next door, over the fence, an arc of water shot through the air, followed by a squeal of children's laughter.

'It must've been horrible, Sarah.' He put his arms over her shoulders and kissed the back of her neck. 'I like who you are.'

'You do?'

'Yes. Very much. Come on, let's do something.'

'What?'

'I don't know.'

After a great deal of consideration she turned her face to him. 'You could start by feeding me. I'm starved.'

He laughed.

'I know. We'll order Chinese.' She kissed his chin. 'And ice-cream.'

# 20

Sarah's gathering flowers from the wood to put in the cottages. I keep seeing her, moving between the trees, stopping to bend down, then gone, out of sight. I want to be back in the wood beside the Emperor Pond, to go further, to where the best flowers are, to the badgers' den, to show her where the woodpecker nests. I catch another glimpse of her, a bunch in each hand, hemlock and wild grasses. She lifts them up to her face, breathing in sweetness I can only guess at, then she's gone again. I close my eyes, the inside of my lids stinging, but it only serves to focus my mind on the feel of the chair.

'Thank you for showing me this.' Doc sits on the edge of my bed. There isn't anywhere else.

'Mum has a box she keeps in her bedroom. Mother's Day cards, pictures he drew, one of his baby teeth. I thought I'd give it to her.'

'I'm sure she'd like that.'

'You don't think it'll just upset her?'

'A little, perhaps, but I'm sure she'd rather have it than not. How did you feel when you found it?'

Sarah again, moving through the trees. 'He believed in fairies that come and take your teeth away. In King Kong, and that spinach gives you muscles. He believed in wishes blown on dandelion seeds. *Not a real wolf.* He was just a kid.'

'Yes.'

'He wrote me a note once. It said "I wish you were dead". Guess he was pretty miffed, huh?'

'Do you think he meant it?'

'Absolutely.' I try to organise the thoughts in my head, pare them down to just one. I can see Tom's arms wriggling on the bed, his feet kicking under my body, his tiny fists slamming down on the mattress. 'But I was stronger. I used to knuckle his head, you know what that is? It's when you make a fist and roll your knuckles over someone's skull. And Chinese burns on his ankles and arms, elastic-band flicks and marble catapults that left bruises like love bites.' I pull away from his stare. 'You think that's awful, don't you?'

'Sounds like typical brother stuff.'

'I suppose I forgot how weak he was, coughing and wheezing all the time. He's not like that any more. It's him who's stronger, or I'm weaker. I don't know.'

'How do you explain that, that Tom could've changed?'

'I can't.'

'I want you to think about it, think about why Tom is changing, becoming stronger.'

He waits for a reply, but when I don't say anything he claps his hands on his knees and stands up. 'Come on. I think it'll do you good to get out of this room for a while.'

It's weird, going out with Doc. I crouch down low in the car because I don't want people to see us. He takes me to a pub called The Grey Mare. There's a small courtyard out the back that looks like nobody uses it. They've tried to make it nice, plants in pots, but someone has forgotten to water them. There are butt ends in amongst the shrunken leaves and more around the kitchen door. Crates in a stack. He sits on a picnic bench next to a stone wall. There's a hole, like a spy hole, and through it I can see St Mary's church and the graveyard. Doc gets some drinks, a pint of lager and a Coke for me. He has a menu tucked under his arm. Sandwiches, jacket potatoes, lasagne in a pot.

'I'm not hungry.'

No lecture. He orders ham sandwiches for himself, says I can have one if I want.

'Have you been here before?' Doc asks, taking a gulp of lager.

'They don't let kids inside.'

'I thought it would be good to get out, change the scenery.'

A man is digging a grave. He removes his cap, wipes the sweat off his forehead with it, and puts it back on. 'How long will it take for me to remember?'

'I don't know.' Doc presses his glass along the edge of his beer mat. 'Let's take it one step—'

'I'm tired of waiting, I'm sick of it hanging over me all the time.' I try to summon an image of the floating island in my mind, see its rough grass spiking from the water like whiskers. And, every so often, a pulse of water, gas escaping. 'I just want it done. You could hypnotise me, take me back to the day of the accident.'

'I don't think it would work.'

'Why?'

'It's unreliable. You might recover a memory, but it probably wouldn't be accurate.'

'How else am I supposed to remember, just sitting here, talking, it isn't going to work.'

'It needs to happen gently—'

'You've no idea what it's like, have you? Pissing myself every night. Every night now. And I don't sleep; a few hours, that's all. I feel like a freak.'

'Listen, there's something I want you to try. I think it will help.' He pulls a notepad from his satchel and a pen from the inside pocket of his jacket. He takes the top off and puts it on the table next to me. 'I want you to write down in one list all the bad things about being in the wheelchair. Then, when you've done that, I want you to write down the good things—'

'It's stupid.'

'Try it.'

'I don't want to.'

He takes the pen and draws a table, *good* in one column, *bad* in the other, then turns the pad around to me. 'Bad first. What don't you like about being stuck in that chair? You can't do sports, right? You used to play basketball at school?'

I shrug. The pen's posh, fat between my fingers. As I finish writing 'basketball' other things come to me, like not being able to have a bath without Mum there, the stairlift, not being able to go outside, like today, in the woods with Sarah. Sarah. The pen hovers, spelling out her name on the air above the page, but I don't write it down. Doc's waiting. Kids at school, Davey, Gareth and Conker, hanging around at the centre with the Sunshine kids. When I'm finished the list is long.

'What about good? Think carefully. Is there anything about being in the chair that makes your life easier?'

'None of it's *easy*.'

'Easier.'

'No.'

'Think about it for a second.' Our eyes meet, but he's not letting me off this time.

I sigh, shrug, tap my fingers on the table. Then it comes to me. Just one thing. I write it down.

Doc turns the pad around to read what I've written. 'Anything else?'

'No.'

'OK. Why did you write "Mum"?'

'Sometimes she's cool. Nice, and I think it's because of the way things are. I guess she feels sorry for me.'

'What sort of things does she do that make you feel good about being in the chair?'

'I wouldn't put it like that.'

'How then?'

'Instead of something she does can it be something she doesn't do?'

'Yes.'

'She doesn't ignore me.' I shake my head straight away. It's not what I meant. Or is it? 'Don't tell her.'

'I won't.' A long pause. 'You think she doesn't ignore

you because you're in a wheelchair? She spends more time with you?'

'Tries to. After Tom died she went part-time, took on a manager, so she could spend more time at home. But it's hard sometimes, harder than going to work. She's used to it though. She looked after Tom when his asthma was bad. She was up all hours of the night sometimes. She stayed in his room with him.'

'Does she ever stay in your room?'

'For a while she did, after the accident. In hospital, then again at home.'

'When was the last time?'

'When I fell . . . when I went in the lake, a couple of weeks ago.'

'How did it make you feel? Her being in your room with you?'

'OK. She held my hand because she was worried. I pretended to be asleep.'

'Why?'

'Because if I opened my eyes, I figured she'd leave. I didn't want her to. I wanted her to stay because I felt, dunno, safe.'

'You felt as though nothing could happen to you.'

'Yeah.'

The waitress arrives with Doc's sandwiches. He hands me one on a napkin and takes the other in both hands. He bites down in the middle of the bread and sucks up a bit of lettuce that dangles from his bottom lip. We seem to have said a lot in a short space of time, stuff that feels important, only I can't figure out why.

'We're talking a lot about Mum today?'

He looks at me, wiping his hands on a napkin, weighing me up the way he does right before he's got something big to say. 'Have you ever heard the words "secondary gain", Matt? In hospital, perhaps?'

'No.'

'Do you know what it means?'

I carve a circle into the algae on the picnic bench with my fingernail.

'It's the idea there might be a benefit to you being in the wheelchair, a pay-off. You wouldn't be aware of it necessarily, but inside yourself, deep inside, there's something keeping you in the chair because it's giving you what you need. Mum spends time with you, she's affectionate towards you—'

'I'm NOT trying to get her attention. You think I'd do that? You think I'm just a kid, sucking up to Mummy—'

'We all need approval, Matt. Have you considered you may feel guilty that Tom's dead and you're not? It's not uncommon in people who have survived an accident where others have died. By making yourself vulnerable you're protecting yourself from that guilt. Subconsciously.'

'It doesn't feel like it's inside my head. Any of it.'

'I'm not saying that you're imagining anything. You understand the difference? I'm saying I think there's a pay-off to you being in the chair. When that pay-off doesn't exist for you any more, when there's something you want more, so badly it drives you mad, that's when you'll be free of the chair.'

'Walk?'

'Possible, but I can't give you any guarantee of that. It might happen, it might not.'

The sun grates on my skin. I breathe out slowly, feeling stranded somewhere between what he's saying – which sounds implausible – and wanting, with all of my heart, to believe it. I think of Sarah, like a taste of something sweet on my tongue. 'I want to try to be, you know, normal.'

'OK, then. Let's keep going.'

But we don't, of course, and we end up just chatting about this and that while he finishes his lunch. Afterwards, he takes me back to the house. As I watch him drive away, I sense the atmosphere between us has changed, more in the words we haven't said than those we have, but something is different from what it was before. And next time I see him, I know it'll be worse.

# 21

I drape the scarf over my face, gasping silk into my mouth. Silk on my cheeks and eyelids. Sarah on my cheeks and eyelids. I close my eyes for the kiss, feeling a surge in my groin as my cock reaches for my hand. Gripping, pulling back on the foreskin. Sarah's hand. There are rings on her fingers, nails varnished the colour of peaches. A whisper, something I can't hear. It doesn't matter. Getting hard on her nipples. She wants me to touch them so I do, I get up and pull her to her feet so we're standing. My cock nuzzles her belly. She looks into me, her breaths are mine. Then I do it. I take her nipple into my mouth.

'You're not dressed.'

The words are strange.

'What on earth are you doing?'

I open my eyes, light slamming into my fantasy. The

scarf falls from my face into my lap. Sarah. Dressed. She's holding a pair of my socks and a T-shirt.

'Nothing.' My hand's frozen under my chair blanket. She tugs on it. I pull back with my other hand, but it isn't enough, I need both. She laughs, a game. 'Sarah! Don't! NO!'

Too late.

'Isn't that . . . that's my scarf.'

A long, slow second.

'I've been looking for that for ages.'

And here it is. My brain won't work. It feels thick and fat, like cheese. She stares at it. We both stare at it. Tick-TOCK. Tick-TOCK.

'We'll be late for the picnic,' she says, smiling away from me. My face burns. She drops the socks and T-shirt on my bed and busies herself opening my curtains. 'I bought some stuff you could take, batten cake, pasties.' She turns to face me. 'Sausages.'

My eyes fix on the shape of her nipples under her T-shirt.

'Ten minutes.' Another smile. 'Oh and . . . you can keep the scarf.'

She closes the door behind her, leaving the heavy cloud of her knowing behind. I breathe it in, open mouthed, and laugh out loud. She knows. She *knows*.

Straight away it's our secret. She doesn't say anything when I get downstairs, or when I help her load the picnic stuff in the car. She takes the basket off my lap, smiling at my smile, but she doesn't say anything. I want to ask *what do we do now, now that I love you and you know*? But I don't. I just sit beside her in the car, big breaths rising and falling in my chest. She drives fast, the momentum pushing me towards her, then away. At the next bend, if we touch, she loves me. A brush against her sleeve.

'Nice day for it,' she says, popping a fresh stick of gum into her mouth.

'Nice.'

'It was supposed to rain.' She looks up through the windscreen. 'Doesn't look like it's going to though, does it?'

I rub my face, whiff the scent of cock on my fingers.

'Robert, Dr Mason, said he might come. That's canny of him, isn't it?'

The feel of Velcro ripping inside me. I see it now, what my mind and body don't want to see. Me, on a blanket, propped up against a tree, Manic Mike with jam around his mouth, parents and carers huddled together. Chit-chat and story session, Simon Says and horse shoes. Wheelchair rounders with beanie bags.

'Don't you want him to come?'

'I don't care.'

'I thought you were getting on better?'

'We are.' We turn on to the site, a few other cars. A black Labrador, coat gleaming, walks off a ramp from the boot of a big four-by-four. 'Just can't imagine why he'd want to come to this.'

The Sunshine bus is further down, parked near picnic benches that overlook the viewpoint. They always use this view for postcards, at night with lights around the edge of the lake and the moon on the water, or in the daytime with sheep dotted on the hills. Only it never looks right, as though they've been put there on purpose, like extras on a film set. In real life it's just a big hill with a steep descent to the lake, no perfect blue skies or fabulous cloud formations.

I see Manic Mike's red wheelchair and Rebecca's hat flapping in the wind. They're my age, which is why I always get stuck with them. No one seems to care that I'm not gaga. Sarah turns off the engine and looks around the car park.

'Maybe Doc changed his mind,' I say, hoping it might be true. I want it just to be us, me and Sarah away from the main group, talking in whispers. 'We could go for a walk?'

'I think we'd better let everyone know we're here, don't you?'

She gets out of the car and opens the boot. In the mirror I see Doc's silver Estate pull up. He gets out and walks towards us, shouts something.

'He's here,' she calls to me.

I watch them talking, Sarah curling hair behind her ears. He looks different, a haircut, jeans. He comes over, gives a little knock on the window and opens the door.

'All right, Matt?'

'Super.'

He raises an eyebrow, amused, but not unfriendly.

It takes ages to get everything out of the boot. Doc helps carry it down. I turn on the radio to drown out the sound of their voices and the wind, whipping around the car. Maybe it'll rain. When I open my eyes again Doc's coming back up the path alone. He wheels my chair around to the door.

'Why'd you come?'

'Rather I hadn't?'

I pull the chair into position. 'I have to be here. You don't.'

'And let you suffer it alone?'

I smile at the thought of him being here for me. 'Won't people wonder who you are?'

'Tell them I'm your uncle.' He taps me playfully on the head.

'Granddad more like.'

We set off towards the group. Rebecca and Manic Mike are chucking beanies at each other. They stop, gawp, then pull stupid faces and waggle in their chairs like geese. Sarah spreads a blanket out on the ground not far away from them, diving at the corners to stop it blowing up. The other women watch.

'Won't be a minute,' Doc says. He goes to help her.

'Your daddy's got big ears,' Rebecca says.

'Yeah?' I stick my tongue out at her. 'And you've got a face like a badger's arse.'

She giggles, waggles some more. Manic Mike throws me a glare.

Eat first. Play second. Sarah brings me a plate. Jam tart with damp pastry. A sandwich with the crusts cut off. Cold chicken leg.

'I'm not hungry, thanks.'

She puts the plate on my lap anyway and sits on the blanket beside me. I watch her suck a sausage off a stick. She's looking at Doc and smiling. The Labrador from the car park, overweight, tail wagging, has buried its nose deep in Doc's crotch. He tries to ignore it, nodding at Manic Mike's mum who's standing next to him, holding a chicken leg up near her mouth like a question mark. Sarah turns to me, wipes her mouth.

'You can see for miles,' I say, taking a bite out of a cheese and onion sandwich. Onion breath. Cool. 'See our house from here, I reckon.'

'Yeah?'

'Yeah. I'll show you, if you like?'

Rebecca drops her jam tart on the grass and starts wailing.

'Her mum'll do it,' I say, when Sarah gets up to help. She gives Rebecca hers off her plate and the crying stops. The other carers, mums, a few of the dads, watch, leaning their heads together like they're sharing a secret. I want them all to get lost so there's just us and the birds wheeling above our heads. Someone turns on a radio, the sound nearer one minute, further away the next. A blanket flares up in the wind, sending paper plates cantering across the grass and down the hill towards the lake.

'What's your c-carer's name?' Manic Mike asks. 'Is it Emma?'

'No.'

There are crumbs on his lap, ketchup on his T-shirt. His head rolls around and settles back on me. 'What . . . who . . . what?'

'None of your business.'

'Is she your s-sister? Is she your aunty? Is she your t-teacher?'

'She's my girlfriend, all right? Her name's Sarah. Now fuck off.'

'G-g-girlfriend.' It takes a while for it to sink in. 'M-matt and S-s-sarah up in a tree, k-k-k-'

'Ah, piss off!' I wheel around him and head towards Rebecca's blanket, but Sarah isn't there any more. I scan the groups of adults, then the car. She probably went ahead to the viewpoint when she saw me talking to Manic Mike.

I wait until there's no one looking and then wheel myself along the narrow path. It's only just wide enough for my chair, but rocky, and I have to concentrate on the picnic bench at the end to keep the wheels straight. There are two benches, side by side on a level piece of ground close to the edge, but I can only see one. Sarah must be at the other, sitting, waiting for me.

The music grows fainter. I start to sweat about halfway along, but it's too far to go back. My right wheel hits a root and for a second I think I'm going to tip over on to the grass bank. It's steep, knuckled with rocks. A few yards on I see a nest, a tight knot of scorched grass and a single egg that's cracked. Another ten feet.

'Sarah?'

I wheel past the first bench, but she isn't at the second one either. A steep face of rock above me. People have scratched their names into it. Tracey loves Dean. Kelly sucks cock. An empty bottle of 20/20 and a condom with a knot in the end.

'Sarah?'

I start to feel sick. My arms and fingers sting with pins and needles. The path behind me is empty, only voices, high-pitched, then softer, but not looking for me, not counting heads. I go over to the edge, as close as I dare. It's steeper than I thought. My hands, covered in a film of yellow dust from the path, tremble on my wheels.

'Where *are* you?'

A herring gull floats up the face in front of me, balancing on the wind, its amber eye fixed. Then it veers away, slicing through the air, smaller and smaller until it's just a speck over the surface of the lake.

*Two boys rowing out to pitch a flag.*

A laugh from underneath me. I edge forward. I might fall. I could shout, but no one would hear. I listen for footsteps skidding on the rocky path. Nothing. Just me. Then I see them on the shore. Doc and Sarah. They're playing skimming stones. Sarah laughs at Doc's effort, two skims and a plop. She kicks the pebbles on the shore with her feet, finds one she smoothes over in her hands. It skims four and she cheers.

'Hey!' The wind swallows my voice. I look at the route down to where they are, a steep path and steps. The shore's all tree roots and pebbles. All I can do is watch and think about what Doc said about the chair having a pay-off. Not now it doesn't. Not here. Watching. Wanting. Stuck in the chair and all I desire in the world is out of reach.

## 22

'Will you stay for a while when we get there?'

'Sure.' Sarah doesn't look up from the map. She's marked the route in highlighter pen.

'I mean not just to say hello. They'll probably do lunch, you'll stay for lunch?'

'You're worried about seeing your dad, aren't you? What do you think's going to happen?'

I shrug.

'I'll stay for something to eat, but then I'll go off for my results. I won't be gone long.'

'How long?'

'As long as it takes me to drive into Newcastle, drive to the college, pick up the envelope and drive back.' She chucks the highlighter at me. 'You'll be fine. They want to see you, not me.'

'Why do I have to take a gift?' I throw the present Sarah bought for Danny up in the air and head it like a football. It squeaks when it hits the deck.

'You'll break it.'

'It's a hippo that makes noises when you throw it. How could I break it?'

She picks up the mangled mess of wrapping paper and Sellotape from the floor and hands it back to me. 'Danny'll like it.'

'How do you know?'

'Because he's a baby, babies like things that make noises. Anyway, it's a good idea, a nice gesture. Like a thank-you for being invited.'

I raise an eyebrow.

'Right, well, you'll have to map-read, but I think I'm pretty clear on how to get there. Can I trust you to keep us right?'

'You mean will I deliberately turn the map upside down and get us lost? There's a good chance.'

She looks exasperated.

'Yes, yes, I'll keep us right. I told you anyway, I'll remember the way once we get going.'

We said we'd be there by 12.30 p.m., for lunch, but because of Sarah's phobic desire not to be late we'll arrive early. At this rate, we'll be there for the bit before lunch; lunch; and then whatever Dad's got planned for afterwards. He didn't mention us doing anything on the phone and I wanted to ask, but didn't, of course, so it could be anything. Or nothing. Fortunately, before we even get on the motorway, we get stuck behind a tractor on the road out of Loweswater and have to slow down to a crawl. Sarah winds down her window and tries to see past it.

'You shouldn't overtake.'

'I'm not going to.' She leans over me to get a tape from the glove compartment, settling on one that doesn't have writing on. She puts it into the cassette player. A crackly, static sound then the first song starts, except it's not technically a song at all because it doesn't have words.

'You're not serious.'

'John Coltrane.' Her fingers tap the sides of the steering wheel. '*Jazz*, darling.'

'Since when do you like jazz? Sounds like something's being strangled.'

She smiles but says nothing. I wind down my window and stick my head out to a rush of warm air. It feels nice and I open my mouth to let it in.

'You'll swallow a fly.'

'Maybe I will. Flies carry bacteria on their feet, did you know that? If I do swallow one and I'm ill, you'll have to take me back.'

The tractor turns off the road and we pick up speed. I close the window.

'You might enjoy yourself, Matt. Have you even considered that as a possibility? You said it's been a while.'

'We didn't know what to say to each other last time. That's how it'll be, talking about things that don't matter because neither of us knows what to say.'

'When was that?'

'Two months after Tom's funeral. He came to Loweswater and we went to a pub for lunch. Have you noticed that's what people do when they don't have anything to say?'

'What?'

'They eat.'

'That was very soon afterwards, though, wasn't it? I imagine you were both feeling pretty raw then. It'd be uncomfortable because of that.'

'For who?'

We fall into a silence, parted briefly to attend to our own thoughts. Mine are focused entirely on the complexity of watching her without being noticed, which is difficult because of the confined space. Any lift or turn of my head in her direction is immediately visible and once or twice she turns her eyes to me as though she's assumed I'm about to say something. Finally, after a great deal of shuffling, I get myself into a position from where I can inspect her unobserved. She's taken care with her appearance, a suit jacket over jeans, and earrings I haven't seen before. And she seems happy, whatever thought she's concerned with turning up the sides of her mouth into a delicate smile. Looking at her, I get the sense of being on a fast down-hill ride, the world outside buffeted into a thin, green blur. It's as though we're suspended on the road rather than travelling along it.

'You all right?' she says, glancing across.

'Yeah. I was just wondering what you were thinking about.'

'What I was thinking? Actually, I was wondering whether your mum and dad still talk to each other.'

I know this isn't true, but it's OK. 'They used to before Tom died, not often. Now they argue. They blame each other – him because he thinks she should've been there to stop us from going out on the lake, her because she thinks it's his fault she wasn't. She was at work.' He remembered her words. 'Someone has to pay the bills.'

'I thought you were minted.'

'Why would you think that?'

'You think everyone lives in a house like yours? Anyway, "*You're just some lackey we hired because we can afford it.*"'

Her impression of me makes me laugh. 'Did I really say that?'

'Yep. So I sort of assumed what with that and the house you must be rolling in it.'

It hasn't occurred to me she might have this view of us as being rich. I wonder if she dislikes rich people, the way some people do. 'The house is worth a fortune, probably, I don't really know, but only if she sells and she won't because of him.'

'Didn't they settle all that in the divorce?'

'They're still married.'

'Oh.'

'If she divorces him she'd have to sell and split the proceeds with Dad and Laura. She doesn't want them living off her inheritance. It won't be like that for ever. She's only postponing the inevitable.'

'I think if it were me, in your place, I wouldn't want to live in that house. Not after what happened.'

She touches my hand, a brief second, but I carry on feeling it. It's like an embrace, holding me so tight I can't breathe.

'Sometimes I feel that.' I rest my head back against the seat. 'On the one hand it's the only house I've ever known, but then when Tom died everything changed.'

'Would you move? I mean, if it was up to you?'

'I haven't thought about it. Perhaps.'

She lights a cigarette.

'Do you think you've passed, then?'

'My A levels?' She shrugs. 'Hope so or I'm up shit creek.'

I laugh.

'I'll be happy with a C and two Bs. Or a B and two Cs. Christ, I'll be happy with anything as long as I pass. I should do OK in photography.'

'I think you'll get an A.'

'I like your optimism.'

'What will you do if you get the grades you want?'

'Get drunk.'

'After that.'

'I don't know. I thought I did.' She shrugs. 'France was the plan. Get a job and study over there. Or somewhere closer to home. I'm not sure. I'll see.'

My mind races with the prospect of her departure, a reality that somehow I've managed not to think about. I look out of the window, ashamed and unprepared for the anger that grips me. I don't want her to go to university, or anywhere.

'You could stay.' My voice is pathetic and I blush. 'I mean, stick around, take a year off or something.'

'Maybe.' She taps ash out of the window and turns up the air-conditioning. 'It's this next turn-off, right?'

I nod without thinking, fingers scrabbling to find the page on the map. It's signposted anyway. Hayden Bridge. I remember the place now, it's a village, but not picture-postcard. Looks like it ought to be in the middle of a city. There are council houses with street names which are all the same except for the number, Garth 21, Garth 23. On the other side of the road there's a big concrete factory skirted with iron railings and barbed wire. The posh end, where Dad lives, is at the other side of the village past a pub called The Dandelion. I remember walking to it with Dad and Tom. There's a beer garden and a climbing frame Tom dangled upside down from. And an old collie dog that's probably dead by now.

'Century Avenue.' Sarah slows down. 'What number?'

'That one.' I point at a house several down. I remember it because of the fir trees at the front, one on either side of the porch. We pull up on the road and Sarah fetches my wheels from the boot. There's a pink bicycle with streamers on the handlebars and a yellow, sit-in truck on the drive she has to move out of the way.

'Want me to let them know we're here before you get out?'

'No. In the chair first.'

I twist around and allow myself to fall back into Sarah's arms and from there into the chair. As she's putting my feet on the steps she looks at me and smiles. I smile back.

'With any luck the wind'll change and you'll get stuck like that,' she says.

I widen my smile until my cheeks hurt.

'Come on.'

'Look who it is!' Laura. Mumsy, high-pitched. Danny's on her hip. She picks up his pudgy hand and waggles it at us. 'You must be Sarah? I'm Laura.'

'Pleased to meet you.' They shake hands, but it's a bit of a fumble because of Danny. 'And Matt, you've grown. What a young man you are!'

She bends down to kiss me and I get a whiff of sweet

perfume. Laura's small, tiny features, tiny waist, tiny hands. It makes Danny look huge, like a baby giant. He gawps at me, face like a squashed raspberry.

'We've some rockery stones at the side of the house, I'm afraid. We're about to re-landscape out the back. I'll open the garage.' She calls through the house for Dad and then disappears. A few seconds later the garage door rolls up.

'It must be on remote,' I say. 'That's handy.'

Sarah throws me a look.

'*There* he is,' Dad says, as though I've been lost. He waits at the other end of the garage while we negotiate our way through the junk. There's stuff I recognise, his tools, fishing stuff, the rest is all kid-related, a Wendy house without a roof, a big fire truck and, perched on top, a giant panda that looks like it came from a fairground.

'Hi. Sarah, isn't it? Did you manage the journey OK?'

'Fine.'

'No problems?'

She shakes her head.

'Good to see you, son.' He touches my head. 'There's a feast. I hope you're hungry.'

We follow him outside to the back garden where there's a large patio table covered in an assortment of buffet-type food. Paper plates, plastic forks.

'Well, I know I'm starving,' Sarah says, filling the silence. 'We didn't have any breakfast so we'd be hungry when we got here. This looks terrific.'

'I wish I could take the credit for it, but it's all Laura's hard work, I'm afraid.'

He looks older, tufts of grey just above his ears. Laura

calls him from the kitchen. He apologises and skips into the house.

The garden is trashed. The grass looks urine-scorched, but they don't have a dog so it must be kid damage. Charlotte, who appears not to be here, has put crates and bamboo sticks all over the lawn, arranged as show jumps, and the grass between has worn away to earth. I think about what Laura said – re-landscaping it, like it's a bloody park.

'Say hello to your Big Brother Matthew,' Dad says, reappearing behind us.

He drops Danny on to the lawn. Danny crawls towards one of the show jumps. Dad picks him up again and brings him closer, but as soon as his arms and legs hit the ground he's off again.

'Like a wind-up toy,' I say.

'Yes.' Dad laughs. 'Daniel? Would you like to show Matt your special thing?'

I'm presuming the special thing isn't in his nappy, but that's where Danny heads, both hands down the front of it.

'When we've eaten,' Laura says. More food. She puts down two large trays, one with pizza, the other with hot dogs on it. 'Tuck in.'

There's too much and what's worse is that Laura obviously doesn't have any intention of eating any of it. Dad takes a slice of batten cake and gives half to Danny.

'Well,' Sarah says. 'This is terrific.'

A long silence. I put an assortment of the food on to one of the plastic plates, not because I'm hungry, but because I can't think of anything to say. Sarah looks at the food on her plate, a swirl of pastry with green paste on the top.

It makes me think of that film, *Bridget Jones's Diary*, when they're all at a party and nobody knows what to say, so, kind of like a conversation starter, Bridget introduces people by tagging on an interesting fact about them.

'Sarah takes pictures of rocks with lichen on them.'

Sarah coughs.

'Oh,' Laura says. 'That's nice.'

'I'm probably going to study photography at uni this autumn,' Sarah explains. 'If I get the grades I want.'

'A levels?' Dad asks.

He's trying to work out how old she is. A wasp hovers over the food, dozy in the heat. It lands on a sticky bun and gets stuck on the pink icing.

'Would you like some wine, Sarah?' Laura fills three glasses. For me there's Coke in a plastic tumbler. Danny gets orange juice in a beaker.

'I'll have some wine,' I say, but it's too late and Laura hands me the Coke with a mumsy smile.

'What about you, Matt?' Dad says. He takes a sip of his wine.

What about me?

'GCSEs next year, isn't it?'

'Yeah.' Danny finds a worm and pulls it at both ends. Saliva dangles from his mouth, a single, silver thread that sways from side to side in the soft breeze.

'You've done well to catch up—'

'Danny! No. Dirty.' Laura picks him up and wipes his hands with a napkin. 'He's into everything. Aren't you, little tinker man?'

'Probably getting restless,' Dad says. 'Or hungry. You hungry, mate?'

'He could have a bit of pizza,' Laura says.

Silence again. Dad's forgotten what he was saying.

'Oh,' Sarah says. 'Matt? The thing you got for Danny?'

She pulls it out of her bag and hands it to me. The timing's all wrong and Danny drops the pizza on the floor to take the present.

'A gift? Matt, that's so sweet of you.' Laura clears a space on the table and puts Danny on it so we can all watch him unwrap it. He can't manage it, of course, so Dad helps him.

'It's a hippo,' I say. 'It squeaks.'

'Thank you very much,' Laura says cheerfully. 'What a lovely thought. He'll absolutely adore it, won't you, darling?'

Danny looks at me and then solemnly hands the hippo to Laura.

'Well,' Sarah says. 'If you'll excuse me, I'll leave you all to enjoy your lunch. Better make tracks.'

'You haven't eaten anything,' I say.

'You're going?' Dad says. I can't work out if he says it because he likes her or because he's terrified he won't know what to do if I need to take a piss.

'I'm afraid so. Off to pick up my results. I won't be long.'

'Ah, right.' Dad gives her a fingers-crossed sign. 'Good luck.'

She waves them off when first Dad, then Laura, get up to show her out. She goes back the way we came in, a thud as she trips over something in the garage, then the car engine starts and fades.

'All this,' Laura says, glancing at all the uneaten food. 'Won't you have any more, Matt?'

'No, thanks.'

'Take it into the nursery,' Dad says, picking Danny up and jiggling him on his knee. 'Is it time? Is it time, young man? Going to show Big Brother Matthew what a clever boy you are?'

Danny chuckles. I wish he'd stop calling me that.

'Hold on to him a sec, Laura, I'll get the camera and we can get a picture.'

Laura bounces him on her knee and starts to sing in a shrill, ear-drum-bursting tone. 'If you're happy and you know it, clap your hands . . .'

Dad returns with the camera – the same one he's had for years, the same one that used to take pictures of me and Tom. I take a gulp of air, feeling suddenly sick.

'If you're happy and you know it, and you really want to show it . . .'

The Coke is warm. I take a sip, but it makes me feel worse. My ears feel blocked the way they do right before you faint. I don't want to faint. Danny's gurgling, spewing out dribble. Please don't faint. I take a paper plate and start to fan myself with it.

'Watch this,' Dad says.

'On the lawn, Andrew.'

They move away, the three of them. It dawns on me, as they arrange themselves and Danny, what's about to happen, but it doesn't hit me until the action starts to unfold. Dad's got his arms out to the side, several feet in front of Danny, Laura is supporting him around the waist. One tottering step, another. Danny is walking.

'See, Matt?' Dad asks. 'Did you see?'

I want to react, but I'm caught between thinking that

it's deliberate, an attack on me for not being able to walk, or it's just some sick oversight. Dad's grinning. Laura's beaming. Danny chuckles triumphantly. *If you're happy and you know it, clap your hands.*

Clap. Clap.

'He's like a train when he gets going,' Dad says, coming over. 'Let's get a picture of you together.'

'No.'

'Come on. We don't have any pictures of you and Danny. Hold him on your lap, just for a second.'

'No!'

Laura freezes, staring at me like I just took a shit on that clean, eiderdown mumsy world of hers. She takes Danny inside. Dad's looking at me with a pained expression.

'What? Sorry, all right? I don't like having my picture taken.' The wasp squirms on the icing, exhausting itself in its efforts to be free. I pick up the bun, flick the wasp on to the table with the corner of the napkin and squash it with my glass.

'Jesus, Matt.'

'I put it out of its misery.' He doesn't understand. He'd rather I let it die a slow death. 'Are we going anywhere this afternoon?'

'Where did you want to go?'

'I don't know. I thought you'd have something planned.'

'There's a farm round here we go to sometimes. Has rabbits, guinea pigs—'

'*Baby animals?*'

'There's no need to be like that. There's only so many places you can take a fifteen-month-old child.'

'I meant us. By ourselves. We could go somewhere *I* might be interested in.'

'Where?' He sighs. 'I don't know what you're interested in.'

'It isn't astronomy.'

'What, then?'

A long silence. He doesn't really want to know and I hate him for it. There are important things, stuff about Doc and Tom and Mum that need to be said, but instead we're sat in the baking sun watching flies suck on stinking hot dogs.

'Why won't you let Mum sell the house?'

'I'm not stopping her. I want her to sell.'

'So you can have the money.'

'So you can move somewhere else where you don't have to wake up every morning and look out on that dreadful lake.'

'I don't mind the lake.'

'She says you're seeing someone, a counsellor.'

'He's a psychiatrist.'

'Is it helping?'

'We talk about you.'

A long pause. I can hear him breathing.

'And your illness?'

'You mean my legs, do we talk about my legs not working and whether it's all in my head or not?'

'Is it?'

Silence. He looks into his lap.

'Just because I'm here with Danny and Laura, Matt, it doesn't mean . . . it doesn't mean I don't care. That I don't love you.'

His words are meaningless. He's completely zonked out on Danny, hasn't written or phoned or come to visit for months and months. He's here, teaching Danny to walk, selling photocopiers and making shapes out of privet bushes, washing the car on Sunday afternoons, changing nappies. Like all the other dads on this street and in this village, he's pretending to be Santa on Christmas Eve, buying life insurance, tinkering with things in the garage. I bite down on my tongue. I'm just a splinter in a past that has a dead son and another who's broken. He doesn't know what to do about that.

He doesn't know what to do about me.

Nymph. You wouldn't think something with such a beautiful name could be ugly. The moon moves through the water, sharpening the stalks on the pondweed, sending others into darkness like the earth on its axis. Night and day. Day and night. I tap the glass, sending the nymph into spasm. Does it sense me watching, waiting for it to change? I turn the jar around until I see its dark shape again, leaning in to see through its skin to the part it hides. What does it feel? Nothing. It doesn't have that kind of brain. It only watches me watching it.

'I brought us some hot chocolate,' Sarah says, setting a mug down on my desk. She lifts it to her mouth, blows, and picks the skin off the top. 'Do you want me to fetch your pyjamas?'

I look at my bare chest, pleased by the shadows the moon makes on my skin. 'I'm fine.'

'So are you going to tell me what happened? You hardly said a word in the car.'

'I never asked you about your results.'

'An A and two Bs.'

'Brilliant.' I laugh. 'I told you. I said . . .' I try to sustain my enthusiasm but it fades. 'Sorry, Sarah. I am happy for you.'

'What happened with your dad?'

'Nothing.' I glance at her, meet eyes filled with determination. 'Nothing. We sat, ate, drank. Watched Danny on the lawn. It was just as you saw it was when you came back.'

She kneels down beside me. 'Then why do you look so destroyed?'

'Don't, Sarah.' I take a deep breath and blink away tears.

'Talk to me.'

'There's no point.'

'Please.'

'I just didn't feel part of it, OK? I don't feel part of anything.'

'Dad?'

'Everything's just going on around me and I'm left behind, pissing myself, stuck in this chair. Everyone's getting on with their lives except me.'

She squeezes my hand. 'It must be hard for you to see him with his new family. I hadn't really thought about it, but Danny must've been born not long before Tom died?'

'They brought him to the funeral.'

She takes my hand and lays it across hers, absent-mindedly stroking the fingertips.

'He screamed his head off in the church, you know, that horrible bleating sound newborn babies make. Laura took him outside, but I could still hear him. I couldn't hear anything else, nothing of what the vicar said. I just kept looking at Tom's coffin, thinking how small it looked, seeing that and nothing else, hearing that awful bleating and nothing else.'

'To have gone through all you have, to still be . . . I just wish there was something I could do.'

'There is.'

She looks at me.

'You could give me a hug?'

She does it without hesitation, her whole body suddenly wrapped around mine in a tight embrace. My face is in her neck, her mouth on my arm. I squeeze her tighter, welcoming the warmth of her body against my bare chest, and further, beyond skin, to the centre of me.

# 23

It's the first time Doc hasn't asked how I feel. That's usually how it starts, or how it ends. But not today. He brings me a glass of water, swimming with ice, and sits down in the chair opposite. The clock on the mantelpiece chimes.

'You got it fixed,' I say.

'Yes.' He smiles. 'You look tired, Matt. Are you sure—'

'I want to do this.'

'We could talk about your visit with Dad? Make that our session today?'

'No. I just want to get on with it.' I pick at a nail, torn deep into the cuticle. 'It's funny, all this time I've been worried about what I might remember. But now, the worst thing, will be not remembering anything.'

'Let's focus on getting rid of the nightmares. Beyond that there aren't any—'

'Guarantees.' A bluebottle circles at the other end of the room. 'I know.'

'Have you got any questions before we get started?'

'I lie back on the couch and you dangle a watch.'

'No. Well, not quite, though you're welcome to lie down if you'd find it more comfortable.'

I look into my lap, legs, thin, useless, held in skin that won't shed.

A glance at his watch, but not from impatience. His sleeves aren't rolled up. He doesn't have paper or a pen. The phone's unplugged at the wall, curtains drawn halfway.

'Remember, hypnotism is merely a deep state of relaxation. You'll be in control, you'll be aware of everything that's happening around you, my voice, the room . . .'

'I understand.'

He stands up to give his armchair a shove in my direction. It moves easily, the wheels thudding over ridges on the floorboards like a train. Then he sits down, shuffles. Our knees knock, a whiff of his aftershave.

'Ready?'

'Yes.'

He asks me to close my eyes and let my head fall back. The muscles in my neck are tense. He tells me to relax my head, instructing each part of me, chest, arms, fingers, back. It takes ages. He even does my legs which makes me smile inside, but I keep going, listening to his voice until that's all there is. Knees, ankles, feet, toes.

'Slow, deep breaths,' he says.

His voice is heavy, like sleep. Several minutes pass, or several seconds, I can't tell. The clock ticks. I feel heavy and light at the same time, floating and falling. It's like being carried, I'm aware of my weight, of going some-where, but I don't know where. For a second I think it might've worked, but I can still hear Doc breathing between words, my mind's still moving around the room, the fly's still circling. I imagine it's me, landing on a wall to look down, a boy and a man, ice in a glass that's melting, then lifting off, wheeling tight around a fan on the coffee table, landing again.

'I want you to think of a favourite place, Matt, some-where quiet where you can be by yourself.'

My mind goes instantly to the wood where I went with Sarah. The path's clear, not overgrown. I look inside to the shade, smell fern on my clothes, hear sounds, bees and birds, see leaves lifting up in the breeze. I can't remember saying it out loud, but Doc's with me. He tells me it's the school holidays and I don't have to think about school, or homework, or getting home. The sun's shining, bright, hot. Cooler inside. The birds are loud, sounding alarms above my head. I can't see them, I hear them. Jackdaws, starlings, blackbirds and thrushes. I take a breath, nostrils filling with the smell of damp bark and earth, different grasses sweet-ened by a recent downpour.

'What else do you see, Matt?'

'Cocoons. They're camouflaged on the ground, but once you know what to look for you can find them, easy.'

'Butterflies?'

'Moths. Moths make a cocoon. Butterflies make a chrysalis. These are moths.'

'What about you? What are you wearing?'

The camp's well hidden, but I know how to find it –

a tin can I use as a marker on the path, then right, three large trees and a thicket of brambles.

'Matt?'

'T-shirt. Jeans, school shoes.'

'No trainers?'

'Too small. I need new ones.'

I drag at the T-shirt around my neck, then pull it off over my head, using it to wipe sweat off my brow and cheeks. My fingers are sticky with sap from where I've snapped branches of fern to make the camp. A blister on my thumb I'll pop later. I roll up my T-shirt and tuck it into the waistband of my jeans. There's still a way to go, but I move freely, swinging my arms and legs in a rhythm that feels good. We spent too much time on the camp just to have it wrecked. Anyone who found it would claim it as theirs, but it's ours, mine and Jack's.

'Where's Jack now?'

'Gone home to get some stuff for our stash. His brother keeps cans of lager in the garage. When he's done that and had his tea he'll come back. I'm not having any.'

'Why's that?'

'I'm going to cook on the fire.' I lift the rucksack off my shoulder. It's heavy, rubbing on my bare skin. Finger buns, and hot dogs you can eat cold, but I'll heat them up. I've got a pan. The camp looks impressive, easily large enough for two and well constructed. No mistakes. We cut the branches just the right length, tied them together with strips of bark to make the frame. Jack said it wouldn't work, but it does just fine. I pull the small Union Jack out of the side pocket of my rucksack and tie it to the camp door with a bit of leftover bark then I get on with clearing a patch of earth for the fire. I need to find big stones to make a circle like they do in Westerns, but Doc keeps asking questions, distracting me.

'Matt?'

'I've got to get the fire ready.'

'You've worked hard. There's lots of time to sort out the fire.'

'OK.'

'Where's Mum?'

'At work. I'm in charge.'

'You're looking after Tom?'

'Yep.'

'Where is he?'

'Er . . . dunno. Inside. On my computer, I think.'

'Playing games on his computer?'

'Not his, *mine*. He'll say he's not been on it, but I know. I look at the history and it tells me what programs have been used.'

'I see.'

A rustle behind me on the path. 'Sssh. Someone's coming.'

Whoever it is doesn't know how to creep up on someone. I get inside the camp and pull fern over the entrance. Then I see him, the top of his blond head poking out of the side of a tree like a toadstool.

'What are you doing here? You're not allowed out.' I climb out of the camp and busy myself moving stones again. He tries to help, but they're too heavy and he stumbles. 'Go home, Tom.'

'I found your camp,' he says, sing-songing in wheezy, nasal breaths. 'That makes it mine, too, doesn't it?'

'It's nothing to do with you. You see that flag? That means you're trespassing.'

The images blur in my head, whirling fast like they're getting sucked up by a vacuum cleaner and spat out again. When they come back into focus I'm not at the camp any more. I'm standing on the shore with the flag in my hand and it's later, dusk.

'I got bit,' Tom says, running a finger over a raised red bump on his wrist.

'You always get bit.'

I skim a stone across the lake, three bounces then it plops. I look around for another flat one, kicking over several which are too heavy, too round, nearly right, but an angle or a bump that won't do. Then I find one. I turn it over on my palm, might make it all the way to the island. It does five bounces and plops short.

'Why won't you let me sleep out in the camp with you and Jack tonight?'

'Because you're too young.'

'I'm seven.'

'You'll get scared and start crying and I'll have to bring you back.'

'No, I won't.'

'You sleep with the light on, dumbo, you think you'd be all right in the woods where it's pitch black and there are animals that might attack? You'd wet your pants after five minutes.'

'Please, Matt.'

'Quit bugging me.'

'PLEASE. I'll do anything. I'll give you my Mallard passenger train.'

I laugh. 'Wow, that does it, I can hardly resist. NOT.'

He starts to bubble. Not proper crying, he's learnt to hold back proper tears because they interfere with his breathing and make him wheeze. But it's there all the same, the scrunched-up face getting redder and redder. I pick up another stone and throw it so it lands just by his feet. He looks up, a moment's surprise, then he starts piling stones together to make a steeple.

'You won't get a stone on the island,' he says. 'It's too far.'

'Watch me.' I pick up another stone, not to skim, but to throw. I give it everything, feeling the wrench in my shoulder, but it doesn't reach.

'Told you.'

'Doesn't matter. I'll row out, plant my flag at the centre.' I pick it up off the ground beside me. Tom's humming a tune, making like he hasn't heard.

'Did you hear what I said?' I say, turning to him.

'You always say you're going to go to the island, but you never do. Besides, you can't go.'

'Why?'

'Because you're not allowed. And,' he looks at me, 'you said you were scared.'

'I'm not. I never said that.'

'You did. You said it before.'

'When?'

He doesn't answer. His steeple topples over. 'You haven't got a boat.'

'There's the dinghy. I'll take that.'

It's still in the garage, a red Jupiter hooked on to the

wall. It was a present from Dad when he visited last year, but we only went out in it once – me, Dad and Tom. Mum says we can't go out in it alone and she won't do it, no way, so it stays where it is. I look at the island, judging the distance. Mum won't be back from work for another hour at least, time to get there and back.

'I'll tell Mum.'

'No, you won't.'

'You'll get wrong. You'll be grounded.'

'Stop whining.'

He follows me as I stride up the garden to the garage. The door's stiff, a nail slotted through a latch instead of a lock. It's dark inside, windows laced with cobwebs. I take a step forward, startling a beetle from its hiding place behind a stack of terracotta plant pots, arranged in sizes, biggest at the bottom, smaller, smallest leaning over at the top like the tower of Pisa. The dinghy's right at the back, still tight with air. I look around for the oars before clearing a route behind me to the door.

'Are you really going to do it?' Tom asks.

'What does it look like?'

'You have to take me with you.'

'Go inside!' He's in the way. He can't help. I move several heavy compost bags to the side, stirring up a cloud of dust that gusts out through the door.

Tom coughs.

'Where's your inhaler?'

He pinches his nose with his thumb and forefinger, something he does when he starts to wheeze. I pause, worried he might be on the verge of an attack, but he'd be coughing a lot more and he isn't. He picks up an old airplane model out of a box on the shelf beside him. A Spitfire I did years ago, wings snapped off.

'Put it back.'

'Take me with you, Matt.'

'No.'

'Why?'

'You can't swim.'

'I'll be in the boat.'

'You're not strong enough to row, you'd just be slowing me down.'

I tug on the dinghy, releasing it from the wall. It falls on top of me, narrowly missing a garden fork. I hold it up above my head until I get back outside, then check it for holes, smoothing over the plastic with both hands. Intact. I lift it up above my head and carry it to the shore, Tom trooping along behind, dragging the oars. I set the dinghy down on the water, holding on to it by the piece of rope that's tied to a ring.

'Give me the oars.'

'No.'

'Tom, give me the oars!'

'I'm coming with you.'

If I let go of the dinghy it'll start to drift and I don't want to have to take my shoes and socks off. I pick up a stone and throw it at him, hitting him on the thigh. He lets out a high-pitched squeal, but, surprisingly, stands firm. He waits for the next one, but instead of throwing another I drag the dinghy back to the shore. He spins around, runs a few strides in an effort to escape what he knows is coming, but starts coughing instead.

'All right!' I yell. 'Bloody hell, you can come. Just stop larking about or you'll bust a lung.'

'You swore.' He grins, wipes his nose with the back of his sleeve.

Sometimes I think he puts on the whole coughing, wheezing thing just to get what he wants. If Mum's around, I swear he'll pretend to gasp, heaving his chest up and down and sucking on his inhaler until she brings him something, a game, tea, sweets, anything to distract him so he isn't thinking about his breathing.

He insists on getting in the dinghy still holding the oars. I keep it steady while he climbs in then get in beside him and snatch them back. The first few feet are shallow. I use the lake bottom to push us off. Tom holds the flag, white knuckles clasped tightly around it. He looks small, a breath in a gale.

'Hold on with both hands.'

It feels like a dare, a ripple of excitement inside me that echoes on the water. Only now I've gone through the process of saying I'll do it, getting the dinghy and putting it on the water, there's the reality of the island. When we get closer, I see that it's broken up into several sections, some underwater, others as much as two feet above. I row silently, fixed on the distance we have to go, not far, but already the shore seems a long way off. The house, garden, jetty, the tops of the holiday cottages. I see the road behind our house, and the hills beyond them. Tom's looking at the island.

'Do you think it's true?' he asks.

'What?'

'You know. About the island. About—'

'Monsters?' I laugh. He's talking about a version of the Loch Ness story parents invented to stop kids going out to the island. Everyone knows its rubbish. His teeth start to chatter. I knew he'd freak. 'I'm not going back, Tom.'

'I don't want to,' he says, defiant. 'I'm not scared.'

'Course not.'

I turn to look at the island. Light glistens off reeds caked in black mud. It's like a hairy wart on the back of the water. As we get closer I pull the oars in and let us drift. The smell's more powerful than I imagined it would be, a rotten-egg stench from brown and green vegetation. Some of the plants have thick stems, poking out from the mud like arms, and round leaves, like palms. The undersides are slick with slime and snail eggs. Elsewhere the plants are mainly reed-like, wound into knots like cotters. I grab a handful and pull us in.

'Hold it steady. I'm getting out.' I stand up, taking the flag off him. The dinghy rocks, veering sharply to one side. 'Hold it *steady*!'

'Don't rock it!'

'I have to get out, don't I?'

It's so simple. No need to get his knickers in a twist, but he does nothing to help. NOTHING. I try again, but the boat slips away underneath and I nearly fall on to Tom.

He screams.

'You're such a baby.'

'You're rocking it!'

'You have to counteract my weight. Concentrate. You have to hold on to the sides.'

Finally he does as I tell him and, with a giant leap, I manage to get myself on to the island, landing chest down in the mud. My fingers sink into the warm sludge, but it feels pretty solid underneath me, to stand, walk, easy. I roll over, marvelling at the state of my clothes. No going back now, that's for sure. There are flies everywhere, midges, bluebottles, mosquitoes probably. I feel them biting, my neck, arms, ears, nose. One gets inside my mouth and I spit several times to clear it. I scan the surface of the island, locating the centre first, the spot for the flag, then look nearer, for something suitable to tie the dinghy up to.

'Pass—'

The dinghy's gone. I hear him whimpering.

'You idiot!' He could've held on to a bit of the island, or shouted for me, something, only now the stupid sod's gone and left me stranded. He looks small, hunched.

'Tom!'

The breeze furrowing the water is hardly anything, barely noticeable from land, but out here, where the water's deep and dark, it moves across the surface like thousands of tiny waves, pushing him further away. I can't see his face, but I can imagine what it looks like. I shout again, but he doesn't reply.

'Use the oars, bring it back around.' No answer. 'Grab the oars!'

He's twenty feet away, maybe slightly more, but it might as well be a mile. I look at the stretch of water between us, growing, dark, deeper than I've ever seen. I could lower myself in, or jump, dive. No time. I close my eyes and take a step forward, falling, then a terrific splash. It takes ages to surface and when I do I have to get my bearings. Tom's still there, a better view of him now. His chin's tucked in tight to his chest, bone-white cheeks puffing in and out.

'Stay there. I'm coming.' I don't know why I say that. Stay there. Like he's capable of doing anything. I start to swim; breaststroke, so I can see, but Tom doesn't move. He doesn't speak. Mum says that's how you know a really bad attack, not when he cries, or he panics, but when he says nothing. When there isn't enough air for anything.

I get along beside him pretty quick, treading water. I could pull the dinghy back to the island, or back to shore. Too far. Or get in. The options seem many, and confusing. Somewhere in the distance I can hear the grumbling engine of a boat, but I don't see it. There's no time. He doesn't have his inhaler and my legs are already getting tired. The quickest thing to do is to get in and row us back, but if I rock the dinghy I risk freaking him out even more.

'I'm going to try and get in, Tom. OK?'

His eyes are wide, pupils large. Another breath, lips puckered. When they're white there's no more time. I put as much weight as I can on to the side of the dinghy, but it scoots me backwards. Tom lets out a strange sound, several sharp breaths that hold nothing, then he seems to settle into a rhythm of wheezing again.

'Tom, listen, you have to put your arms out to the sides, OK?'

He shakes his head.

'You have to balance the dinghy out so I can get in.'

He closes his eyes, opens them again. He's terrified. I'll make it all OK. I see us by the jetty, climbing out on to the shore, me rushing to the house to get his inhaler. I'll make it OK. I look around, no boats, no people on the shore. It's getting dark.

'Ready?'

Tom puts his arms out to the sides and I take a deep breath, hold it in and push up. My arms scrabble at the side of the dinghy, slipping, sliding back, on again, off, then it starts to tip towards me. I feel the weight of Tom, but it isn't enough. The dinghy is light. A splash. Darkness.

When I open my eyes again I'm fighting with the dinghy. My breath's gone, streaming out of my lips in a gush of bubbles. When I surface I'm in open water, the dinghy behind me.

'Tom!'

I swim over to the upturned dinghy, smacking it away, but he isn't behind it. The water's still, a flat, featureless expanse. I brush back my fringe, look left, right. Then it hits me, slamming into my chest like a giant wave. He's gone down. I take a breath and go under, meet black. I can see my hips, knees, then nothing, just a well of tar that stings my eyes. I surface again, coughing.

'Tom!'

My mind whirls. No sound. No cry for help. Then an arm. His face surfaces, turned up for air. I swim forward, but there's too much water and it's too heavy. He's down again. I dive, a brush of his arm, or leg against my foot. I snatch, handfuls of nothing until my hand hooks on to something. The weight is a shock and the surface seems to slip away, dragging me down. I have to get his head up so he can take a breath. We surface, both of us coughing, his arms thrashing. He lands a blow to my right ear.

The dinghy's close. I manage to grab it with one hand.

'Don't struggle!' He's spluttering, that means air. Breathing. He tries to grab the dinghy. 'I can't hold you. Don't struggle!'

I lose him. I'm shouting now, under the water, mouth streaming bubbles. He's lost in the black. Each time I try to stay down longer, but my chest burns. I have to surface. I try to call out again.

'Help!' I cough. Water gets up my nose. I tread water, taking in a breath. Another. Then another. I have to go back down. Now.

Now.

A car up on the road. Too far away. It's dark. No one can see us. I'm alone. I picture Tom's face, pale against the gloom, sinking. I see the lights on the shore, houses in the village, ours in darkness. Dark. Tired. The dinghy's moving away. I try to rest my legs, not to kick, but my chin drops below the surface and I suck water up through my nose.

'Tom! Tom! Tom!'

'Matt.'

I don't know how long Doc's been saying my name. I open my eyes, meet his staring back. His face is close enough for me to see the tiny pores on his nose, the stipple on his chin.

'Take a minute.'

'Where . . .'

'You're awake.' He passes me water, but I don't want to drink.

'He's dead.'

'Yes.'

He stands up to switch on the fan and returns to his seat, hands clasped.

'Was I talking? How long? I feel funny.'

'You've been right here, sitting beside me. You've been explaining to me what you remember.'

I gasp, a strangled breath I've held too long. My chest's sore, like I've been breathing pins.

'It's normal to feel disorientated. After you've rested we can begin to talk through what you've remembered.' He stands up, goes over to my chair and wheels it to within reach.

'That's it?'

'You're exhausted.'

'What am I supposed to do now?'

'Rest.'

'No.' I push the chair away. 'I want to talk.'

The room's darker, but it isn't night yet. I look at the clock, an hour has passed though it feels much longer. Doc's quiet for a long time. It's raining outside, an uneven patter on the glass which sounds like it doesn't know whether to stop or keep going.

'Why did I survive? Why not Tom?'

'He couldn't swim.'

'But I could've saved him.'

'Do you really think you could have dragged Tom out of the water and got him into the dinghy?'

I feel the weight of him in my hands. Dead weight. It feels like I've been holding it for a long time, like the memory, and I've known all the time what happened and how Tom died, but I couldn't see it. Couldn't see what was right in front of me.

'You couldn't even get yourself into the boat, Matt. How could you have saved Tom?'

'I could've tried harder.'

'It might seem that way to you, but in those circumstances—'

'This is where you tell me it wasn't my fault. A terrible accident. "You were tired, you were a long way from the shore." Thanks, but "it isn't your fault" doesn't change it.'

'No, it doesn't. I believe you did everything you could to save Tom, but he drowned. He drowned because he fell into the lake and he couldn't swim.'

'He shouldn't have been there.'

'You were responsible for him on that day, but it doesn't make what *happened* your responsibility.'

'I could've gone down for him again. Seconds. That's all it was. Seconds.'

'Yes.'

'And all I could think was stupid sod, falling in the lake, he shouldn't have been there. He could've grabbed the oars, he could've held on, he could've—'

'He wasn't strong enough. It's OK to be angry with him.'

'No, it isn't.' I look at him. 'Now, maybe, but not then. Not when he needed me.'

A long silence.

'I can't alter what happened, Matt. I can't tell you that it won't stay with you for the rest of your life, or that you won't always feel some pain at—'

'Then what *have* you done? You made me remember how my brother died. Big achievement. Thanks.'

'The past, however traumatic, is a part of who we are.'

'I'm still in the chair. I'll still have nightmares. All you've done is change them.'

'What happened to you is a part of who you are. You have to forgive yourself.'

'That's your pretty picture of the future? I'll just wake up one morning, and go "Hey, yeah, it's OK, I let Tom drown, but I forgive myself"?'

'No, I'm not suggesting that at all.'

'You've been so busy thinking of ways to get me to remember that you never stopped to think *if* I should. Think Mum'll ever forgive me? Do you think she'll be able to look at me, ever, and not blame me for what happened? I wish I'd gone down with him.'

'But you didn't. You survived. And you can move on.'

'No. When I'm eighty, I'll know that Tom would be seventy-three. A dad, a granddad. An architect, a fisherman, a lawyer. I'll always have a dead brother. Every birthday, every Christmas. And every time I look at Mum, I'll know what I did to her.'

'It wasn't your fault.'

'You should've told me the truth.'

'I did.'

'No, you didn't. You said I'd walk.'

'Matt, I never said that. There's no such thing as a miracle cure. It's going to take time.'

'Oh, I've lots of that!'

'You're still blaming yourself.'

'I'm still in the chair.'

'Yes, well, perhaps those two things are connected. I want you to think about that. You've got to believe that what happened on the lake with Tom wasn't your fault.' He makes me look at him. 'Can you do that?'

# 24

'Let's do it by the fire,' Sarah said.

It was early evening, still warm, too warm for a fire, but he lit it anyway. Sarah fetched the bottle of white wine they'd opened at lunchtime and poured two glasses. The kindling hissed, spitting orange sparks, a few that shot forward and fizzled out on the slate hearth. He waited for the flames to build and then doused them with a sprinkling of coal.

'I'm waiting.'

He turned around to see Sarah drinking out of her glass with one hand, the other unbuttoning her blouse.

'Going to get your kit off, Dr Mason?'

Too bloody right. He knocked back his wine in two large gulps and, still holding the empty glass, pulled his T-shirt over his head.

'Look at you,' she said, laughing. 'You're all tangled up.'

She set his glass down on the hearth with hers and slowly removed the rest of his clothes. When he was naked he reached under her skirt and pulled down her pants. Her excitement quickening, she kicked them off, undid her bra and pushed him back to sit astride him.

He guided his cock inside with fumbling jerks then, watching him through half-closed eyes, she began to rock. He covered her mouth with his palm, letting his fingers fall inside to be sucked and licked. She was so beautiful and so unusually silent that he didn't want to close his eyes, so he watched her, intent, gradually taking him up to the point of coming and, with a smile, dropping him down again. Her skin was pink from the fire and when he found her nipple with his mouth it felt hot on his tongue. Finally, when the head of his cock burned with frustration, she reached for his hands, holding them for balance while she rolled and drove herself on to the end of her climax and the beginning of his. They stayed, moving gently back and forth, for several minutes afterwards, him listening to her breaths lengthen, slow, and finally return to normal.

Outside it had grown dark, but he hadn't been aware of it, or the ringing of the phone that seemed, suddenly, to encroach on his senses. He heard the answering machine kick in, his own voice on the message, then a click as whoever it was hung up.

'I'm burning,' she said.

He rolled her away from the fire so she lay at his side, and gently kissed her on the forehead. Anything he might say now would sound clumsy, but he wanted, all the same, to say something. The moment passed and she got up, asking him if he wanted a drink of water.

'Please.' He sat up, resting against the sofa and smiled to himself.

When she returned she had two tall glasses of iced water. She handed him his glass and sat on the floor beside him to put her blouse back on.

'Are you OK?' he asked.

She shrugged. 'No. Yes, I am. It's nothing.'

'So it's something.'

'Oh, what the hell. Yes. It's about Matt, actually.'

'You know I can't—'

'I know, confidentiality, but this is important. I can't talk to Gill about it and there's only really you who can tell me if I did the right thing.'

'What's happened?'

'We were having breakfast on the terrace yesterday and he was quiet, you know what he's like, but this was different. He's hardly spoken a word to anyone since your last session. Just sits, staring at the floating island.'

'I saw it was back.'

She nodded. 'It's been coming up for days. I thought it was that. It's bound to affect him, right? So anyway, we're sitting there and all of a sudden he says he wants to go.'

'To the *island*?'

'Yes. I didn't know what to do. I tried phoning you, but you weren't in. He said he wanted to go so he could plant a flag for Tom. I knew Gill would go ballistic if she found out, but he was . . . well, really insistent.'

'What did he say? Exactly.'

'Tom had always wanted to go, and he never got there, and it would help him – Matt – to draw a line under what happened. He said it's what Tom always wanted and if he could do it then it would be like he was doing it for Tom.'

'How did he seem?'

'Hard to tell. Calm. Anyway, I managed to get him in the dinghy and row us across and I got out and planted the flag. Bit of a struggle really, I nearly fell in, but I didn't want to say I'd do it and then not go through with it. He didn't talk and I was busy, you know, trying not to go arse over tit. But then, when I finally turned round, he was just sat there, tears streaming down his face.'

'And afterwards?'

'Nothing. Very subdued. He did say it had helped but that's not how it looked. Do you think I did the right thing?'

'Oh, yes.'

'Really?'

'It's bound to have churned him up, it would anybody, but at least now it sounds like he's facing up to it.'

'I wasn't sure.' She blew out. 'What a relief. It's so hard sometimes, to know what the right thing is.'

He kissed her on her head and they settled into a comfortable silence, resting side by side against the sofa to watch the fire. Every so often she'd rub her feet, her toes small and neat against his.

'Oh!' She got up, disappeared into the kitchen, returning a few moments later with her portfolio tucked under her arm. 'I completely forgot about this.'

Still half-naked, her pubic hair flirted at him from the hem of her blouse.

'I was going to show you my work, remember?'

'So you were.'

'You still want to see it, don't you?'

'Of course.' The cover, spread across his bare legs, felt cool on his skin. 'It doesn't open.'

'You have to push the sides together.'

'You'll need a new one,' he said, finally managing to undo the zip. 'You can't possibly go to university with this old thing.'

She smiled. 'I'll get dressed.'

The first couple of photographs showed a man on an allotment, elderly, in his seventies. In one he was digging, sleeves rolled up to reveal thin, muscular arms. It was surprisingly moving to see what Sarah had seen, the emotions in each task the man attended to, pride, concentration, a deep sense of contentment.

'These are really very good,' he said, when Sarah came back into the room. She put her skirt back on and moved to an armchair to watch him. 'Very good indeed.'

'Thanks.'

He leafed through to the next section, black and white. These were different, but again, one person, an old woman sitting on a terrace outside what looked like a retirement home. 'I like what you've done with the background, the sign on the door, NO VISITORS BEYOND THIS POINT.'

The doorbell rang. 'I'll get it,' Sarah said. 'Look at the next one. I think you'll be surprised.'

He got up to pull on his jeans and moved on to the sofa. In the next photograph the woman was closer to the camera, a broad, toothy smile.

'Who is it?' No reply. He rested the portfolio on the sofa beside him and went into the hall.

It was Elizabeth's face he registered first, a smile, a flicker of unease.

'Hello, Robert.'

He stepped forward, not with any idea of what he was going to do, and there the three of them stood, the two women registering each other for what seemed like five minutes or more, but was only seconds. He put a hand on Sarah's shoulder. A mistake. No. Yes. He was supposed to say something. What?

'I'm Sarah.' She offered her hand to Elizabeth.

'Elizabeth. Robert's wife.'

Silence. Watching in frames, he saw Elizabeth take in his bare chest, the top button of his trousers, still undone.

'I left my coat,' Sarah said, after what seemed like a long time. She turned away from the door and went upstairs.

'Why didn't you ring?' he asked.

'I did. You must've been busy.' She raised her eyebrows. 'Are you going to invite me in?'

He stepped aside and she walked past him into the hall.

'I thought you were in London.'

'I was.'

He picked up a sweatshirt that was lying over the banister and put it on.

'I wouldn't have thought she was your type, Robert.'

'Sarah does some cleaning for me now and then, that's all.'

'Oh.'

Shit. Shit. Shit.

She wandered into the lounge, took in the changes,

233

turned, smiled. He watched her, moving around, cautious, sniffing the air like a cat back from the vet. She was dressed in black, a wide skirt, her long, dark hair shining. In the kitchen, after glancing out of the patio doors to the garden, she pulled out a chair at the table, sat down, and crossed her legs.

'So . . . how long have you been fucking the cleaner?'

# 25

Elizabeth squeezed past him to the cupboard and took out two mugs. She put the kettle on, then got herself a glass of water. Her proximity alarmed him. Here she was, moving around, knowing where to find things, taking over. He stood at the door, astonished by how peculiar it felt.

'Work's underway as you can see.' Several of the kitchen units were on the floor, their contents, plates, saucers, piled high on the table. 'They've only just started on the units.'

'I'm surprised you're staying here for it. Must be hell.'

'It's not so bad.'

'I noticed you'd had the windows done.'

'It's what we agreed.'

'Oh yes, I know. I wasn't saying . . . It looks good.'

'So do you.' He tried to determine what was different, summoning an image of when he'd last seen her. At the station, sitting on her suitcase on the platform, pale, tired. 'How's Julia?'

'Fine.' She smiled. 'Young.'

He imagined them together, moving between bars in Hampstead, laughing, heels clicking on the pavement. Julia showing her older, married sister what she'd been missing out on.

'Sorry about that,' she said. 'It's no business of mine who you're seeing.'

He took the mug of coffee from her. Her top lip was trembling.

'You must be wondering what I'm doing here.'

'It's your cottage, too.'

'Can we sit down?'

She led the way outside. It felt cool, a low sun. He brought out the cushions for the chairs.

'Thank you for the birthday card.'

Sending one appeared to have been the right thing to do. He'd hesitated for a long time. Birthdays had become so etched with grief.

'My parents came down for the weekend. We went to the theatre. And then on Sunday we drove to Cambridge. You know how Mum's always said . . . sorry, I'm rambling, aren't I?'

'You go to the theatre a lot?'

'Quite a lot.'

'What else do you do?'

'What?'

'What else do you do? I imagine it's quite lively where you are.'

'Not really.'

'Bars?'

'Yes.'

He waited.

'This feels remarkably like an interrogation, Robert.'

'I'm simply trying to understand how your life's changed.' Was he hell. He wanted to know who the men were, if there were any, and how she was meeting them. 'So you go to these bars, clubs . . .'

'On occasion.'

'With Julia?'

'Yes, with Julia. I dress up in leather and fishnets and drink vodka till three o'clock in the bloody morning. Is that what you want to know?'

'Sorry.'

'I'm not seeing anyone. I came *here* to see *you.*'

Her nails, once long, had been cut short. No wedding ring. Make-up, more than usual, to mask tiredness, perhaps. She looked, suddenly, very tired.

'I didn't know if I should come. Perhaps it was a mistake. In the end, I just got in the car and—'

'You *drove*? From London? It's miles.'

She made as if to speak, but looked out over the garden instead. It was horribly overgrown, lawn crowded with the happy faces of daisies, thistles growing out of cracks in the patio.

'I've been working,' he said, by way of explanation.

'Here?'

'A boy in the village. And I'm trying to write a paper.'

She knew from experience not to ask too many questions about his work. He wondered why he'd brought it up. What he really wanted to know was why she'd come, but she wasn't ready to tell him and he couldn't bring himself to press her. 'What about you?'

'Oh, I'm trying a new glaze. There's a gallery in Hammersmith that takes quite a few of my pieces. They're doing an exhibition in a couple of months.' She pressed her hands together.

'What's going on, Liz?'

'There's something I came here to say and I think I have to say it now or I'm afraid I won't manage it.' She fingered her necklace. 'I wanted to know, I mean, I wanted to ask whether it's too late. For us.'

'Too late?' He laughed. '*You* sent the divorce papers.'

'Maybe because of that, it's made me ask myself whether it's what I really want.' She reached for his hand, covered it with her own. The warmth moved him. 'Whether it's what you really want?'

For a moment he wanted to pull her hand to his face, but he stopped himself. 'It wasn't so long ago you were telling me you'd sleep with anyone, be unfaithful, just to get pregnant.'

'I was angry.'

'So was I.'

'I was upset, Robert.'

'*So was I.*'

'You're right.' She shielded her face from the sun. 'I said a lot of things that hurt you. I know that.'

'So what's changed? You feel differently now?'

'You're not making this easy.'

'Well, I'm sorry, but I took it from your decision to divorce me that things were pretty final.'

Silence.

'What are you saying? You can love me, just me, no child? I'm enough?'

'You always were.' She closed her eyes. 'I love you, Robert. I never stopped.'

For a while he couldn't answer. He found himself standing up, walking slowly to the bottom of the garden. The wallflowers were dying, leaning heavily into the fence. He crouched down, picked the head off a daisy and crushed it between his fingers. She looked so fragile. Had she really spent all those months away from him, loving him, building up to this one day?

She waited for him to sit down again. 'Whatever we said to each other, we can get past it.' She searched for his eyes with her own. 'I'm sorry, Robert. Please believe—'

'Don't. I don't blame you, Liz. Christ.' All his efforts to turn what he felt into anger had failed. 'I have tried.'

'If you've moved on . . .'

'No, that isn't it.' Sarah. He heard it again, the sound of the front door slam as she left. God. 'It's just it's a hell of a shock. You can't expect . . .'

'I know.'

'How long are you here?'

'I hadn't thought. I've booked in at the hotel for tonight.'

'There's no need . . .' he stopped. 'Yes, perhaps that's best.'

Had Elizabeth shown up a few weeks ago and said this, would his response have been different? And if so, why? Because of Sarah?

'There's not been a day gone by that I haven't thought about you,' she said.

'Not so I knew.'

'There never seemed to be the opportunity—'

'To pick up the phone?'

'The last conversation we had we were arguing about possessions. Who gets the sofa, who gets the bed, who gets the fucking coffee percolator . . .'

He looked at her, surprised by her sudden outburst of anger.

'What was I supposed to say? By the way, I still love you?'

'Yes. Jesus, Liz. Our marriage isn't something you can fix with a bit of Elastoplast. Besides, love isn't the point, is it? It didn't stop us getting into a bloody mess. It didn't prevent our marriage being torn to pieces, or you walking out. I couldn't give you a child and you felt you had to choose, be a mother or be my wife. You chose.'

'I want both.'

'You can't *have* both!'

Silence. Despite the pain it had caused, there'd been a decision to make about their future and it had been made. It had been a relief to find that clarity. There had been, at last, a clear line.

'I thought it might be strange being back here,' she said. 'Sad. We only ever came here to grieve.'

'That's not true. We were happy here, too.'

'What I meant was, it doesn't feel sad, particularly. Even with all we were going through, the treatments served a purpose. They brought us together.'

'And tore us apart.'

'If we could've stopped blaming each other—'

'I didn't blame you,' he said.

'You resented me for not wanting to give up, for driving us so hard.'

He stared into his mug. 'You couldn't look at me, remember? You said it'd got to the point where every time you looked at me you felt pain. Nowhere else to go when it gets to that point, is there?'

An image flared in his mind of their last row, suitcases opened out on the bed. She'd accused him of robbing her of her only chance to be a mother. It wasn't up to him to call it a day, he didn't have that right.

'I thought your decision to walk away was selfish,' she said. 'About how much *you* could take, but I know now you were only trying to save our marriage.'

He gave a hollow laugh. 'By doing the one thing guaranteed to end it.'

'It can't have been easy to say it.'

'I inflicted a sentence on you, that's how you put it, wasn't it? That by denying you more treatment I took away what glimmer of hope you had left. Only it wasn't just me who was saying stop, the consultant said it too. He made it clear there wasn't any point continuing. You just weren't ready to hear it.'

'So it fell to you.'

'I was fighting for something I thought was more important than a child – us. If we'd have carried on, there'd have been nothing left. Only there wasn't anything anyway, obviously.'

She swallowed. 'I've felt so lonely without you.'

Her words struck him with such resonance that he couldn't, for the moment, give her any indication he understood. But he did. Her presence, the mere fact of her sitting here with him, gave him comfort.

'I need a drink,' he said. 'Will you have one?'

He wanted to put off the awkwardness of her leaving to stay the night in a hotel. But he'd need that time. They'd talk some more, inevitably, but then she'd go. Dinner, tomorrow, or something. They'd go out maybe. He'd have to talk to Sarah, but not now. He went to the kitchen to prepare two strong whiskies. At least there was some ice in the freezer. He tried to release the cubes, but his hands were shaking, no use, and the tray slipped out of his grip. In the end he smashed it against the tap which loosened several pieces and sent them skidding across the work surface. He threw the tray into the sink and took a deep breath. Wasn't it what every marriage aspired to, not in your twenties and thirties, perhaps, but at some stage, to bury every hope and fear in the other until you no longer lived outside each other at all? Surely a marriage based on such understanding, even if sexless, was better than no marriage at all?

He looked around for the stray ice cubes. As he bent down to retrieve one from the floor he glanced through to the living room. Sarah's portfolio was on the sofa. He picked it up, shuffling several photographs together that had slipped out, and put it out of sight. The room was still warm from the fire. On the rug in front of it he saw the cushion he'd put under Sarah's head after they made love, the soft indent still there. He patted it out, hastily collected the drinks, and took them out on to the patio, ice chinking with every step.

## 26

'Hey! You're not old enough to drink.'

Sarah snatched the wine out of Matt's hand and returned to the bed where she sat, cross-legged, against the wall, and poured herself another glass.

'What's wrong?'

He came further in and closed the door, an unwelcome intrusion into what she'd come to regard as her private space, but she wasn't in the mood for making a big deal out of it. She wanted to drink, not talk.

'Sarah?'

'Nothing's wrong. I'm getting drunk.'

'Why?'

'Because I want to.' She'd left her portfolio at the cottage. Shit. 'Look, I just don't feel like company.'

He didn't leave. She opened the bag of booze – six cans

of Stella and two bottles of Jacob's Creek on special offer. She examined the label, twelve per cent proof, with any luck she'd get so far up Jacob's Creek she wouldn't know night from day. There was a great deal of comfort to be had from getting solidly drunk. She looked at Matt, pale, eyes bloodshot and swollen.

'How are you?' she asked.

He shrugged.

'Have you eaten anything?'

'Mum's out. There's a film at nine, Ewan McGregor, you said you liked him, so—'

'Did I? I don't remember.'

On leaving Robert's she'd got into her car, intending to return to the Logans', but she'd changed her mind and accelerated past the house. She hadn't known where she was going, only that she wanted to be out of Loweswater. After a while she realised she was heading towards the main road out of the Lakes from where it was only a short distance to the A69, the dual carriageway that would eventually take her back to Newcastle. Regardless of the fact she hadn't packed, hadn't told Gill, and was owed nearly two weeks' wages, the thought of seeing the city break on to the horizon made her stomach swell. She'd pictured Mum and Nanna in front of *EastEnders*, trays on laps, Josh in a cloud of dope smoke in his room, but when it came to putting herself in the frame, it didn't work. She didn't belong there any more, too much had changed. Or she had.

Matt sat in front of her, fingers drumming the arms of his wheelchair.

'What film is it?' she asked.

'*Moulin Rouge.*'

'I'll pass.'

She blew the dust out of an old coffee mug on her bedside table and filled it with wine. He took it from her, stared at the contents for a moment, then gulped it down.

'Steady, can't have you whacked out of your tree. Your mum'll have me shot.'

'I have drunk alcohol before, you know.' He looked at the bag. 'Lager, usually. Anyway, she won't be back till late. I think she's got a boyfriend. Someone at work.'

'Has she?' Sarah covered a belch with her hand. 'Unlucky for her.'

She thought of asking him how he felt about it, but sod it, she wasn't Robert. He offered his mug for more wine. She hesitated, then filled it to the brim.

'Can I have one of your cigarettes?'

'No chance.' She lit one and blew the smoke towards the open window. 'Filthy habit.'

He glanced around her room, taking in the clothes piled high on a chair, make-up scattered on the dresser. In the beginning, she'd taken great care to ensure her room was tidy, but after a few weeks she'd begun to relax, leaving the door unlocked, tidying up only now and then.

'Have you still got my scarf?' she asked.

He blushed.

''S all right. Just wondered whether you still had it.'

'Yes, it's . . . somewhere.'

He was almost certainly a virgin, probably never even been kissed. She knew what it was like for kids who had something wrong with them. At Bensham Comprehensive there'd been this kid, Simon or Stephen, she couldn't remember, from her English class, anyway. He had one ear slightly larger than the other. The lasses called him Frankenstein. You didn't need to be in a wheelchair, just different.

'I didn't mean to embarrass you. I'm in a funny mood, that's all.'

'I'm not embarrassed.'

His eyes wandered. His shyness was touching, and attractive, she thought, though that'd be the wine talking.

'When girls get upset, it's nearly always because they've had a fight with their boyfriend or he's done something to make them feel bad.'

'Right.'

'Is that why you're upset?'

'Lesson for the future. Don't do stuff that makes girls feel bad.' She took a long drag on her cigarette. 'Let's just say I'm one of those girls who attracts it.'

'It?'

'Trouble.' She swallowed. 'Married men.'

'How many married men have you been with?'

'Oh, cheers, you make me sound like a right slapper!'

'That's not what I meant.' Another flush up his neck. 'Sorry.'

'I don't seek them out, if that's what you mean. Two, since you're asking. The first time I was too young, missed the signs, didn't find out he had a wife until we'd been going out for ages. I suppose I believed him when he said he was going to leave her.'

'Did he?'

'No.'

'And the second?'

'Uh?'

246

'You said there were two.'

How easily Robert had explained her away. How little he must've thought of her. Her mind had gone over the entire relationship, from the first encounter to a few hours ago, making love by the fire. She could still smell him on her skin. *So how long have you been fucking the cleaner?*

'You're not drinking,' she said.

Matt turned his mug upside down. Empty. She reached into the bag and handed him a can. 'From now on you're your own responsibility. Just don't throw up.'

He laughed and she joined in. After a while she didn't know what she was laughing at any more, but it didn't seem to matter. Her lips tingled and she lay back on the bed lighting one cigarette after another. Matt told jokes, rummaged through her tapes until he found Abba. They sang along, words slurring together. She felt better, no question, but every so often she'd look at her mobile and think of Robert and the pain returned.

'Hey?' Matt snapped the ring pull off his can and chucked it at her. 'I thought we were getting drunk?'

'We are?'

'No sense in you getting wasted by yourself, is there?'

It was dark outside. At some point – it seemed like a long time ago – Matt had gone to the kitchen to fetch candles and spaced them out on saucers around the room. Shadows flickered across his face and neck. He stretched his arms above his head, showing a flash of stomach, and reached for another can. Perhaps it was the light, or the drinking, she didn't know which, but somehow he'd matured. He seemed older, physically strong, clever, a pretty wicked sense of humour. She liked him being close, felt the long, empty minutes when he disappeared to the toilet. Now, door closed again, she was sure she didn't want it to be opened for a long time, and that if it was, all they'd created within the four walls would vanish and there'd just be Matt, in his room, fending off nightmares. Her, alone, thinking about Robert.

'Well . . .' She opened her bedside-table drawer and rooted around for a pen. 'If you're serious about drinking we should make it serious, don't you think? Have you ever played shotgun?'

'Shotgun?'

'I'll show you.' She arranged a pillow behind her and laid a can of Stella horizontally across her palm. With her other hand, she took the pen and held it poised over a point near the bottom. 'You make a hole here, put your mouth over it and then, in one movement, you tip the can vertical and release the ring pull.'

'Why?'

'Because the lager comes out in this massive rush and you have to drink the whole lot in one go or get soaked. And because it makes you drunk really fast.'

'My can's already open.'

'I'll go first, then you can get another one and do it with that.'

She made the hole, took several deep breaths, and leaned forward. She could feel Matt watching, eyes wide and shining. Shit. They'd be really plastered at this rate.

'Do it, then.'

'OK, OK. Just building up to it, that's all.' She heard him groan frustration, then took another breath and released the pull. She had to swallow fast, but even so, a fair bit of lager, foam mostly, dribbled down her chin and on to the collar of her T-shirt. When she'd finished she belched loudly.

Matt cheered. 'Mint! Now me.'

'The secret –' she was out of breath – 'is to make the hole big enough. You don't want to be sucking it out.'

He made a hole in a fresh can, glancing at her several times to see if he was doing it right, then he turned the can up and released the pull. He only managed half before he threw his head back and spluttered. Sarah booed loudly. His T-shirt was soaked, but he was laughing.

'I think I could burp the alphabet now,' she said. She did a spectacularly good 'A', followed by a pretty impressive 'B'. Matt joined in, some good efforts, apart from 'G' which neither of them could manage.

'Stop!' she fell back on to the bed laughing. 'I'll be sick.'

'Sarah?'

'What?'

'Thanks.'

'What for?'

He shrugged. 'I'm having a good time.'

'Me too.'

A silence. He held her gaze.

'You know, if we're going to do this properly, we have to play the game that goes with the game.'

He frowned. 'That makes sense.'

'I'm drunk.'

'Oh, OK. What game?'

'We tell our secrets. Sort of like a truth or dare. You tell a truth about yourself and I try and top it with a truth about myself. If you can't think of anything, or you chicken out, you have to finish your drink.'

'What sort of truths?'

'A story, a fact about yourself that's embarrassing, or stuff no one else knows – like my middle name, I could tell you that because it's embarrassing and I haven't told anyone else. Only you have to top it with something worse.'

'I don't have a middle name.'

She groaned.

'Only kidding. I get it. So what is it?'

'Bettina.'

'That's terrible!'

'It was my great-grandmother's name, OK?'

His shoulders shook with laughter.

'Right, your turn. Try not to exaggerate.' She took a can of hairspray from her dresser. 'This is the bong. When you have the bong, you talk, and vice versa.'

'The *bong*?' He took it from her and held it up to his mouth like a microphone. 'I can't think of anything.'

'Then you have to drink. The *whole* can, no spitting it back in.'

'OK, OK.' He closed his eyes. A minute, two. 'Right, I've got something. When I was in hospital they made me see this physiotherapist. Even though I couldn't move, I still had to see her, every day. She was awful, really bossy and ugly, too. God, you've never seen someone as ugly as this woman. She was called Miss Quigly and she had all this hair which she piled high on her head. And she had bad breath, really bad, like something had crawled into her mouth and died. Anyway, I called her the Nazi. One day, like when I'd been in there a week, she said I had to get out of bed and into a chair. I'd been stuffing my face with chocolates all morning, watching MTV,

you know, then she comes along and starts yabbering –'
he held his forefinger under his nose – 'Vat are you
doing? Out! Out of ze bed!'

Sarah laughed.

'So she grabs me under the arms, spins my legs off the
side of the bed, and says I've got to lean into her. But she
stinks, right? And I go all dizzy from getting up too quick.
All I can smell is her, her breath on my face and it's this
yacking horrible stench. Next thing I know I've thrown
up all down her uniform. Chocolate-coloured vomit.'

'Urgh, God! Good one. OK, now me.' She took the
bong. 'I need glasses, normally it's contact lenses 'cos my
eyesight's rubbish—'

'I never knew that.'

'No interruptions. That's a rule, by the way. Anyway,
yeah, before I started using lenses I had these glasses, thick
jam-jars they were, with pink, plastic frames. Couldn't see
a jot without them, only I looked like a right nonce, so
whenever I went out on the town I used to leave them
off. One night I was skint. I had about five pounds in my
purse which was enough for three half-lagers and my bus
fare. So I get on the bus, dolled up to the nines, can't see
a bloody thing, and I drop my money all over the floor.
The coins scatter everywhere, under the seats, every penny.
The bus is packed with people going to the Bigg Market
and of course they all cheer, don't they? So I sit down,
without picking my money up, and I think, I'll just wait
until my stop and use the time to identify where it is so
I can get it, casual, you know, on my way down the aisle.'

'I'd no idea you were so *vain*.'

'Sssh! I'm not vain. Anyway, this wasn't about vanity it

was about survival. So I think I see a 50p, and that's my bus fare home. At this point it's all I've got in the whole world and drinking, night out, forget it, all I care about is getting home. The bus gets to my stop and I stand up first so I can get the 50p. Only when I pick it up it's not 50p.'

'What was it?'

'The top of a beer bottle. I'm so embarrassed, the whole bus is cheering and laughing because I've just picked up a beer-bottle top and put it in my purse. I had to *walk* home, in the rain.'

'That's the best you can do?' He took the bong to begin the next round.

After round five they'd worked their way through nearly all of the cans and opened the second bottle of wine. Matt shook his head when she tried to fill his mug. He was smoking one of her cigarettes, or rather letting it burn down between his fingers. Occasionally he took a puff and coughed until his eyes streamed.

'Right, final round,' she said. 'Confession. You know, I think I'm right out of stuff I can confess.'

He nodded at her drink, but she waved him away.

'OK, OK. Comfortable? Ready? *OK.* The married man I hooked up with? He was my art teacher at school.'

'Your *teacher*?'

'Julian. Mr Harrington to everyone else. I was fourteen. I used to have long hair, all the way down my back, only one day I got sick of it and cut it all off. I made a right mess of it and then Josh, my brother, had a go. He said I had sideburns which were uncool so he took them off with a razor, only he went too far and I ended up just about shaved. I guess you could say I looked different. Julian noticed me then. I used to see him drawing on this pad in class, looking at me, drawing some more. He used to set everyone off on a task and sit at his desk and sketch. One day he waited until everyone had gone out for break and he showed me. Drawings of me, pages and pages. He said I had amazing bone structure.'

'Shit.'

'We used to have sex in the storeroom.'

A long pause. Matt was still, mouth open.

'It was where he kept all the paints, paper, the busts from pottery group that were waiting to be glazed. I used to think it was pretty ironic, you know, being surrounded by all these weird self-portraits, my classmates looking down at me while I shagged the teacher. He started taking me out in his car after school. He had a BMW with electric seats.'

'You shagged him because he had a nice *car*?'

'Hey, don't judge. You don't know the first thing about it.'

'Sorry.'

'I loved him.' She stopped, corrected herself. 'I thought I loved him. It didn't matter about the car, OK, or the fact he was the first guy to notice me. He didn't treat me like the boys my age; they thought I was scum.'

'Why?'

'Because I was fat.'

'You're not.'

'I was then, all right? He had a wife called Emily and a daughter, Karen. When she was born he showed me pictures. Can you believe that? Pictures.'

'Why didn't you break up with him? Or tell someone?'

'I wasn't being *abused*, Matt. We were together for nearly four years. He was young, not long out of university. It wasn't so hard to believe he could like me.'

'What happened to him?'

She lit another cigarette, threw him the packet. 'I told you. He didn't leave his wife. End of story.'

'I'm sorry,' Matt said.

'You're not allowed to be sorry. No pity. Another rule. Actually I'm making them up as we go. Your turn.'

It was warm, heat oozing from the radiator into the smoke-filled room. Too warm for central heating, but Gill liked it that way. You got used to it.

'There's these kids at school. Davey, Gareth and Conker. When I got out of hospital and went back I had a different routine, go into class early, leave after everyone else had gone, avoid the crowds, you know? One day Mum was late picking me up and they were waiting for me.'

He glanced at her, but she said nothing.

'They took me across the road to Brent Industrial Estate and chained my wheelchair to a lamp-post. At first I thought they were just going to leave me there, but then Conker undid the zip on his trousers. Next thing I know, they're pissing on me, all three of them, arcs of yellow piss in my face.'

'Oh, Matt.'

'No pity, remember?'

A long pause. She wiped her cheek and found tears.

He wheeled forward and rested a hand on her leg. 'You think I told you that so you'd *cry*? You think that's what I want?'

'No.'

His voice sounded brittle as though by telling the story he'd hoped to deny the pain. It was what she'd hoped for in speaking about Julian – to let the words come, seemingly without effort, in a way that would diffuse their meaning.

'Your turn,' he said.

She shrugged, lifted her glass and finished her drink.

'Then I guess it's me again.' He took a deep breath.

'You don't have to, Matt. I didn't take my turn so you've won. Game over.'

He blinked. 'Do you believe in secrets, Sarah? I mean, do you think there are some things that should stay buried?'

They weren't playing the game any more. 'Depends what they are.'

'The ones you daren't even tell yourself.' He looked at her. 'The day we went to the island. I told you I wanted to plant a flag for Tom, but that wasn't why I wanted to go. I thought if I went out there, saw it again for myself, I'd know the truth.'

'But you do. I thought you and Doc—'

'I'm still in this chair. I still have nightmares. Doc said being hypnotised doesn't always work, because sometimes you remember stuff that didn't happen. So maybe I remembered what I wanted to believe happened. There's no independent witness. Tom can't tell us.'

'No, Matt. It takes time. You have—'

'I think I killed him.'

Silence.

'It isn't true,' she said.

'How do you know?'

255

'I know.'

'How?'

'I just do. You did everything you could to save Tom. He was your brother. You loved him.'

'I was fed up with him most of the time.'

'So what? Want to know how many times I could've strangled Josh? I've lost count, that's how many. That's what it's like, Matt.'

'I'll never know. I'll never be able to believe that what I've remembered is the truth, nor can I prove it isn't. Makes a joke of it all, really. I could've killed him, no one would know.'

'You know this is the drink talking.'

'Maybe.'

'Not "maybe" at all. It's ridiculous. Christ, Matt, don't you think you're hard enough on yourself? You've already got yourself down as a madman, now you're a murderer? Like hell you are.'

'Yeah.' He leaned forward. 'Want to know something else? I've got another secret.'

'No more! I've had quite enough secrets for one evening, thank you.'

'I love you.'

She stared at him. 'Yeah, right. You're drunk.'

'I do.'

She brought herself forward to the edge of the bed. 'I don't know what to say.'

'You think I'm a freak, don't you?'

'No.'

He blushed fiercely.

'I don't. Not at all.' She slid off the bed on to the floor

and shuffled towards his chair. He was breathing quickly, pupils large. She knelt in front of him and without another word, kissed him, long and hard, on the mouth.

'Wow,' he said, when she'd finished. 'That was . . . amazing. Like static.'

'God, I'm drunk.' Her head felt heavy. 'Well, you win. Beginner's luck, mind, but fair dos, you win. Jammy sod.'

'Win?'

'The *game*, you nonce.' She crawled to the bag of booze. 'So you want another one, or what?'

# 27

Last night she'd seen a glimpse of the real Matt, the one who didn't hide, who laughed, who made her laugh. Today, sober, she saw that person had seeded and grown. She sat next to him at the patio table, where he looked as though he'd been all morning, pencils spread out around him, several sketches started and abandoned.

'Matt, about last night . . .'

'Wasted, weren't we?' He smiled widely. 'I thought I'd puke.'

'We were very drunk.'

His lips were dry, cracking at the corners. He began shading a section of tree trunk he'd copied from one of the photographs she'd given him but, unhappy with it, he scrunched the paper into a ball and tore a fresh sheet from his pad.

'The thing is, Matt, I was feeling pretty mixed up.'

He brushed some coloured pencils aside, several falling off the table and rolling into the cracks between the paving stones.

'I wasn't myself.'

'That drinking game's mad, isn't it?' he said. 'You were off your trolley.'

'I was, that's right.' She looked at him, tried to get some sense that he understood. 'People do some pretty crazy things when they're drunk, you know?'

'Yeah.' He smiled at her again. 'It's OK, you don't need to apologise.'

'I crossed a line. You understand . . .'

'Y'know, I woke up this morning with so much energy.' He looked at his picture. 'It's weird, because I thought I'd be knackered. I mean, my head felt like it was in a vice when I first woke up, at dawn; I listened to the birds for a bit then dropped off again. Then, when I woke up later, I felt great.' The lead on his pencil broke. He picked up a fresh one and blew on the end. 'Anyway, I've been waiting for you. I've been thinking. I want to do physio. I remember the exercises from hospital. Will you help me?'

'Of course.'

'I'll draw them, if you like. I could do that. Then you can memorise them. Because you have to want to get better. It's like Doc said, it's down to me. I've got to focus on what I want and if I put the work in, then, who knows, I might be normal again.'

She smiled. 'Normal?'

'You know what I mean.'

'I think it's brilliant you want to do something.'

She waited, but he didn't make eye contact. There was an intensity about him, in his concentration on the drawing, in the way he spoke. Of course she'd help, it was her job. Somewhere, in all the shit with Robert, that'd been overlooked.

'When do you want to start?' she asked.

'Now, if you like?'

She laughed. 'Let me get over my hangover first, yeah? I'm popping out for a while, thought I'd take a walk. Do you want anything before I leave?'

'I know some great places you probably haven't been to.'

'Maybe another time.' She put a hand on his shoulder. 'Probably best to save your energy.'

'Yeah, course.' He looked annoyed with himself as though it was stupid he hadn't thought of it. 'Physio takes it out of you. I should rest.'

She left him drawing and went to her room to get dressed. She'd make a real effort with the physio, maybe even pop into the library and see if they had anything she could read about it. This was a growing shoot and needed to be encouraged, but first, she had to clear her head. With no distractions, she could focus completely on Matt.

With the same determination she got in her car and drove, turning off whenever the way ahead looked too popular. She passed through a village, turned left where there was no signpost. Finally, reaching a narrow track, she pulled up beside a long stretch of hedgerow and got out. She was high up, looking down into a valley with a few farms.

She started to walk. After a few hundred yards she spotted

a stile and climbed over it into a field. The footpath, worn away to earth, cut diagonally through long grass to a hill. She rolled the sleeves on her T-shirt over her shoulders. The air was thick and warm. Thunder cracked over her head, followed by a moment's silence, then rain. She kept walking, pushing ahead until she reached the top of the hill.

'It's coming down, huh?'

A young man sat, knees up, on a stone wall that cut across the middle of the hill in a straight line apart from a few places where it had collapsed, leaving gaps. He looked familiar, but she couldn't place him.

'Sarah, isn't it?'

Finding someone else in what had promised to be a secluded spot felt like an imposition.

'I'm Gavin. The Bird of Prey Centre in Harley?'

'Oh.' She did recognise him. 'Yes.'

'Gavin Firth?'

He looked different. Cleaner.

'You're supposed to say, "Ah, yes, how lovely to see you again, Gavin."'

'I didn't think anyone would be here.'

He glanced at her T-shirt. She was wearing a black bra; all her white ones were in the wash. It hadn't been obvious at all before it rained. She folded her arms.

'It should clear in a bit.' He took in the view. A mist was forming, rolling out like a sleeping bag on the fields below them. 'Where've you walked from?'

'Nowhere.'

'Nice place.' He unscrewed the cap off a bottle of water, took a drink, and wiped his mouth.

He had a rucksack and wore heavy boots caked in mud.

'I meant I brought the car,' she said. 'It's on the road back there.'

'That's the spirit.'

She sat on the wall several feet away.

'I thought you'd have come back to the centre. With that kid, what's his name?'

'Matt.'

'Yeah, that's it. So he's your brother then?'

'No.'

'Boyfriend?'

'I'm his carer.'

'Oh.'

He threw a leg across so that he faced her and proceeded to stare, rudely, she thought. She remembered now, the brashness. He was confident, good-looking, and he knew it.

'So what'd he do?' he asked.

'Excuse me?'

'Well, I'm sat here hoping for a bit of conversation and not getting any, so to speak, and you've got a face that says you'd quite happily rip my testicles off, which either means you've got this big aversion to men you meet on hills, or all men are wankers and I'm just in the wrong place at the wrong time. The kid piss you off?'

'No.'

'It's a fella, though, right?'

'Why do you assume it has to be a fella? Not that my mood, or my reason for it, is any of your business.'

'Just making conversation. You're not dressed to walk and you look like you've had the roughest night of your life—'

'Do you have a point? Sorry. I'm quite angry, I'm afraid.'

'You're quite forgiven.'

She forced a smile. 'Do you walk a lot, then?'

He didn't answer at first. He was flirting, holding on to pauses. 'No,' he said. 'Do you?'

'No.'

'Begs the question as to what we're both doing stuck on top of this hill in the rain, then, doesn't it?'

'What's your excuse?' she asked.

'I'm thinking of becoming a hill farmer.'

'Really?' She turned to face him. 'And give up birds?'

'Only ones with feathers.'

'I thought they were your passion.'

He looked surprised.

'It's obvious from how you talk about them,' she added.

'I like the speed. Power, you know? When you watch them fly at peak fitness, it's incredible. I've got a Red Kite and two Harris Hawks.'

'Yours?'

'Perk of the job. One of the hawks, a youngster, I took her out this morning for the first time. That's why I'm up here really, wanted to check it out as a flying spot. Took me more than two months to man her.'

'*Man* her?'

'Get her to accept my fist, accept food. It's about trust, see. If she trusts me, she'll find quarry and bring it back. If not, see you later. She's a clever one, though, only a week on the rabbit lure – it's like a pad that looks a bit like a rabbit. Sorry.' His eyes shone. 'I tend to rattle on.'

'Passion.'

'Yeah.' He cocked his head to one side. 'I don't suppose you'd like to go to a party with me tonight?'

'Come again?'

'A party? You know, drink, dance? Get chatted up by nice young men who go walking on hills.'

'Are you always so forward?'

'What you see is what you get.'

She smiled at this.

'What? I make a joke?'

'I can't go to a party with you, Gavin, thank you for asking.'

'Why?'

'Because we just met.'

'For the *second* time.'

'I'm not in the habit of making dates with men I meet on hills.'

'I'm sure that's true. Even so, the answer is "yes". Or you could go so far as to elaborate and say, "I'd love to".'

He looked fun. And young. 'Where's the party?'

'Friend of a friend's. A few of us are meeting at The Pot and Glass first about eight.'

'I'll see what I'm doing.'

'Lots of other people there, chilling, drinking. That means it's cool, I might try it on with you, I probably will, but you needn't feel obliged to give in.'

She pushed herself down from the wall and walked a few steps backwards, smiled, and turned back the way she'd come.

'Where are you going?'

'Home.'

'You can't. You haven't said "yes" yet.'

She laughed. *Some* guy; she didn't know the first thing about him. A date that wasn't really a date. Maybe she'd have a good time. It was something to do and what had she done since she got here? Found another married man to get screwed up by, that about summed it up. She wouldn't give herself time to mope about Robert. Besides, she'd passed her A levels, got good grades, and hadn't, as yet, done anything to celebrate. Her heart thumped hard in her chest. She ran back to the car, smiling to herself, and checked her reflection in the rear-view mirror. Wet hair, face the colour of ash and, she looked down at herself, the bra. Oh God, the bra.

# 28

The alcohol had made him drowsy. Elizabeth was putting on her coat.

'Don't go,' he said. 'Why don't you stay a while?'

He wondered why she wasn't drunk, or tipsy at least. She didn't seem to be, then he remembered – he'd had most of the wine; she'd hardly touched hers.

'I don't want to fight, Robert.'

He signalled for her to sit beside him. 'I don't want to fight either.'

He wanted them to go to bed, together, for no other reason than he felt exceptionally tired and didn't want to be alone. She sat down again, fumbled for the light switch on the lamp behind them, and settled into a silence.

He'd tried, that morning, to work on his paper, but by mid-afternoon he was restless, constantly checking his watch and willing the hours closer to evening. He'd not arranged to meet up with Elizabeth until seven p.m., but by five he was walking through the village to the hotel. It was both infuriating and telling that he'd not been able to use the time by himself to think. He'd never been able to think about the problems in their marriage with any clarity, not without her. It was as though he needed her to give his thoughts direction.

But for a time, over dinner, he'd felt himself relax. They'd steered away from the subject of their marriage, turning instead to the safer ground of work. She seemed to be doing well, had launched a website, and had taken on a few sessions at St Martins. She looked good, laughed deeply, her eyes shone. He couldn't remember the last time he'd seen her so at ease. He hoped it was because she'd found some peace. Listening to her talk reminded him of the woman he'd fallen in love with, and by the time he asked for the bill he was feeling invigorated. Now, though, they were back to the usual subject.

'Was there a point when you thought "I'll stop there"?' she asked.

'The consultant said it was worth us going to five, so we did.'

'It was the third treatment for me.'

'The *third*?'

'I thought that'd surprise you. We were at the National Glass Centre in Sunderland buying something for my mother's birthday. Do you remember? It was the day after egg collection. I could barely walk I was in so much pain. We were walking down that long slope to those double doors. Felt like miles.'

'You could've said something.'

She shrugged. 'I was afraid you'd try to talk me out of going on. I'd got it into my head we'd do it and keep doing it until it worked. I didn't care how much it hurt or what our chances were, as long as there was some hope. That was enough.' She looked into her lap. 'I hated you at times, you know. Sitting in the waiting room reading the paper while I lay in the next room like a slab of meat. I kept thinking "There's nothing wrong with me. It's him, and he's getting off scot-free."'

'Hardly.'

'I know, it's just how I felt. I said some pretty awful things to you and I can't ever really take them back, can I? But what I said about sleeping with someone else . . .'

'You were desperate.'

'It hurt you.'

He shut his eyes. 'Not because you were threatening me with adultery, but because I agreed with you. I felt I had no right to stand in the way of another man and what he could do. Anyway, it doesn't matter any more.'

'No, it doesn't. Can't we both just say sorry and get on with our lives?'

'I don't know.' He looked at her. 'Can we?'

'I have to be honest with you. I want us to have a future, that's why I came, but . . . I haven't let go.'

'Oh, Liz—'

'I haven't given up.' She ran her fingers through her hair and brought them back to cover her eyes.

'Adoption? You weren't on for it before.'

'No.'

'What, then?'

'Donor sperm.'

'We're separated! One minute you want a divorce, the next . . . Christ, haven't you had *enough*?'

'The chances of it working are quite high. Better—'

'We discussed it a year ago. I told you then I couldn't do it.'

'He'd be yours, Robert. In every way that matters, he'd love you—'

'We've been here before. What about when he's a bolshy teenager and in the middle of a row he says, "You're not my dad"?'

'Why would he say that?'

'Because it's true.'

'So we don't tell him.'

'Lie?'

'It isn't a lie. Look, you're there at the birth, walking the floor, changing nappies, teaching him to ride a bike, you're there in every way that matters. He doesn't have to know where the sperm came from.'

'Things have a way of coming out.'

'How?'

'Look at us, it isn't so hard to believe we could be here again. Divorce on the cards. He's yelling at you, he says "He's still my father" and you say, "Oh no, he isn't."'

'I'd never do that.'

A long pause.

'A few years ago we'd have said we'd never argue over a coffee percolator,' he said. 'But we did. After a few drinks, if you were angry, you don't know what you'd say.'

'You're talking yourself out of it.'

'I can't believe we're talking about it at all.'

'Lots of couples never tell the child. You think they're living a lie? They're changing nappies, Robert, getting on with it, planning the Christening, taking—'

'You can't see beyond the baby, can you? I *can*. I see a screwed-up teenager who finds out everything he thought he ever knew about himself is a lie. And suppose you do keep it a secret? You're taking away his legal right to contact his biological father when he gets to eighteen.'

'But don't you see, Robert? It would solve everything.'

'No, it wouldn't. Babies don't save marriages.'

'They do if the only thing wrong with the marriage is infertility.'

'Was it the only thing? I seem to remember we hadn't made love for six months.'

'It's our best chance.'

'So we have five, six goes at donor sperm and then when that doesn't work, what? Six goes at donor egg, donor embryo? Where does it *end*?'

'It ends with a baby.'

He heard laughter outside, a bottle fall over and roll on the pavement.

'Are you really willing to throw away all that we have together, Robert? To give up the chance of being a family because you can't accept someone else's genes?'

'What do you mean, "all that we have together"? *You* sent divorce papers. Let's at least keep some perspective.'

'I was confused.'

'And now you're not?' He got up and poured himself another glass of wine. 'You make it sound as if I'm being asked to look after the neighbour's poodle while they go on holiday. This is a life we're talking about. Another man's—'

'You really think you'd reject the child because it didn't come from you?'

'I've thought about it, Liz. Standing in the treatment room while they fetch the donor's sperm, holding your hand while they inseminate you with it. It's like you threatening to sleep with someone else to get pregnant. A more sophisticated, high-tech version of shagging the postman. It doesn't matter what the ethical way of thinking about this is, it comes down to a gut reaction. You can't argue with that.'

'Think of it as a gift. We need a third person—'

'To succeed where I can't.'

'To bring us together.'

'To replace me.'

She stood up. 'We're not getting anywhere.'

'Liz. Don't think I don't see that it's the logical next step, but for a couple with a sound marriage, not for two people torn apart by desperation and sheer, bloody misery. Look at us. Maybe, with time—'

'I haven't got time! I'm thirty-nine.'

They fell into silence, Elizabeth at the window looking out, Robert staring at her back. After a while she went into the kitchen, filled the sink, and started washing up.

'Just as well we never bought a dishwasher,' he said, leaning against the door. 'What would you have done then?'

'Polish silver.'

'We don't have any.'

She turned around to face him, wiping her hands on a tea towel.

'I'm sorry,' he said. 'I'm tired. Did we get anywhere?'

'No.' She folded the towel, unfolded and folded it again. 'You've made it pretty clear what you think. I should go.'

'Don't stay in the hotel tonight.'

'Why not?'

'Because I don't want you to leave, not like this.'

'I'll sleep on the sofa then.'

He raised an eyebrow. It was ridiculous for them not to sleep together, and equally ridiculous that they should. 'I think we can lie together in the same bed and not let it go to our heads, don't you? We never found it difficult before.'

She slipped off her shoes and positioned them neatly underneath the radiator. 'Do you remember what it felt like in the beginning, when we first decided to try for a child?'

'It's a long time ago.'

'We wanted to be a family so between us there'd be this incredible little person whom we'd love as much as we loved each other. It wasn't complicated, Robert. We just wanted to be parents.'

She touched his arm as she passed. He stood in the kitchen, listening as she climbed the stairs. For several minutes he felt unable to move, so exhausted, so terribly fucking tired of it all. There was always his infertility, always the pain, never a second just to breathe. He locked the patio doors, resting his forehead on the cold glass. As he went through the house, checking doors and windows, he felt the weariness grow inside him, fat and heavy as a tumour. Here he was going through his nightly ritual of locking up, following Elizabeth up to bed, after hours spent talking without conclusion. It was familiar and in that familiarity, there was a comfort he didn't want to acknowledge.

'I left the bathroom light on for you,' she said, when he reached the top of the stairs.

'Thanks.' He watched her pad barefoot along the landing and go into the bedroom where she pulled up her skirt to take down her tights.

He turned into the bathroom and locked the door. Yesterday he'd made love to Sarah; he'd allowed himself to think about what it might be like to have a future with her. And here, now, his wife was pleading with him to use donor sperm. He rubbed the skin under his eyes, turned off the light, and followed her into the bedroom. She was already in bed, hands crossed over the top of the duvet. He undressed silently, hesitated at his underpants, then removed them. They'd slept naked together for eight years, no reason to stop now.

'This is nice,' she said.

The ease of her closeness, her smell, the way she tucked her bottom pillow under itself to make it higher. 'Yes.'

She found his ribcage and rested her hand there. He closed his eyes, certain that if he opened them he'd see her hand cover his whole body, casting a shadow like a cloud moving over a valley.

'We ought to try for a good night,' he said quietly. 'Talk some more tomorrow.'

He turned away from her, listening to her breaths gradually deepen. Only when she was asleep did he feel able to let go of the tension that held him, close his eyes, and follow.

# 29

'Nobody home?' Gavin tapped the top of her mobile phone with his beer glass. 'Come and dance, Sarah. It's a party, remember?'

She'd resisted calling Robert, but checked the screen regularly to see if there was a message. Nothing. Her head felt thick. They seemed to have been there hours, wandering from room to room, talking to Gavin's friends, an OK bunch, younger than him, but as the conversation had centred almost entirely on football or various types of water sport – none of which she knew anything about – she'd said little. That was probably why she felt so drunk. She looked around for her glass, gone, another one finished or put down somewhere. She tried to remember where the bathroom was. She went through the kitchen where a young lad, twelve or thirteen at most, was being sick into a saucepan.

Gavin was beside her again. The music kept changing volume, quiet for a few seconds, head-splittingly loud the next. He said something she couldn't hear, and took her hand. She followed, past a group of lads leaning up against the stereo in the living room. Up the stairs. A couple were sprawled about halfway up, the girl's top and bra pushed up to her neck.

'Gavin, I need to pee.'

'In a minute.'

'Gavin?' She tugged on his hand.

'It's up here, I think.'

He led them into a bedroom where there were two singles, one very obviously occupied by a couple, the other empty.

'This isn't the bathroom.'

'Just come in here a sec.'

'No!' Her head was swimming. She staggered backwards, knocking into someone on the landing.

'Hey!'

Gavin laughed. She wrenched her hand free and concentrated on planting her feet on the stairs. At the bottom she met a group of girls coming in the front door, speaking all together. She shoved them aside.

'What's the big deal?' Gavin was behind her, his voice full of disbelief. 'I thought you'd want to.'

Her cardigan was still inside. To hell with it. She had her bag. She had money to get home.

'Sarah! Slow down, will you? I got it wrong, yeah? I just wanted to take you out.'

'Why?' She was standing in the middle of the lawn, heels sinking into the grass.

'*Why?* You're asking me why I wanted to take you out? Are you always this suspicious?'

'I'm not thirteen. I don't go to parties and expect to be mauled.'

'I hadn't planned on "mauling" you. I thought we were getting on.'

'I've hardly spoken to you all night. You know someone in there asked me whether I fancied a beer and a fuck?'

'Ah, that'll've been Charlie.' He drove his hands into the pockets of his jeans. 'Never was very good at chat-up lines. What did you say?'

'I said I don't like beer.'

He laughed and fell into step with her. 'So what do you like? I'll take you wherever you want to go.'

'I'm going home. Alone.'

'Anywhere you want.'

'Paris.'

'Paris? Paris, France?'

She kept on walking, then, realising he'd stopped, she turned around. He'd pulled out a crumpled five-pound note and some change from his pocket. 'We'll need to pop to the bank, oh, and I haven't got a passport. Apart from that—'

'You don't have a passport? Haven't you ever been abroad?'

He kicked a stone with his foot. 'I went to Ireland once, on a boat.'

She crossed over the road. It was dark now, hard to say whether she was headed in the right direction for town, but she'd keep going until she saw a taxi.

'I'd love to travel, though, you know? There's loads of

places I'd go, maybe go travelling for a year, or more, and just see where I ended up. Maybe I'll do it, tomorrow.' He ran a few steps to catch up with her. 'You could come if you like.'

'Just pack a suitcase and off we go.'

'Yeah.'

'You're very sure of yourself, aren't you?' She liked the fact he hadn't been anywhere and didn't have any money. 'What about your job? I suppose you'd just pack it in, ring them on the way to the airport?'

'It's just a job.' He put his thumb out for a taxi, but it sped past. 'Are you cold?'

'No.'

He took off his jumper anyway, showing a whirl of dark hair around his belly button, and handed it to her. 'Suits you, that does.'

'Huh?'

'Your dress. Red. It's nice.'

'Thanks.' She took a deep breath, relieved to be sobering up. His jumper was warm and smelled nice. He walked beside her, balancing on the kerb, turning to walk backwards so he could look at her. Several times during the evening he'd done just that, looked without looking away. It was nice to be admired, and with such confidence.

They crossed over the road, nearing town now, and headed towards the taxi rank. Gavin was talking. A question.

'What?'

'I said my flat's just around the corner. Why don't you ring for a taxi and wait at mine? Looks like the only people getting one are those who've booked.'

He leaned into her, encouraged by her smile, and kissed her lightly on the lips.

His flat was above a take-out pizza place, closed, but the smell of fat was everywhere. She followed him up the stairs and into the kitchen, one of those galley types. Half the lino floor was ripped up to reveal bare concrete.

'What do you want?' he asked.

'I don't think I'll bother.' She pulled her mobile out from her bag. One bar on the battery. Enough for one call, but as she scrolled through to the address book, the screen disappeared into darkness. 'Shit. Where's your phone?'

'One drink.' He slid past her to the cupboard, brushing a hand around her waist. 'I've got —' he opened the door, catching a pot noodle that fell out — 'vodka, something that looks like it's a liqueur, a funny sort of green, anyway, probably quite nice, or . . . er . . . vodka? There're glasses in that cupboard there. Fetch them, would you?'

She stepped over a large wicker basket on the floor. Something had been sick on the blanket. 'Do you have a dog?'

'Cat.' He glanced at the basket. 'Big cat. He'll be out chasing mice.'

She gave him two glasses and wandered into the living room. There was a large stain on the carpet, something once liquid that had dried into a thick crust. Plates on the floor, a fork she nearly stepped on.

'I like what you've done with the place,' she said, when he came back with the drinks. She sat down on a brown armchair, the only item of furniture that didn't need something removing from it.

'Cleaner's day off. You got your own place?'

'I live with the Logans.'

'He's *that* kid? Shit, I didn't realise. Logan, yeah. His kid brother drowned, right?'

'Last summer.'

'I remember it. Plastered all over the news. Isn't it a bit weird living there? Talk is he's seeing a shrink.'

'Psychiatrist.'

She took a sip of her drink. It was incredibly strong and she coughed.

'Sorry, there wasn't much Coke.' He got up to put some music on, running his finger along a line of CDs and shouting out suggestions. Ironically, considering how he lived, they appeared to be in alphabetical order. 'What music do you want?'

'I don't mind. Whatever you want.' She looked around for the phone.

He took a CD out of its case, put it in and pressed play. The Kaiser Chiefs' 'I Predict a Riot'. Figured.

She rubbed her heels, sore from the straps on her sandals, and looked along a shelf behind the TV. There were half a dozen DVDs and a few hardbacks, which seemed to be mostly about falconry. She picked one out and flicked through the pages.

'Any chance I could get you interested?' he asked, touching her shoulder.

'What?'

'In falconry.'

'Oh. I don't think so. I like the idea of it, though.' One of the pictures showed a man standing next to a large bird on the ground, its wings spread out like an umbrella. The caption said it was an American Bald Eagle.

'It's called mantling. She does it to protect her prey.'

He stretched an arm around her shoulder.

'I should go.'

'You haven't finished your drink.' He handed her glass to her. 'It's hot in here now, don't you think? That's the trouble with this room. Too small. You put the heating on and it's boiling after five minutes.'

He leaned back from her, lifting his T-shirt over his head. The skin was pallid, drawn tight over lean muscles. On his breastbone a few dark hairs lay flat and long, cat-like. Further down, towards his belly button, they were rough.

'Where's the phone, Gavin?'

'Broke.'

'What?'

'Come on, Sarah.' He rubbed her ankle, removing the sandal. 'Hey, your feet are gorgeous.'

'Not a chance.' She lifted her foot to his chest and pushed him away.

'You were up for it earlier.'

'Is the phone really broken?'

'Just stay a bit, you'll never get a taxi now anyway. Pubs are chucking out.'

'Where is it?' She put her sandal back on and wheedled past him, checking every visible flat surface, moving clothes, lifting magazines.

'Chill out.'

She went into the kitchen, saw no sign of it. 'Is it in the bedroom?'

'I don't know,' he said. 'Let's go see.'

'I mean it, Gavin. I'm about three seconds away from screaming the bloody place down.'

'You know, you're pretty uptight.' He rolled into a kneeling position and put his T-shirt back on. 'It's in the hall where you came in.'

She rang Directory Enquiries, got the number of a taxi firm, and asked to be put straight through. Behind her she could hear Gavin moving around. The music stopped.

'Must be living with the Addams family that's made you weird. You know they're a joke, don't you?'

'It'll be here in five minutes.' She picked up her bag. 'I think I'll wait outside.'

'Everyone knows it. Husband ran off, kid cops it, wife's a nutter, and the other one, Matt, belongs in a home for retards.'

'Oh, for God's sake, Gavin, grow up. You're the joke. Maybe one day, somewhere under all this scum, you'll find that out for yourself.'

She didn't wait for a reply, but as she closed the door to his flat and made her way down the stairs to the street, she heard music again, rising from a muffled thud to ear-splitting maximum volume.

# 30

I've been ready, swimming trunks and towel in a bag on my lap, since seven. We have to be at the baths before eight if we want an empty pool because on Friday mornings they do life-saving classes. I look at my watch. 7.52.

'Right,' Sarah says. 'I think I'm ready. Do you have everything you need?'

'You've still got your slippers on.'

'Uh?'

'Slippers.'

'Oh.' She gulps another mouthful of the coffee I made her. Strong. 'Right.'

'We don't have to go if you don't feel well.'

She hasn't bothered to put on make-up, because she's hung over or because we're going swimming, I don't know which. She takes her mirror case out of her handbag and pinches her cheeks.

'You can make yourself sick, you know. You stick your fingers down your throat and—'

'Yeah, thanks, Matt.' She drops the case back into her handbag and kicks her slippers in the air one at a time, catching them in her hands. 'I'll be fine. I'll be swimming a hundred lengths, you'll see, bombing off the diving board . . . do they have a diving board?'

'A big one. I'll hold you to that.'

'I'd expect nothing less.' She slings her bag over her shoulder and grabs the car keys off the counter. 'Come on.'

Outside it's already warm, a haze of glassy heat spread across the garden. The car smells of rubber. It's only a short drive to the swimming baths, but the traffic's heavy and when we turn into the car park there's a queue waiting to get through the barrier.

'Looks like everyone's had the same idea,' Sarah says.

'These'll be for the children's pool. We're in the adult one.'

Even so, I feel a moment of panic. I got Mum to check the times, but she could've got it wrong. We park and go inside. There's a small, glass booth just inside the door where a large, blonde woman sits. A badge pinned to her blouse says 'Brenda Buchan'. She's sorting the rubber locker bands you put on your wrist into piles – green for women, blue for men, white for children.

'We're here for the assisted swim hour,' Sarah says. 'Are we too late?'

Brenda doesn't look up straight away. 'Fifty-eight, fifty

nine, *sixty*.' She glances at a large, round clock on the wall above a snacks machine, then at her watch, as though to emphasise we're not here when we should be.

'Are you the carer?'

'Yes. We've not been before—'

'You might get twenty minutes if you're quick.' She passes one green and one white band through the hatch. 'You need to be here at eight precisely if you need the winch.'

'Thanks, Brenda,' Sarah says. 'Perhaps if you'd be so kind as to tell us where to go so that we might be *even* quicker?'

I clear my throat to suppress a laugh, but it doesn't work and Brenda's eyes dart to me.

'The shared cubicles are to the right of those double doors.' She points with her eyes. 'Chris will tell you what to do when you've got changed.'

Shared. The word plants itself. Somehow I didn't think that far ahead. I should've got Mum to put my trunks on this morning under my jeans. As we go through the doors and along the corridor to the changing rooms my mind scurries from one image – Sarah taking off my pants – to another – Sarah taking off hers.

'She must mean here,' Sarah says.

The door has a sign with stick symbols of a mother and child. Inside, there are little kids with armbands, pale-skinned and pot-bellied. Warm air and a strong smell of chlorine. A girl in a purple swimsuit stops mid-waddle at the sight of me, just as a woman's voice from inside a cubicle shouts, 'Lily, don't run.'

'Can I help you?' Chris, it turns out, is female, beefy and large-breasted.

'Yes,' Sarah says. 'We'd like to get changed.'

Chris leads us to an area behind the showers where it's quieter, five empty cubicles.

'Right.' Sarah takes the bag from my lap. 'I'll get changed first and then you.'

'Oh, OK.'

She goes inside the cubicle by herself and locks the door.

Of course. Stupid, Matt. I hear the clink of her belt and the zip on her jeans, followed by the softer sounds of blouse and bra and pants. A few minutes later she appears in her bikini.

'I'd have bought myself a swimsuit if I'd known,' she says. 'Is this all right, do you think?'

Lush. 'Fine.'

'Come on then. Now you.'

And in we go. Without me having to say, she lets me get on with the easy stuff, turning away to put the items of clothing I hand her in the bag. She folds my T-shirt into a tiny square, shakes it out and does it again. Somewhere outside someone's using a hair dryer. It starts, stops again. When it's time for my jeans and pants Sarah closes her eyes, blindly tugging on them until they're off my ankles. I feel like one of those mind-teaser puzzles, tilting and swivelling until all the balls fall into the holes.

When we're ready she stuffs the bag into a locker and goes to find Chris who takes me through a side entrance to the pool. Sarah's got to go a different way so she can dip her feet in the verruca water. She waves at me, grinning when we meet up again on the other side.

'I don't think we'll need the winch to get in,' Sarah

says, when Chris starts to unstrap it. 'If you could help me get him so that he's sitting on the edge, though?'

Chris looks doubtful and for a second I think she's going to start spouting about some health and safety regulation, but Sarah sounds confident. We go to the shallow end and the two of them lift me off the chair and sit me down on the cold tiles.

'I'll get in,' Sarah says and lowers herself off the steps further down. 'Shit, it's freezing!'

I laugh. She wades across and rests her hands on my knees. 'Ready?'

'Yep.'

With Chris supporting me from behind and Sarah in front, I roll forward into the water. I make a big splash.

'I don't—'

'I've got you,' Sarah says. 'You're all right.'

The sensation is weird at first, like I'm going to sink, but I reach for the sides. Sarah holds me around the waist.

'OK?' she asks.

'It's cold. Bloody hell.'

'Do you think you can use your arms?'

I nod and I feel Sarah's hands slip from around my waist.

'We've got an inflatable ring,' I hear Chris say.

'He's fine, thanks.' Sarah looks at me and I nod.

'You're breaking all the rules,' I say when Chris is out of earshot.

'Like you care. Try to swim?'

I focus on a stretch of water and go for it. Front crawl. The water's cool on my head. After a few swings of my arms I think about stopping but it's easier than I thought it'd be. A doddle. I turn my head to the side and take a breath, stretching out with my arms until my fingers touch the wall at the other side of the pool. When I turn around Sarah's swimming towards me, mouth open in surprise.

'It's easy.' I laugh.

'That was brilliant!'

'It's amazing.' I smack the surface of the water with my hand and laugh again. 'I mean it isn't difficult at all. I just use my arms. Watch.'

I set off again, ducking my head right under this time, and try breaststroke to pull myself through the water. In no time at all I reach the other side.

'I bet I could beat you in a race,' I say, when she settles at the side next to me. She arches her back to wet her hair, breasts surfacing. 'It must be 'cos my arms are strong, you know, from the chair.'

She squeezes the bicep on my right arm. 'Yeah. Not bad, I suppose.'

'You're impressed, I can tell.'

'Big head.' She splashes water in my face.

'Hey!'

I make a lunge for her, diving under the water to grab at her ankles. She comes up for air, shrieking, smacking water at me. 'Stop! Matt!'

'I'll get you!' She makes it as far as the steps, but I get there at the same time and pin her in. 'You look like a drowned rat.'

'Thanks.' She coughs. 'You like it here, then? I thought it'd be more fun than doing those silly exercises you had to do in the hospital.'

'Yeah. You're heaps better than the Nazi.' I want to kiss her, but I stop myself. 'Thanks.'

'You're welcome.'

'It's like I'm gliding.' I push myself off the steps and float on my back. 'It feels . . . normal.'

She laughs. 'Take it steady though, huh?'

'I'm all right. You don't have to worry about me.'

'OK.'

'What about you, feeling better?'

'I haven't thrown up for at least an hour so yes, I think so.'

I come back to the side. 'What was it like, the party?'

'Rubbish. Do we have to talk about it? I've been trying to forget it happened.'

'Why?'

She leans forward and pinches my nose. '*Because* I had a crap time and Gavin turned out to be a tosser.'

'Gavin?'

'The Bird of Prey Centre.'

'Oh, him. I could've told you he was a tosser ages ago. When did he ask you out?'

She tucks hair behind her ears.

'Did he try it on with you?'

She groans and drops her head under the water, blowing out bubbles. When she surfaces she's holding a gobful of water in her mouth which she squirts at me.

'Oh, now you've really had it!'

She pushes off the side, a race, but she's not quick enough and I get in front. I reach the other side a few seconds before her, but start to whistle, like I've been waiting ages.

'You win,' Sarah gasps, treading water.

A cleaner moves along the gallery above our heads,

289

wiping down seats. She glances down at us, seeing a girl-friend and boyfriend larking about because, here, in the water, that's what we look like.

'We should do this every day. It's fun.'

'Yeah.' She smiles. 'It is. Only next time we'll have to get here earlier. I think it might be time for us to get out.'

Chris has climbed off her chair at the other end of the pool. She checks the time from a large watch she carries around her neck and starts to unstrap the chair winch from the wall. The long arm swings out over our heads. I think of saying to Sarah that I'll just push myself out of the pool, but the sides are higher than my shoulders. I'd never manage it. The waterproof seat drops into the water, straps and buckles to hold me in.

'People are watching.'

Sarah looks, sees the group of teenagers at the far end of the pool waiting to get into the water.

'Stuff them,' Sarah says. 'Come on. We'll have you out in no time.'

She steps back from me as the winch takes my weight. Its machine noise is loud, echoing around the pool. I see my legs again, like something dead being lifted out by a crane. I close my eyes and keep them closed until the noise stops.

Sarah climbs out and picks up our towels from a bench. One she wraps around herself, the other she puts around my shoulders, pulling it tight under my chin. Water from her hair drips on to my face.

I want to say, 'I hate this, I hate this chair.' The kids are in the pool now, laughing, splashing, diving off the board. One of them, poised to jump in, looks across and elbows his friend. Then we're gone, back the same way we came in, Sarah going one way, me the other.

But it was good in the pool. No, it was brilliant. Racing, laughing, mucking about. Like being normal again. I think about what Doc said, a constant playback in my head. *When you want something badly enough . . .* I do. Sarah and me to be going out together. Properly. We'd go to parties and she'd be there with *me*, not with Gavin, the tosser. It could be like it was in the water, all the time. Only better. I just have to want it badly enough.

# 31

The air held the threat of thunder, but the sky was clear. Robert dressed the chairs on the patio with cushions he'd brought out from the kitchen.

'It's not much,' Elizabeth said, setting down a tray on the table.

Iced water, salad and some bread.

'I should've gone to the supermarket.'

'This is fine.'

They sat down, neither inclined to tuck in.

'What I said, Robert, about how I feel, I meant it. I do want *you*. I've always . . .' She put a hand up to cover her eyes. 'Oh, God. I hate this.'

'Liz . . .'

'I just can't understand your arguments against it. If this were fifteen years ago, before they'd discovered how to inject sperm into an egg, we wouldn't be having this conversation. It'd be donor sperm or nothing.'

'I married you. You first and foremost. If it's only us, isn't that enough?'

She was staring at the ice in her glass.

'Don't you remember what it was like before IVF?' he continued. 'We were happy, we enjoyed each other. Our lives didn't always revolve—'

'But I had the *expectation* we'd have children, it was in the future, not snatched away from me.'

'We could have a different life.'

'I don't *want* a different life.'

'I just don't think I can do it any more, Liz. I haven't the heart for it. More disappointment, more heartache . . .'

'You don't have to.' She paused, took a deep breath. 'I want to . . . I'm pregnant, Robert.'

He opened his mouth to speak, but no words came.

'I was inseminated with sperm from a donor and it worked.'

'You're *pregnant*?'

'I had a scan. I've seen the heartbeat. It's sixteen weeks, I didn't want to tell you before in case I lost him.'

A life. A third heart beating only a few feet away. His mind raced through a series of practised responses. All the times he'd imagined her telling him she was pregnant – at work, on the phone, waiting till he got home. In one version he'd even rung the clinic himself. But this. The facts wouldn't string together. She was pregnant, but it wasn't his. That meant a man, someone she'd found and slept with. It was what he'd dreaded all this time and so it was several more seconds before the meaning of her words registered and he heard 'Donor'.

'Donor sperm?'

'Yes.'

He felt winded. 'Him. You said "him".'

'It's a boy. A baby boy, Robert. I was going to tell you when I got here, but I wanted to know how you felt. I thought if we talked it through—'

'You've already done it.'

'We can be a family.' She searched his face. 'No more treatments. No more waiting. This is it. We can finally move on.'

'I don't . . . you've been here two days and you're telling me *now*? All the talking . . .'

'I know you've got doubts, but I promise you they won't mean anything when the baby comes. You'll be a father.'

The heat of the sun lay heavy on his head.

'Oh, it was awful and yet it wasn't. I've so much to tell you. First, I was convinced it'd work first time and when it didn't I felt like the world had ended, and without you . . . But it doesn't matter, none of it matters any more. I'm here now and the three of us can—'

'Oh, Christ.' He couldn't catch his breath. 'You went to a clinic on your *own*?'

'You haven't heard me, have you? Robert, I'm pregnant.'

'You got treated, then came here to talk me into it.'

'No, not talk you into it. I—'

'Why the divorce? Why send—'

'I didn't plan it this way.' She looked out over the garden. 'I really did think we'd reached the end and I had to do whatever I was going to do on my own. But I knew, I think I always knew, I couldn't do this without you.'

'Oh, Jesus.' He stood up, feeling snared by the heat.

'Come and sit down.'

He leaned over the table, feeling the cold metal cut into the palms of his hands. Somewhere in the distance a lawnmower buzzed.

'I did this for us.'

'You didn't *ask* me. How could it be for us when I didn't know anything about it? This isn't a new sofa, Liz. This is a child.'

'Our child.'

She'd thought so little of his views, of his input, that she'd disregarded them completely.

'Don't you see? Everything we've been through. It's *over*. Doesn't that mean anything? I thought when I told you, when you finally had it in front of you, you'd be pleased.'

He said nothing.

'What's wrong?'

'I didn't have a say in this.'

'Would you honestly have told me not to do it if you'd known it would work?'

'You acted *alone*. Didn't you think I might want to be needed?'

'I've never made you feel you weren't needed.'

'You just did.'

Silence.

'Robert, all the time I've been here you've talked about what IVF did to our marriage, how it tore away at everything. You said yourself how different we were before. Don't you see we can get back to that now? Finally, there's a baby. I did it for us.'

'You did it for yourself.'

She leaned back in her chair, moved by the force of his words. 'So it's all right for you to tell me I have to give up, because you're taking the decision, but when I do this, actually get pregnant, you can't accept it.'

'It wasn't your decision to make.'

'Likewise.'

'This is completely different.'

'The hell it is. You might show a bit of gratitude. It wasn't easy, going through it on my own.'

'*Gratitude?*' He brought a fist down on the table, sending knives and forks clattering on to the paving stones. Afraid of his anger, he went inside. How far along was she? She'd told him, but he couldn't remember. Not enough to show, though he could hardly bring himself to look at her.

She followed him into the kitchen. 'If it's pride . . .'

'It isn't pride.'

She leaned against the fridge, stepped aside when he moved to open it. No wine.

'It doesn't matter how we got here or what I did to get us here. It's done.'

'It matters to me. What about the donor?'

'What about him? They gave me a list. Do you really want to know?'

'I told you I couldn't do it. Jesus, Liz. You made this decision, this enormous, fundamental decision concerning our lives, without me. You took away my choice.'

'Because I thought you'd take it for what it is. A fresh start.'

'What if I don't want anything to do with it?'

She was startled, looked away. 'The baby exists, whether you want it to or not.'

'You should've *asked* me.'

'For God's sake, listen to you. You're behaving like I had sex with this guy!'

He found a half-bottle of brandy in a cupboard and poured himself a glass, taking it through with him into the living room.

She followed and sat on the sofa opposite him. 'I admit, at one point, I thought we had no future, but I did this because I chose *you*. Through it all that's never changed. I stuck by you when we found out you had a problem, I stuck by you through the treatments, when I could have found someone else. I could have had three children by now.'

'You want me to be grateful? That you didn't leave me years ago?'

'No. I want you to realise that however brutal it might sound there's a reality behind this. I *chose* us; all I've done is a result of that choice and it wouldn't have happened at all if I didn't love you. This child exists because of that.'

'And it makes me responsible?'

She threw her hands up in the air. 'This isn't a trap, Robert. In the end you have to come to your own conclusion. You can decide whether you want to be a part of it, or not.'

This was probably her last chance to conceive. But to do it without consulting him, when she knew he was against it, and then turn up suggesting they start again – where did that leave him? The baby existed because she loved him, because he was infertile, because she'd stuck with him all the way through her thirties. She had, despite his fears, forsaken all others.

'I can't talk about this now,' he said. 'I need time to think.'

'What—'

'*Think*, Liz. Not talk. We ought to leave it for a day or two. Talk again when . . .'

'You're right,' she said, after a long silence. 'Yes. Maybe it's best. I'll stay at the hotel tonight, leave first thing in the morning.'

# 32

Robert paused outside, took in several breaths and let them out again slowly, and then entered the pub. A thin man, who'd been sitting at the end of the bar, took off a pair of large-framed glasses and went through the hatch to serve him.

He doubted Sarah would show up. He expected to be given instructions for how he should return her portfolio, so he was glad she'd agreed to see him. He took a seat in a small alcove in the lounge and rested the new case on the seat beside him – he'd driven to Carlisle and bought it this morning, not knowing whether it was the right thing to do, and then spent an hour transferring her photographs. He stretched out his legs under the table and tried, as he had done on the drive over, to organise his thoughts.

'Hello.'

He looked up, startled. 'Sarah. I didn't see you come in.'

She hesitated and then sat down, lighting a cigarette. Her eyes flicked over to the barman, back to him.

'Thank you for seeing me,' he said. 'I wasn't sure whether you'd come.'

'I need my portfolio.' She took in the new case. 'You shouldn't have done that.'

'I wanted to.' He reached for her hand which she withdrew at his touch. 'What do you want to drink?'

'I don't know. She picked up a beer mat and tore at a corner. 'I'll go for whatever that is.'

'Carling.'

He went to the bar. She looked beautiful, sulky, and something else, different. Younger. He watched her cartwheel the beer mat between her hands and wondered how much he'd have to explain. She deserved to know it all, and yet something made him want to hold back. He suddenly wished for a longer breath of time between them, but that wouldn't be possible. Or fair.

'Here.' He handed her the drink and set down the fresh pint he'd bought for himself. 'Sarah, these last few days have been a bit of a shock to me.'

'To *you*?'

'I know how it'll sound now, in the light of what's happened, but I didn't lie to you. That's important. I really did think it was over. Liz and I aren't . . . together, not in the sense—'

'You're together by definition. It's called being married.'

'Separated.'

'Bit of a technicality, don't you think? Considering

she's probably at home cooking your bloody dinner.'

'She went back to London this morning. Look, everything I told you was true except for the timing. I've received divorce papers, but it hasn't gone through. I told you it had because I assumed I was talking about something that was inevitable. As far as I was concerned our marriage was over. And as for her turning up like that, I had no idea.'

'Bummer that, isn't it? Getting caught.'

He told himself he had to continue, if only because she had every right to be angry. 'I want to explain—'

'I don't want you to.' She picked up her cigarette packet and drove her thumbnail along the side. 'It doesn't matter.'

'It does to me.'

She smacked her cigarettes down on the table. 'Why didn't you just tell me it was for fun? I could've dealt with that.'

'Because that's not the way it was.'

'No. You were just fucking the cleaner.'

A long silence.

'I'd no idea you heard that.' He pulled at his collar, the skin underneath hot to his hand. 'You must've been terribly hurt—'

'Don't flatter yourself.'

'I'm sorry. I panicked. I didn't know what to say. I suppose I wasn't ready to explain to her who you were.'

'Obviously.' She looked at him squarely. 'So you've patched things up. That's what you really want to tell me, isn't it? Get together for a little chat so you can give me

301

the "I'm giving it another go with my wife" speech? Spare me. You're forgetting, I've been there once already.'

'I haven't agreed anything with Elizabeth.'

He saw now, how she'd see this. Two betrayals. Two married men who'd had their fun and moved on. He took in her expression, chin pinned to her chest.

'I don't blame you for being angry, Sarah. For what it's worth, everything I told you about my marriage was true. I don't know how I can make you believe that. I made one mistake which was to tell you I was divorced before it was official. I regret that deeply.'

'Did you fuck her?'

'No.'

She looked at him.

'No. That's the truth.' As though the presence or absence of sex decided whether his marriage with Elizabeth existed or not. 'She came to tell me she's pregnant.'

'Oh, congratulations.' She clapped. 'I hope you'll all be very happy.'

'It's not mine. I'm infertile.'

'Infertile?'

'Yes.' And there it was. Like gas escaping. 'Before we separated I said no to donor sperm, I said I couldn't ever foresee being comfortable with it. She did it, went to a clinic, got treated, without my knowledge.'

The door burst open and a crowd of office workers from the nearby industrial estate lined up at the bar, each talking over the top of the others. He tried to make himself heard.

'I never agreed to it, Sarah.'

'Bloody hell.'

'We separated. The end. Then she turns up here and tells me she's gone ahead.'

She shook her head and picked at the beer mat again. 'So she wants you to get back together, have the child and live happily ever after?'

'Something like that.'

'That must've been quite a shock.'

'She took away my decision. I didn't, Christ, it doesn't matter, what matters is her doing something like that without my—'

'Why are you telling me this? It's between you and her.'

'Because I want you to understand that this child wouldn't exist if it wasn't for me, for my infertility. She did it for us. That's what she says. It makes me responsible, or maybe it doesn't. I don't know. Either way I think too much of you to drag you into it. I wanted you to understand that I wasn't, just, you know . . .'

'Using me?'

'Yes.'

He felt her reach across, the smallest touch on his head.

'Look, you really think you should be held to account for something she did on her own?'

'I don't know.'

'What are you going to do?'

He shook his head. 'I have absolutely no idea.'

'You really didn't have sex?'

'No, we didn't. That was true in the past anyway, before we split up.' He could see her attaching too much importance to the fact. Or was he attaching too little?

'She went and did this, knowing how you felt. That's pretty fucked-up, Robert. Anyway, it's not my business

303

really.' She paused. 'Shit, it's not like we were making plans. Nothing depends on our relationship, I mean, we'd hardly got going. It's not like I expected either of us to change our lives to fit in with each other. What did we honestly think was going to happen? That you were going to carry my books, meet me after classes, get drunk with a load of obnoxious students?'

'No, of course not. I wouldn't want to be a drag on you.' He breathed out slowly. 'I just wanted you to understand it, us; it was important to me. I wasn't just spinning a line to get in your knickers.'

'The way I remember it, it was me trying to get into yours.'

They shared a smile.

'What I mean is, everything that's happened between us meant a great deal. I've hurt you and I'm incredibly sorry about that, and you'd be quite right to tell me to bugger off –'

'I'm not sure I want to.' She shrugged. 'I don't know. But it's pretty obvious we need to take a break.'

'Would you have dinner with me tonight? I mean, just as friends?'

'No.'

'Right.'

'It's not what you need, Robert. Or me. You need to talk to Elizabeth.'

'Yes. I know.'

'And I have to get back. Gill's got to go into work.' She paused. 'I'm already late.'

He stood up, helped her into her jacket, and handed her portfolio to her. Someone had put music on and a girl sat on a stool by the bar surrounded by the large group of office workers he'd seen come in earlier. A card next to her drink said 'Sorry, you're leaving'. He led the way outside, glad for the quiet of the car park. It was raining heavily. She hunched her shoulders against it.

'Typical. Pissing it down.'

He smiled.

'Go. You'll get soaked.'

'Where's your car?' he asked.

'Wouldn't start. I walked.'

'Then I'll give you a lift.'

She tightened her jacket around her.

'You can't walk home in this. What about your portfolio?'

She nodded and moved into the doorway while he ran to fetch the car. Relieved to find her still there when he returned, he opened the passenger door and she jumped in.

'You should've run faster,' she said, affectionately placing a hand on his knee. He struggled to get the car in gear, pulled forward and stalled.

'Sorry,' he said.

He asked about Matt on the drive back, desperately needing something to say to break the strange mood.

'Intense. He follows me around. We went swimming yesterday which was good. I don't know, he seems better.'

He listened, nodded, but by the time he'd reached the house he knew he'd recall nothing of their conversation. He switched off the engine.

'Right,' she said. She opened the door.

'I'll be seeing you again?'

She nodded.

'What I mean is . . . you're OK, aren't you? You're not . . .'

'Heartbroken? Of course.' She tried a smile. 'You need to sort through what it is you want to do, without me as a distraction.'

'You wouldn't try to influence me. I know that.'

'Yes. I would. I'd do all I could to persuade you what you really wanted was me.'

'Sarah . . .'

'I had a great time, Robert. Let's leave it at that.'

He felt something inside him break. It was as though a part of him, discovered by her and strengthened by the time they'd spent together, was being destroyed. He couldn't bear it. Reaching out, he pulled her towards him and kissed her. She met him with the same urgency, opening her mouth and leaning into him. When he finally tore himself away he buried his face in her neck and held her for several minutes.

There were tears in her eyes, but she wouldn't let them come. She got out of the car and walked to the house. Glancing round to pull away, he saw she'd left her portfolio on the back seat.

'Sarah.' He jumped out and ran across the drive. 'You forgot this.'

The security lights came on, flooding the drive with light.

'Thanks,' she said. 'It was nice of you to buy me this. Must've cost a bomb.'

She lifted it up, fingered the handle — too shy or too hurt to look at him. He raised her chin and kissed her again. Deep. Long. Christ, he couldn't get enough. Finally, she pushed him away.

'Goodnight, Robert.'

He nodded and, without looking back, she went inside and closed the door.

# 33

She rested her head against the door. Had she tried to convince him he'd have been swayed. They'd have gone back to his cottage and made love. She lifted her sleeves to her face and breathed him in. Go. Please, go. She listened, holding her breath as the sound of the car crunching over the gravel faded and there was only the house, dark, the soft hum of the fridge. It was right, like this, not to wake up in his bed tomorrow, not to fail with Robert as she'd failed with Julian. Julian had said he loved her, but he hadn't chosen her. Nor would Robert.

'Hello.'

She looked for the direction of the voice and saw Matt, a silhouette at the top of the stairs. She fumbled on the wall beside the door for the light switch.

'How long's that been going on?'

'I thought you'd be in bed.' She checked to make sure she'd left the door on the latch and, resting the portfolio against the hall table, she bent down to untie the laces on her trainers.

'I *saw* you.'

'Jesus, Matt.' She wasn't in the mood for an inquisition. She heard the sound of his fingernails on the spokes of his chair. 'Do you need me to get you something?'

A long silence. The landing was dark. She climbed the stairs halfway. Gill had changed him into his pyjamas before leaving for work.

'A drink?' she asked.

No reply. He wheeled forward a few feet. He looked tired, pissed off.

'The loo?'

'It *was* Doc, wasn't it?'

He'd have been looking out of the landing window. She sighed. Perhaps it was time for a dose of reality. She ought, at least, to be able to come in after a night like that and get some bloody privacy. 'Yes.'

'You kissed him.'

He looked small, hunched in his chair.

'Yes, Matt, I kissed him. I am allowed a private life.'

He said nothing. Stared.

'Why don't you invite someone over from school instead of sitting here all night by yourself?'

No response. She threw her hands up and went down the stairs to switch off the light, plunging the hall, and Matt, into darkness. She closed her bedroom door firmly and kicked the wastebasket. Nicely done. She needn't have been so sharp.

No, it's what he needed. Asking her questions. A million bloody questions. Where the hell was Gill anyway? Something to see to at work – getting a good 'seeing to' was more like it.

Sarah got undressed, slinging her clothes on to the chair, and switched out the light. The bed felt cold. She couldn't spend every minute of every day with him, that was just a fact. She had her job and then she had her personal life. She already did far more than she was paid to do. It was only because Gill was out so bloody much she did more. And because she liked him. Matt was a nice kid. She turned over. So what if she was the next and only alternative to a porno mag? Just because he was in the chair didn't make him any different to a million other fifteen-year-old boys. It wasn't like he could call into the local newsagent and buy *Hot Blonde Totties* or whatever off the top shelf. Even the items in her room, some moved, others missing. It was harmless. A scrunchie, a spray can of deodorant. Weird maybe, but lots of teenagers had crushes. Sooner or later he'd get over it. As long as she did nothing to encourage him . . .

The kiss. But he'd understood about that. One drunken kiss. It didn't change anything. He was sweet, attractive when he wasn't so bloody depressed. She'd been drunk, angry, she was still entitled . . .

She tried to shut down her mind to sleep, but each time she closed her eyes she saw Matt where she'd left him on the landing, sitting in the dark. The clock ticked. Its lighted face annoyed her. She turned it on to its front and rolled over, rolled back, checked the time. At last, groaning, she threw back the duvet and put on her dressing-gown.

The hall light was still off. She shuffled to the bottom of the stairs in her slippers, heels slipping out on to the cold floor.

Light poked out from the bottom of his door. Still up. He'd probably be reading, or drawing like he sometimes did long after she and Gill had gone to bed. She thought about leaving it until the morning. Shit. No, she couldn't possibly leave things as they were. She paused, fingers lightly touching the door handle, and knocked. Once, quietly, then again, louder.

'Matt?'

He'd probably fallen asleep with the bedside lamp on, pencils scattered over the duvet.

'You awake?' She pushed open the door. The bed, to her surprise, was empty. She looked around the room. He was in his chair beside the window, facing her. At first she thought he'd fallen asleep, or else he would have seen her come in and said something, but as she got closer she saw something was wrong. His chest, bare, was red, spreading up his arms and neck in large, starfish-shaped splotches.

'Matt!' Head tilted back, mouth open. He took a breath, faint, shallow, the skin on his ribcage stretched like bubble gum. She gripped him by the shoulders and shook him. His body flopped forward. As she brought his hand up from the side of the chair a bottle fell on to the floor. Pills.

Oh God.

She tried to remember. ABC. Airway. Breathing. Something else. She examined the bottle. Amitriptyline. It meant nothing. The label said Gillian Logan. She pulled him off the chair, but the weight of him knocked her sideways and he landed awkwardly on top of her. She pushed him off, pain stabbing her side, and rolled him over on to his back. His breaths were shallow, scratchy in his throat. She put an ear to his chest, knowing even as she did so that his heart would be beating. Think. He was breathing. She snatched a pillow from the bed, put it under his head, and ran along the hall to Gill's bedroom. Her hands were shaking. She pressed the button to get a dial tone, accidentally switching it off. She dialled again, fingers jerking at the buttons. Heard a voice.

'Ambulance. Orchard House, Craddock Lane, Loweswater. Orchard House, Cr—'

A woman told her to slow down. Sarah took a breath. Her voice was choked, gasping; she tried again, but was met with a series of questions. Who needs the ambulance? What's his condition? Conscious? No. Breathing. Yes.

'He's taken pills. Ami . . . something.'

The woman wanted to know which pills, spell it slowly. How many? She didn't know. She didn't even know Gill took anything. Why would she? Or where she kept them, or why . . . The call was taking too long.

'We need a fucking ambulance!'

'Sarah, calm down. The ambulance is already on its way to you. Are you with Matthew now?'

'No.' The phone was one of those remote ones. She sprang up off the bed and went back into Matt's bedroom, tripping over his shoes, laid out, as they always were, for morning. He was still. She knelt down beside him and put her ear over his mouth.

'He's still breathing.'

She was supposed to be doing something else. She picked

up his arm, let it drop, slapped his face. 'Wake up, you sod!'

She could hear sirens, but they sounded far away. Another world.

'How is he now, Sarah?'

'How the *hell* am I supposed to know?' She watched his chest, felt seconds pass. 'Why aren't they *here*?'

The faint sound of another breath as it hooked the back of his throat and escaped his lips. She pulled at his hair, stroked his face. Why couldn't she just love him back, she'd be anything he wanted, the love of his life if that's what he wanted, anything but this. It felt like a separate reality, him loving her, a crush and a kiss, which was supposed to mean nothing. She swallowed, aware she'd been crying, but wasn't any more, tears blocked by another feeling that for the moment didn't have a name.

A bang at the front door and voices. Unfamiliar. She went downstairs, losing a slipper on the way, and opened the door.

'Where is he, love?' Green uniform. Equipment in a heavy, white box with a padded strap. 'It's Sarah, right?' He opened out the fingers on her left hand and read the label on the bottle. The smell of outdoors on his clothes. 'Do you know how many he took?'

'They're his mum's. I have to ring her.'

The other man, younger, with bleached-blond hair spiked with gel, climbed the stairs to Matt's room. After what seemed like a long time the two of them followed.

Matt looked small, a blue-grey doll on the carpet. The blond-haired paramedic leaned over him and slapped his cheeks, red and gleaming with sweat.

'Is he going to be all right?'

No answer. The sound of Velcro being ripped. An oxygen mask over his face, dragging the skin under Matt's eyes.

She was steered on to the landing by the elder of the two.

'Wait here.' He had a kind face and grey hairs in his nose. 'How we doing, Graham?'

The sight of the phone resting on the hall table focused her mind. She dialled Gill's mobile number and got the answering machine. There were other things she had to do. Get dressed. Keys. Leave a note. She scribbled a message for Gill and put it behind a magnet on the fridge. A minute, two, maybe more, and the paramedics came on to the landing with Matt on a stretcher. They turned him, up, high above the banister and the stairlift. Then she was in the way, being pushed forward out of the door to the ambulance outside.

They'd taken him straight through. Occasionally there were sounds that offered clues as to what might be happening, the squeak of rubber-soled feet, getting quicker, more of them, sometimes none at all. She'd been asked questions, the same ones as before – the pills, how many, how long since he took them – and had then been told to wait. No Robert, although she'd phoned him when she hadn't been able to reach Gill. She used the payphone to dial Gill's mobile number, but it diverted to the answering machine again.

'Can I get you anything?' Janet. She reminded Sarah of her old PE teacher, same hair, grey, tight curls like metal shavings.

'When can I see him?'

'He's still in resus. I'll see if I can find anything out for you.'

She disappeared through the double doors, volume turned up on voices inside, beeping, then nothing again.

'Sarah.'

'Robert!' She hugged him.

'How is he?' His clothes were creased, like he'd pulled them on quickly from a pile on the floor.

'They haven't told me anything.'

'What did he take?'

'Ami something. I can't remember.'

'Amitriptyline?'

'Yes.'

'An antidepressant. Gill's presumably.'

He walked briskly to the reception desk and spoke to a woman on the other side of it. She heard him say Matt was his patient, and other things, voice lowered. Sarah sat down, eyes fixed on a bubble gum sweet dispenser on the wall opposite. A poster next to it extolled the virtues of fresh fruit and vegetables. Five a day.

'Gastric lavage.' He sat down, folding his jacket over his knees, and turned towards her. 'Do you know how many he took? Think, Sarah. It's important.'

'I don't know. I told them—'

The double doors opened again. A nurse, but not for them.

'Was he conscious?'

'No.' She wiped tears from her cheeks. 'Like I said on the phone, out of it, blue. I found the bottle in—'

'There's a separate waiting room down the hall,' Janet said, reappearing. 'Perhaps you'd like to wait in there?'

315

'Any news?' Robert asked.

'I'll ask the doctor to come and have a word with you.'

The waiting room was situated at the other end of Accident and Emergency, past the doors where Matt was taken on the trolley. Plastic curtains covered the windows. Everything was plastic.

'I'll bring you some tea,' Janet said and left them.

The room had toys, a model of the Starship Enterprise, a robot with arms in mid-swing.

'It looks like the sort of place they take you to tell you bad news,' Sarah said. 'Do you think that's it?'

'I don't know.'

'You should be able to find something out. You're his doctor, you could—'

'They're still working on him, Sarah.'

She swallowed. Her throat felt sore. What did working on him mean? Reviving him? 'People survive this sort of thing all the time though, don't they? You must've seen this before?'

Robert was silent.

'*Robert.*'

'I didn't see it coming. He's my patient, it's my job to recognise—'

'Stop.' Sarah sat on a low, wooden stool opposite him. 'The drug, how bad is it?'

'Bad.' He rubbed his eyes. 'It's a tricyclic antidepressant, dangerous in overdose. It depends how many he's taken.'

A doll, head lolled back, was propped in front of the entrance to a Wendy house.

'Could it kill him?'

'I missed something. Shit, I should've—'

'Stop. Can you just stop blaming yourself for one minute? You didn't do anything.'

'It's my job to assess suicide risk, Sarah.'

'He has a crush on me.' She looked away. 'Matt's in love. With *me*. If you're looking for a reason why this happened, that's it.'

'A crush?' He looked astonished for a moment; clearly the thought had never entered his mind.

'When you dropped me off tonight he was there, waiting. I wasn't in the mood for questions and he was giving me the third degree so I flipped. I told him we'd been seeing each other.' She wiped a tear off the end of her nose. 'It's my fault.'

'Why didn't you tell me?'

'I didn't think it was important.'

'Not important?' He threw his hands in the air. 'You didn't think him falling in love with you was important?'

'Of course I do, *now*.'

'The two people in the world he trusts betray him with each other. I'm his doctor, you're his carer. No bloody wonder.'

'We haven't betrayed him.'

'Try telling him that.' He stood up. 'You should've told me.'

'Why didn't you *know*? You're his psychiatrist, you're supposed to know everything that goes on in his head. Aren't you?'

'I didn't know about this.'

'Then what the hell did you talk about all that time?'

'You're the reason he's been making progress. Don't you

see? You're the reason he's finally willing to consider a life beyond the chair. You're the lynchpin in all this and you didn't say a bloody word!'

She broke down. He came over and knelt in front of her, bringing her head to his shoulder.

'I'm sorry,' he said. 'Of course this isn't your fault.'

'It is. I did this.'

'No, Sarah.' He raised her head to look at him. 'He did it to himself.'

His hand felt stiff on her back. She sniffed, pulling away from him to stand up.

'We've got to get hold of Gill.'

'I'll keep trying her. Do you want to see him, if they'll allow it? You don't have to—'

'No. I want to.'

Robert spoke to the receptionist again and after a few minutes they were allowed through the double doors into resus. A nurse, petite, with short, dark hair, took them to a curtained bay.

'I'm Dr Friedman,' a man said. Robert shook his hand and the two of them moved away to talk.

Sarah slipped inside the curtain. Matt was lying on a bed, bars raised up at the sides. She touched his leg, clammy skin. As she moved up to his hand her fingers snagged on something, a hospital bracelet with his name written in ink. Matthew Logan.

'Matt?'

Wires everywhere. A machine showed heart rate, blood pressure, oxygen levels. It beeped constantly, stopped, and a second or two later gave out a long piercing tone. The numbers flashed.

A nurse appeared at her side, pressed a button and the noise stopped.

'What's happening?' Sarah asked.

'You see this number here? That's his heart. The alarm goes off from time to time.'

'Why? Is he OK?'

'It's just to keep us on our toes. Are you his sister?'

'No. Friend.'

She put a hand on her shoulder. 'Try not to worry.'

Sarah pulled up a chair and held what part of his hand she could without dislodging anything. He had an oxygen mask over his face, warm breath clouding the plastic, and, on the end of one of his fingers, a clip to monitor his pulse.

The curtain moved back and Robert appeared.

'Well?'

'Good.' He straightened up. 'They're going to monitor him, but they won't be able to test the level of poisoning for at least twelve hours. It all depends on how many he took.'

'Gill might have an idea. She'd at least know if it was a recent prescription. Has anyone got hold of her?'

'She's on her way.'

'Right.'

'It's not your fault, Sarah. I'm quite happy to vouch for you if you're worried—'

'I need a cigarette.' She stood up, feeling suddenly nauseous.

He followed her outside. Another ambulance was pulling up, an old woman in a chair, red blanket tucked up to a grey face. Sarah lit a cigarette and pulled her coat around her. She looked down at her feet. She was still wearing slippers.

'Do you know what time it is?' she asked.

'Nearly midnight.'

It felt much later. At some point she'd have to go home and fetch clothes, but she didn't want to leave. 'What am I going to say to her? Her son had a crush on the hired help and that's why he tried to kill himself?'

'You don't know the reason. Only Matt can tell us that.'

'Betrayed by the two people in the world he trusts the most. You said it yourself.'

'What could you have done differently? It's not as if you and he—'

'I kissed him. I got drunk the night Elizabeth showed up and I snogged him.' She took a long drag on her cigarette. 'So, you see, it *is* my fault.'

Robert was silent.

'Did you hear me, Dr Mason? I said I kissed your patient, on the mouth.'

'Why?'

'Because I felt sorry for him. Because I was angry with you.'

He nudged the cigarette bin with his foot. 'If he comes out of this—'

'*If*?' She ground out her cigarette into a pile of hundreds. 'You're keeping something from me. I knew—'

'They think it was a large dose.'

'But he looked better. His colour—'

'That's down to the oxygen. There isn't a lot we can do. Just wait.'

Gill's car sped into the car park, pulling up in an ambulance bay. She got out and ran towards them, heels clacking on the concrete.

'Where is he? Is he all right?'

She dropped her handbag. Robert picked it up and steadied her at the elbow.

'Where is he?'

'OK, Gill. I'll take you to him in a minute, but you have to—'

She pushed Robert aside and smacked through the double doors into the Accident and Emergency waiting room. She was frantic, eyes wide, a film of sweat on her nose and cheeks. She tried to enter through an exit sign and was met by paramedics coming the other way.

'Matthew Logan,' she said to the receptionist. 'I'm his mother.'

'Gill. This way.' Robert took her by the arm and led her through to resus.

Sarah stayed behind. After a time the waiting room became a kind of territory, spaces she'd inhabited, others she hadn't yet ventured into. She counted the floor tiles by her feet, increasing the size to a square around her, four squares, eight. Every so often someone would walk across it and she'd lose count and have to start again. One hour passed, two, three. At some point Robert had rejoined her and fallen asleep, stretched out on the row of chairs opposite. She'd tried all three of the working options from the drinks machine: coffee, which had left a grainy, bitter taste in her mouth, tea the colour of rust, and something called Chocomilk, drinkable, but lukewarm. Eventually, with nothing left to do, she stared at the clock on the wall. It had an almost inaudible tick, until you focused on it and then it became a loud, incessant intrusion.

Janet, the nurse who'd spoken to her when she first

arrived, touched her on the shoulder. She was out of uniform, car keys jangling in her right hand. 'He's stable. Why don't you go home?'

'What does stable mean?'

'It means he's still very poorly, but he's comfortable. There really isn't anything you can do, sitting here. They won't know any more till the morning anyway.'

'OK, thanks. Robert?' She shook him. 'Wake up.'

'What's happened?'

'Nothing. He's stable. We may as well go home for a bit, but I want to see him first.'

It was a few hours since she'd seen Gill and when she emerged, drawn and tense, Sarah nearly didn't recognise her. She was still dressed in her work suit. Her mascara had smudged, leaving two bands under her eyes. Antidepressants. How long had that been going on? It seemed, suddenly, as though Sarah knew nothing about this woman, of her life, other than her absence from Matt's. She looked down, feeling ashamed and angry and not wanting to.

'They want me to fill in some forms,' Gill said. 'History, medications. I wondered . . .'

'Of course,' Robert said. 'I'll come with you.'

A cleaner was polishing the floor in the corridor, slow arcs right and left. Sarah left Robert and Gill at the nurses' station and slipped behind the curtain. Matt was covered up now, cocooned under a thin, white sheet so that just his head and the shape of his body were visible. She touched the outline of his foot, the starched cotton of the sheet feeling like rough skin on her fingertips.

'I'm so sorry, Matt.'

His eyes moved beneath his lids, the flit of some dream played out in fast forward. She watched him for a while; listening to the slow, rhythmic beep of the machine, then let her own eyes close.

When she woke, dazed, confused, it was to the sound of Robert's voice. She looked at her wrist for her watch, but wasn't wearing it. Matt was the same, paler perhaps.

Gill appeared behind them, coat draped over folded arms. 'Dr Mason thinks it would be a good idea for me to have a break. I'll only be an hour. You should both go and get some rest. Thank you for staying.'

Outside Gill went off quickly, running the last few steps to her car. Robert and Sarah walked together. The enormity of how things had changed, in such a short space of time, was only just becoming clear. Of course Robert couldn't continue to give Matt therapy. And nor, now she thought about it, would she be able to continue being his carer. Not after this.

'I didn't tell you, but the other day she freaked out,' Sarah said. 'She was doing paperwork in the lounge, punching numbers into a calculator, and all of a sudden she starts crying. It didn't mean anything to me at the time. I don't know why. I just looked at her and I, well, I was surprised and embarrassed, but I didn't feel anything.'

'Did she talk to you?'

'No. I should've tried, but I didn't. She's always at work, always having to ask me how Matt is instead of knowing herself. He told me he thinks she's been seeing someone, but I don't know if that's true or not. Sometimes I wonder though, if there were no work, no bloke, whether she might find some other escape.'

'From Matt?'

'Maybe it's her way of coping. He's been doing better, happy – or so we thought. Perhaps she only knows how to love him when he's not like that, when he's weak, needy. It's such a mess.'

'Come on. Best if we all try and get some rest now. There's nothing more any of us can do.'

She nodded.

'I'll give you a lift.'

She followed him to his car, rubbing the chill off her arms. It was light, dawn birds singing. She doubted she'd sleep.

# 34

When he got home Robert went to bed, but the snatches of sleep he'd managed in the waiting room at the hospital made it difficult to drop off. He lay for several hours drifting, the way you do when you're expecting the phone to ring. Eventually, he got out of bed, showered and dressed, and made himself toast.

It would be weeks before Matt was given any therapy. He needed to be seen sooner, but Robert knew how stretched psychiatrists on the NHS were. If only Sarah had said something. If only he'd done his fucking job properly, he'd have seen it for himself.

He went into the living room to look at the task in hand, several boxes he'd fetched from the garage which, when erected, would take everything in the living room except the furniture. The rest he'd arrange a removal van for, he didn't even need to be here for that. The work on the cottage was all but complete, small jobs that would take more than a few days, and the final clear-up he'd do himself.

There was a knock at the door. His first thought was that it couldn't be Sarah because they'd left it that he'd phone, so he was surprised to see her standing on the step.

'Any news?'

'No.' She followed him through to the kitchen, and bit her nails while he made tea.

'Did you sleep?'

'I think I might have managed half an hour or so.' She watched him drop two tea bags into the pot. 'I'd rather have a drink, do you mind?'

'No. Of course not.'

They moved into the living room where he emptied the rest of the brandy into two glasses.

'You're packing,' she said.

'Yes.'

'When are you going?'

'A few days, a week, whenever I'm able to sign off with the cottage.'

'Have you decided what you're going to do?'

'I have a house and a practice to get back to.' He sat down and rested his head on his hand. 'After that . . . I don't know. I need to talk to Elizabeth. The relationship we had doesn't exist any more. I think I need to know what's replaced it. If anything.'

'So you're going back to her?'

'I don't know what I'm going to do, but no, I'm not going to move in with her.' He shook his head. 'You know,

I'd got to the point of thinking it's my responsibility. I put her in this position, so I bring up the child. But then I think of her showing up here, doing that, not consulting me, just showing up and saying "Isn't it great, you're going to be a father", and I'm so bloody angry I can't breathe.'

'You've got every right to be angry. What she did just isn't on.'

'But who put her in that position?'

'It's not like you did it voluntarily. It wasn't anything you *did*.' She circled a finger around the rim of her glass. 'How far along is she?'

'Sixteen weeks.'

'*Sixteen*? Why wait so long before telling you? I bet it's a boy.'

'Why do you say that?'

'Because she'd be frightened of bringing up a boy on her own. Rightly so, you should see my mam and Josh.'

'I hadn't thought about it like that,' he said.

'Anyway. It's none of my business. You know, I was worried it'd be weird between us. I'm glad it isn't.'

'Me too.' He'd been surprised by it, and relieved. Ironically it made him want her more.

The phone rang. He jumped to answer it.

'Gill?' Sarah asked, when he hung up.

'Yes. Good news. He's improving.'

'Oh, thank God.'

She tried to find more words, but burst into tears instead. He held her until, a few minutes later, she pushed herself back.

'Just relief.' She sniffed. 'I didn't know. I wasn't sure he'd make it. I thought . . . I really thought . . . God.'

'He's been very lucky.'

'What'll happen to him now?'

'He'll be assessed, then referred. Finch probably.'

'He'll think he's gone right back to square one.'

'I'm afraid he will.' He sat back from her and sipped his drink. 'It has to be like that. You should see him, you know, in a day or two.'

'There's a bad idea. I'm the last person he'll want to see.'

'You need to talk to him.'

'And say what?'

'He's very important to you and you care deeply about what happens to him, but you'll never be able to feel the same way about him as he does about you.'

'No way.'

'It's true isn't it?'

'Of course it is, but how can can I possibly say that to him? Now?'

'You can't be blackmailed, Sarah. The only way Matt'll move forward is if he does it for his own reasons. You have to make it clear what the situation is. You won't be doing him any favours if you leave things as they are.'

'I do care about him. He's clever, gifted. I've never met anyone like him. He's got so much to offer. That sounds so trite.'

'No, it doesn't. Tell him. But you have to explain how it is.'

'Yes. I suppose so.'

He leaned towards her and kissed her lightly on the mouth, wiping her wet cheeks with his thumbs. 'You look shattered. Do you think you could rest now?'

She nodded. He arranged cushions at the head of the sofa and went upstairs to get the duvet from the bed. When he returned she was already asleep, legs tucked up to her chest. He put the duvet over her and sat in the chair opposite, watching her features clench and soften.

It was right for her to go off to university, and without the middle-aged guy with emotional baggage holding her back. It would hurt, though, letting her go.

He rested his head against the side of his chair, looking at her, until finally, his own eyes growing heavier he closed them and allowed himself to drift off.

# 35

'Are you looking for Matthew Logan?' One of the nurses, blonde, plump, paused by the door. She was carrying a pile of bed sheets, chin perched on the top.

'Yes,' Sarah said.

'Down there, to the right. Bay seven.'

'Thanks.'

Bay seven was the last on the ward and like the others had four beds. A smell of sweat and aftershave greeted her as she walked in. All men, adults. Matt was in the bed furthest away, nearest to the window. As she got closer she saw that he was asleep. The transformation from when she'd seen him last was dramatic: different pyjamas, damp hair, combed back. They'd propped him up on several pillows and turned back the sheets. Surprising he managed to sleep at all like that, but he looked peaceful. A trolley moved past, turning on a broken wheel. She pulled up a chair and sat down, listening to the breath escape his dry lips.

'Matt?'

She waited while he registered the voice.

'I wasn't sure whether to wake you, but it's nearly the end of visiting.' She poured a glass of water from a plastic jug and held it out to him.

He stared at her, eyes widening, closing.

'How are you feeling?'

He turned his head away.

'I got you some books from the shop. A John Grisham and another one, looks good, a thriller. Have they told you when you can go home?'

No reply.

'You gave me a shock. All of us.' She put the carrier bag on the floor. 'I imagine you're still feeling pretty rough?'

'Mum said it was you who found me.'

'Yes.'

He swallowed, wet his lips.

'I went to your room to talk to you . . . after . . . anyway, there you were.'

'Were you scared?'

'Yes.' She reached out to him, pulled her hand back. 'I thought . . . I don't think I've ever been so frightened.'

'Have you come to ask me why I did it?'

'No.' She looked into her lap. 'I know why, Matt. I hoped we might talk about it.'

'Want to know something funny?' He tried to turn his body towards her, but only managed to lift himself up a few inches. 'I was dreaming, just now. I was walking along the shore, looking down at my legs and they were strong.

Then I was running, kicking up the water with my feet, leap-frogging over the big boulders at the edge of the wood like they were nothing. You were there. Taking pictures.'

'Matt, there's something I have to tell you.'

'There's something I want to say to you, too.' He blinked, signalling her closer. 'I'm not afraid any more.'

'That's good.'

'I'm not afraid because I love you.'

'Matt—'

'I know I said it when you were drunk and I was drunk, but it doesn't mean anything unless you say it properly. That's what I should've done ages ago. And it doesn't matter if you go with someone else because I know it's completely different to what we've got.'

'We don't have anything.'

'Not yet because I'm not better.' He looked down at himself. 'I don't expect you to want to be with me when I'm like this. But I'm not going to be for much longer, I lost sight of that because I was jealous and I hated . . . it doesn't matter now.' He smiled. 'What matters is that when I'm better—'

'Matt, I'm leaving.'

He looked blank. 'It isn't the end of visiting yet.'

'Loweswater. I'm going back home to Newcastle.'

'Why?'

'I can't be your carer any more.' She stood up to pull the curtain around them and sat down again. 'I've talked to your mum and we agree it would be best if I went home. I'm going to university soon, anyway, I'm just bringing the whole thing forward a bit.' She took a breath and pressed her hands together, resting them under her chin. 'I care for you, Matt, you know I do. I know you think you love me—'

'I do.'

'But I don't love you. Not in the girlfriend, boyfriend sense. I care for you a lot. You're very important to me, but you have to understand that we can only ever be friends. I want that, I do, more than anything.' She stopped. 'I'm sorry. I just can't be your girlfriend.'

'Because of Doc?'

'Because I don't feel the same way as you. It's just one of those things, but I don't want you to stop wanting to get better.'

'Right.'

'Don't waste what you've got, Matt.'

'What have I got?'

'A future.'

'No, I don't. But thanks, thanks anyway. Have a nice life.'

'Please don't be angry.'

'You know what's waiting for me when I get out of here? A lifetime of Mum blaming me for everything, blaming me for Tom, blaming me because I tried to top myself, blaming me because I didn't succeed. Never doing anything for myself, stuck in front of bloody Finch listening to his crackbrained ideas, until finally, years from now, there'll be no one left who cares. I'll just be some sad sicko in a chair—'

'It doesn't have to be like that.'

Silence.

'It's up to you.'

'Yeah, it's always been up to me.'

'Don't you *want* to do something for yourself? Wouldn't you like to be able to walk into that room with Finch and walk out again whenever *you* choose? You can't rely on other people, me, or anyone else. You have to change your life.'

'Oh fuck off, Sarah. You sound like Doc.'

'So your choice is to be wheeled in to one psychiatrist after another, listening to their "crackbrained ideas" as to what's wrong with you? You *want* to be washed and changed and dressed and taken to the bloody toilet for the rest of your life because you're too scared to do anything about it?'

'I'm not scared.'

'The only person you're cheating is yourself. I know you can do it, *you*, Matt. No one else. For God's sake, you're incredible—'

'Here we go.'

'A wicked sense of humour, talented. Good-looking. You can do whatever you want to do.'

'Then why don't you want me? If I'm all those things.'

'I don't know. I just don't. Not in that way.'

The curtain was pulled back.

'It's steak and kidney pie or fish and chips and, for afters, jelly and ice-cream or jam roly-poly with custard.' The nurse looked from Matt to Sarah and back again. 'Which do you want?'

Sarah took it as her moment to leave though it felt abrupt, too little said despite having said it all. At the entrance to the bay she stopped, hoping for some sign she'd got through to him, but he continued to stare into space. The meal was put down on a tray in front of him, but he didn't eat.

She left, walking at first, and then breaking into a run halfway down the corridor. She got as far as the double doors at the end. But she couldn't leave. Not like this. She wanted him to understand and for it not to hurt, but that wasn't possible. She went back, trying to work out what else she could say. At the entrance to the bay she stopped. He was staring at the steak and kidney pie, hunched, shattered.

Then, slowly, he reached for his knife and fork and started to eat.

# 36

I've been trying to think of something to say about Finch. It's taken me six weeks and this is it: Sarah wouldn't shag this guy in a million years.

*You can walk out of that door, Matthew, any time you like, but you can't wheel yourself out. The only way out of this place is to walk.*

I could tie sheets together and abseil out the bloody window, but I let it pass. Finch likes his speeches. When they came to take me for my first session with him I threw a major wobbly and locked myself in the disabled toilet on the ward. I was OK, incredibly pissed off, but mostly I just needed time away from all the noise to figure out how I was going to get out of it. Time to think. Only the nurses thought I might be trying to hurt myself. That's a laugh. The only person who got hurt was Dave, one of the hospital security guards, when he kicked the door in. He actually did it. I still can't believe it. Later, Finch said people who try to commit suicide have to earn the trust of those around them. In other words, nobody was going to believe a word I said until I proved I wanted to get better.

I don't know if I've done that or not, but I know I'm going to walk out of here and it's got nothing to do with Finch or what he thinks. I can't explain it; it's like this restless feeling. It's there when I wake up in the morning and it follows me through the day, each day stronger than the last. I know it's going to happen.

Today I'm going home. Only for one night and still on wheels so no brass band just yet. A red-letter-day though, as Finch calls them – a successful red-letter-day is one step closer to 'normal'. Whatever that is.

'Hello, love.' Mum kisses me on the forehead, setting down fresh pyjamas on the chair next to my bed. I've been thinking about the pyjama thing as it happens – not much else to do in here, but think – and I've decided I'm going to sleep in my skiddies from now on. Pyjamas are for kids.

Mum waits while I tie the laces on my trainers and then we're off, down the corridor and out of the entrance like a prison break.

The town is the same, still heaving with tourists, only now they're the autumn ones – older, big on scenery and walking. They come to gawp at the trees when they change colour, but they're a bit early for that.

I lean my head against the car window, turning to look at Doc's cottage when we pass it. There's a For Sale sign up in the front garden and the curtains are half drawn. At first I thought they'd gone back to Newcastle together, him and Sarah, but I don't think they did. The day after she came to see me I got Mum to bring the photographs she took for me. The ones of the moss and the lichen and the mayfly larva on a stone. I must've spent a good couple of hours tearing them up into tiny squares. I posted them to her, no note. No response either, not that I expected one. Then, out of the blue, a letter telling me all about her student digs in Leicester. She's having a whale of a time. Freshers' week, parties, and a new camera, better than her old one, bought with her student loan. And the photographs, fresh copies, just as they were. No mention of what I did. No mention of Doc.

I got a letter from him, too. A long one. Now that *was* a surprise. It's full of encouragement . . . and common sense and a whole load of waffle about feelings – bog-typical Doc. Reading between the lines I can tell he thinks he fucked up. I don't think he did. All he did was fall for Sarah – and anybody can do that.

We pull up to the house. I've only been gone a month, but I've almost forgotten what it looks like. It hasn't changed much, a few weeds growing up out of the gravel on the drive and the flowerbeds, quieter without their colour.

Mum takes me around the back to the patio table, moved out on to the lawn to make the most of the evening sunshine. The roses are dying out. Petals on the ground, stained brown, withered. Others that haven't fallen yet hang loosely from the stems.

'I got cakes,' Mum says, disappearing into the kitchen. She comes back with two vanilla slices, two chocolate éclairs and a small Victoria sponge.

'There's loads.'

'A treat,' she says, smiling. 'I got carried away.'

I take a bite of a chocolate éclair, cream squirting out the side on to my cheek. Mum laughs and hands me a napkin.

'Are the cottages full?'

'For the next two weeks. Nothing after that. Where's your tea?' She tuts and goes back inside to fetch the pot. When she's sat down again and filled our cups, she pulls her chair closer to mine. 'I've been thinking, Matt. About this place. About lots of things. We could move, you know? Out of Loweswater, somewhere completely different. If you wanted to?'

'Move? You're not serious?'

'I could get another job.'

'But you love your job, you love this house.'

'I love you.' She laughs a little, turning away from me to look across the garden. 'Who's to say I won't like somewhere else just as much. It's a lot of work this house, and, besides, perhaps somewhere without so many memories would be better for us, don't you think? A fresh start. Think about it.'

I look at the island, no more than a fuzz on the surface of the water now, sinking fast. Soon it'll be gone. I know I'll always see two boys in a dinghy rowing out to it. I can't get away from that. But lying over the top of that memory there's another: Sarah standing in the middle of it with a flag in her hand. Good and bad. Mixed in together.

So what do I feel? I can't escape my memories by moving – I'll take them with me. They're in my head not in the house or on the lake. Wherever I go, Tom will follow.

He always did. And that's OK. I'm not even sure I want him not to.

'No. I don't think we should move,' I say. 'I like it here.'

'Oh. Really? OK.'

She looks surprised, and pleased. She didn't really want to move. It's just she's always thought I was afraid of the lake. And at this time of day, when the light's beginning to fade, it does look a bit threatening. It breathes, like a giant lung, sucking up all the colour from the trees and the hills. Everything within its reach. Even me.

But I'm not afraid.

# *Free Food for Millionaires*

## Min Jin Lee

Casey Han's years at Princeton have given her 'a refined diction, an enviable golf handicap, wealthy friends, a popular white boyfriend, and a magna cum laude degree in economics. But no job, and a number of bad habits . . .'

The elder daughter of working-class Korean immigrants who run a dry cleaning shop in Manhattan, Casey inhabits a New York a world away from that of her parents. Ambitious, spirited and obstinate, she's developed a taste for a lifestyle – and a passion for beautiful hats and expensive tailoring – she hasn't the means to sustain. And between the culture to which her family so fiercely cling and the life she aspires to, Casey must confront her own identity, the meaning of wealth, and what she really wants from her future.

As Casey navigates an uneven course of small triumphs and spectacular failures, a clash of values, ideals and ambitions plays out against the colourful backdrop of New York society, its many layers, shades and divides.

'As easy to devour as a nineteenth-century romance . . . Ambitious, accomplished and engrossing.' *New York Times Book Review*

'This big, beguiling book has all the distinguishing marks of a Great American Novel . . . [a] remarkable writer' *The Times*

arrow books

# *The Editor's Wife*

## Clare Chambers

When aspiring novelist Christopher Flinders drops out of university to write his literary masterpiece, his family is sceptical.

However, when he is taken up by London editor Owen Goddard and his charming wife Diana, it seems success is just around the corner. Christopher is captivated by his generous and cultured mentors – but on the brink of realising his dream, he makes a desperate misjudgement which results in disaster for all involved. Shattered, he withdraws from London.

Twenty years on, Christopher has buried himself in rural Yorkshire, with a career and a private life marked by mediocrity. But then a young academic researching Owen Goddard seeks him out, and Christopher is forced to exhume his past, setting him on a path to a life-changing discovery.

'Original and addictive . . . reminds us of the rare pleasure that an intelligent tale with a happy ending brings' *Daily Telegraph*

'A great read with a fantastic twist at the end . . . thoroughly enjoyable and very clever' *Sunday Express*

'Engrossing, romantic and well-observed – not to mention exceedingly amusing – this is a perfect holiday read'
*Daily Mail*

arrow books

# *Honor & Evie*

## Susannah Bates

**Does growing up have to mean growing apart?**

Privileged and beautiful, intelligent and popular, life's gifts come effortlessly to Honor Montfort. If only things were that simple for her prickly cousin, Evie.

Yet in spite of their differences – or perhaps because of them – the bond between Honor and Evie is strong. They are the very best of friends.

But which of them is really best-equipped for the challenges ahead – the one who appears to have everything, or the one who's had to learn to fight? And how will their unusual friendship survive when Honor's charms start working against her will . . . upon the only man that Evie has ever loved?

'Charming and beguiling' Penny Vincenzi

arrow books

# *Rise and Shine*

## Anna Quindlen

### The *New York Times* No.1 Bestseller

It's an otherwise ordinary Monday when Meghan Fitzmaurice's perfect life hits a wall. A household name as the host of 'Rise and Shine', the country's highest-rated morning talk show, Meghan cuts to a commercial break, but not before she mutters two forbidden words into her open mike.

In an instant, it's the end of an era – not only for Meghan, who is unaccustomed to dealing with adversity, but also for her younger sister, Bridget, a social worker in the Bronx who has always lived in Meghan's long shadow.

The effect of Meghan's on-air truth-telling reverberates through both of their lives, affecting Meghan's son, husband, friends, and fans, as well as Bridget's perception of her sister, their complex childhood, and herself. What follows is a story about how, in very different ways, the Fitzmaurice women adapt, survive, and manage to bring the whole teeming world of New York to heel, by dint of their smart mouths, quick wits, and the powerful connection between them that even the worst tragedy cannot shatter.

'A columnist's eye for social nuance and Manhattan manners . . . reminiscent of Nora Ephron' *Independent*

'A writerly achievement, her best so far' *New York Times*

arrow books

# The Whole World Over

## Julia Glass

Greenie Duquette lavishes most of her passionate energy on her Greenwich Village bakery and her four-year-old son, George. Her husband, Alan, seems to have fallen into a midlife depression, while Walter, her closest professional ally, is nursing a broken heart.

It is at Walter's restaurant that the visiting governor of New Mexico tastes Greenie's coconut cake and decides to woo her away from the city to be his chef. For reasons both ambitious and desperate, she accepts – and finds herself heading west without her husband. This impulsive decision, along with events beyond Greenie's control, will change the course of several lives around her.

*The Whole World Over* is a vividly human tale of longing and loss, folly and forgiveness, revealing the subtle mechanisms behind our most important, and often most fragile, connections to others.

'Just when the reader feels sure of an outcome, other forces are set to work, shifting the momentum in unexpected directions. Glass is such an unobtrusive writer, conveying meaning not through insightful asides, philosophical musings or verbal pyrotechnics but through storytelling.' *New York Times*

arrow books

ALSO AVAILABLE IN ARROW

# *Happiness Sold Separately*

## Lolly Winston

Elinor Mackey has lived her life in perfect order: college, law school, successful corporate career, marriage. But suddenly her world is falling apart. Now in her late 30s, she's discovered that she and her podiatrist husband, Ted, can't have children.

When Elinor withdraws from Ted into an interior world of heartbreak and anger, Ted begins an affair with Gina, the nutritionist at their gym – a young woman with an oddball son who adores Ted. Meanwhile, Elinor falls in love with the oak tree in her front yard, spreading out her sleeping bag to sleep under the stars.

Lolly Winston's second novel looks beyond the manicured surface of suburbia to a world of loss, longing, lust and betrayal.

'Sensitive and lyrical, with moments of hilarity and pathos' *Chicago Sun Times*

'A bittersweet, funny novel about the end of one love and the beginning of a new life' *Glamour*

'Elinor's wit, as well as Winston's keen eye for humor in moments of despair, elevate this touching, comic tale above the crowded pack' *People Magazine*

arrow books